Out of Cabrini

Out of Cabrini

A Macbeth Novel

Dave Case

Five Star • Waterville, Maine

First Edition
First Printing: April 2006

Published in 2006 in conjunction with Tekno Books and Ed Gorman.

Set in 11 pt. Plantin.

Printed in the United States on permanent paper.

Library of Congress Cataloging-in-Publication Data

Case, Dave, 1961–
    Out of Cabrini : a Macbeth novel / by Dave Case.—1st ed.
      p. cm.
   ISBN 1-59414-378-1 (hc : alk. paper)
   1. Policewomen—Fiction. 2. Chicago (Ill.)—Fiction.
  3. Drug traffic—Fiction. 4. Gangs—Fiction. I. Title.
  PS3603.A839O98 2006
   813′.6—dc22
                                        2005030123

This book is dedicated to:
Ronald Michael Ryan, Jr.
St. Paul Police Department
August 26th, 1994

Acknowledgements

I cannot begin to thank anyone without first acknowledging my wife, JeanMarie. This whole adventure began with her encouraging me to pursue my dream of writing. It was, and has been, and continues to be a huge sacrifice, in which she shoulders a significant burden. Thank you for all that you have done in the past, and for what you're doing now, and for what you will do in the future. Without you, this never would have been possible.

I've also been blessed with a number of family members who have been very supportive: my mother and father, Peggy and Lester Case; my sister, Juli Case; my uncle, Dr. Thomas Stamps M.D.; Bill and Joan Zupan, Zeke and Kelly Zupan; and Kelly's mom and dad, Donna and Neil O'Keefe. Thank you one and all for believing in me.

I've intentionally left out one family member: my wife's sister, Susan Zupan, who has been instrumental in a number of ways. She labored through a line-by-line edit with JeanMarie and me, and, if that wasn't enough, she has continued to actively encourage me. I'm sure she found me to be more hard-headed than her third-grade students. Thank you.

I've also experienced what I consider to be a most extraordinary career in the greatest law enforcement entity on the face of the earth: the Chicago Police Department. Thank you, George Barzydlo; without you and your family, it never would have been possible. The men and women of the Chicago Police Department are its single greatest resource and I am proud to count myself a member. I've always been fortunate to be surrounded by phenomenal police officers. Thank you, Mike Alexander, Dan Amidei, Jim Antonnaci, Tommy Ayers, John Baranowski, Jake Blake, E. Fred Bosse, Kenny Charles, Jim Darling, Dan Dugan, Ken Johnson, Bill Kushner, Mike Landando, Rich Mancha, Arnie Martinez, Joe Mullins, Jim O'Brien, John Thomas, Matt Tobias and Earl Zuelke. Please forgive me in the event that I left someone out. I cannot begin to tell you how much influence you've had over my professional and personal life. I can't forget Danny's sister, Dee Dee, and her family. Thanks for the support and for the dinner; it was great.

My writers' group that meets at Scotland Yard Books Ltd. in Winnetka, Illinois, has had a substantial influence on my writing. They have seen me mature as a writer under their sharp, critical eyes. Thank you, David J. Walker, Steve Mandel, Libby Fischer Hellman, Eleanor Taylor Bland, Mary Harris, Lisa Kartus and Gordon Macintosh. And a special thank you to Michael Allen Dymmoch, who took it upon herself to complete an exhaustive edit of this manuscript in an earlier form. I learned more from that experience than from any other. Thanks.

I would also be remiss if I didn't thank John Camp for taking the time to help a beginning writer. Time and again you reached out and assisted me. You gave me great insight through our conversations. Thanks for believing in me early.

And finally, to Michael A. Black, fellow sergeant, writer and, most importantly, friend. You were always there, even when I didn't show up. I appreciate your support and, if that's not an understatement, I don't know what is. It's comforting to know you got my back. Thanks, brother.

As you can tell, it takes a village to support a writer, at least this one, anyway. I hope I haven't forgotten anyone in my haste to produce this. I would never let myself prepare this acknowledgement page, having met with rejection so many times. Now that it's here, I've got to rush. Sorry.

I certainly hope you enjoy reading this book as much as I enjoyed writing it. Though some aspects might ring more true than others, it's still a work of fiction. That's my story and I'm sticking to it.

If you're interested in reading more about those Chicago Police Officers who have made the ultimate sacrifice, as Ronnie did in St. Paul in 1994, go to

www.CPDmemorial.org.

There you will find a rich illustration of the Gold Star Memorial and Park that the Chicago Police Department is raising funds to build. It will be beautiful and dedicated to our fallen officers, some four hundred sixty as of this writing. They deserve so much more . . .

Foreword

Cabrini Green actually began in 1942 with the construction of the Frances Cabrini Rowhouses; at that time, it was even referred to as "Little Sicily," since it was initially populated with Italian-Americans. It took twenty years before the whole complex was completed; by that time the demographics had shifted, so that the vast majority of inhabitants were African-Americans. According to the Chicago Housing Authority, at its peak, Cabrini Green was home to some 15,000 residents and consisted of twenty-two high-rise buildings and a section of rowhouses, providing some 3,500 public housing units.

The project buildings north of Division Street are a very light gray and are called "the whites" by residents. All of the whites are very tall, towering sixteen stories. The high-rise buildings south of Division are red brick and are called "the reds." These buildings vary in height; some are as tall as the whites, but many are smaller and more compact (nine to twelve floors). The original buildings, constructed in 1942, are yellow brick, and are referred to as the rowhouses. These are a series of two-story buildings stretching along a city block, with a number of apartments opening onto the various streets that divide the complex.

Cabrini is home to many gangs, the largest faction being the Gangster Disciples (GDs). They dominate the whites, north of Division, and are well represented in the reds as well. The Vice Lords are also present in the complex and occupy several of the red buildings.

The GDs and the Vice Lords are the polar opposite in regard to overall gang affiliations, with the GDs lining up with the major alliance of "Folks." The Vice Lords are affiliated with the other major gang faction, known as "People." These two large factions are at loggerheads, and conflicts often erupt into deadly violence. In a fashion similar to the United Nations/Warsaw Pact, they often establish treaties with other gangs for mutual support. These relationships are most apparent in the prison environment, where that cooperation is paramount. The gangs are led by males who are frequently in their late twenties, and usually have natural-born leadership abilities. Despite their lack of formal education, these leaders often have good organizational skills, not to mention the charisma that allows them to control their gangs from prison.

Frequently, gangs enlist the services of an enforcer, usually a member who is very tough, mean and many times crazy. He is responsible for internal discipline, and metes out discipline for violations. These enforcers usually have reputations that extend well beyond their respective gangs.

Another gang deeply rooted in Cabrini Green is the Mickey Cobras. A smaller gang, most of their members are older, yet they're much more dangerous and prone to violence. Their leadership is also much more ingrained in the community, with influence in many venues not normally available to gangs. Following their example, many gangs have subsequently sought similar influence in the community. The Mickey Cobras inhabited several red buildings on the eastern corner of the Cabrini complex, and they ruled them with little regard for anyone, even the police. This attitude garnered them a lot of attention from the local district.

Chicago is carved into twenty-five police districts, based loosely on calls for service from years ago. Cabrini Green falls completely within the Eighteenth District, which is located on the near north side of the city.

The Chicago Police Department's Detective Division is divided into five Areas, each responsible for the investigations in a number of districts. The Eighteenth District falls within Area Three and, as such, fields the detectives who conduct their criminal investigations. Area Three is also responsible for the Nineteenth, Twentieth, Twenty-Third, and Twenty-Fourth Districts.

Each district is allowed to field a team of plainclothes officers, called a tactical team, or "tac team." Currently, each team is made up of one lieutenant, five sergeants, and forty officers, and is used as a discretionary force available to the District Commander to use as needed, usually to address emerging crime trends within the district.

At the time *Out of Cabrini* was written, tac teams were limited to three teams of eight officers. But the Eighteenth District, with Cabrini Green, needed an even greater presence within the project complex, and subsequently kept an unauthorized fourth team, dedicated to Cabrini. Stacey Macbeth and his fellow officers are a fictionalized representation of just such a team.

Prologue

For fourteen months, Latricia Gibbons' thirteenth-floor apartment in the 1150 North Sedgwick building of the Cabrini Green Projects had been uncharacteristically quiet. The fact that Lonnie Huggins, her longtime boyfriend and father of two of her three children, had been locked away in prison wasn't lost on her. Things were about to change.

Lonnie was getting out.

Chapter 1

The Stud

0415 Hours—Friday

Stacey Macbeth watched in morbid fascination as the piercing-girl pulled Mike Zito's tongue flat out of his mouth with what she had called "forceps," but to him looked a hell of a lot more like pliers. The girl had a face full of metal jewelry and, if she'd done her own, they at least knew she had lots of practice. She was all of five-foot-two, eighty-five pounds and maybe twenty-two years old. Zito, at five-ten, two hundred pounds, should have looked bigger as he reclined under her, awaiting the needle. A flush had crept up his neck, past his face, into his receding dirty-blonde hairline.

Zito's drunk seemed to be fading, had been since he'd planted his ass in the chair, a fifties dental reject from the looks of it. They'd spent the night bar-hopping, starting at Dougan's, a nice cop bar in Greek town, and ended on the near west side at Ira's, a cop bar that stank of decades of cigarette smoke and cheap beer. Zito had been talking about meeting the woman of his dreams or his fantasies, but Macbeth knew he'd settle for a woman who'd just put up with him. Having spent the better part of their overtime checks on booze, Zito was no closer to love or lust, and so they'd decided to take the plunge and get their tongues pierced.

Macbeth had argued that Zito would have to fight women off once he had a stud, and that would be a marked improvement over his current state of scaring them off. Zito was reluctant at first, but when Macbeth mentioned that his girlfriend Erin liked pierced tongues, he came around.

It all had started a few days ago when Zito's most recent squeeze had sent him packing. Citing, among a host of other bad habits, his refusal to quit smoking as the final straw. Zito had been miserable since, and was about to drive Macbeth crazy. Something had to change and, since he hadn't been able to secure Zito any companionship for the night, he now hoped to make him a "stud" in future encounters.

A sweat had broken out on Zito's forehead. His eyes focused on the piercing-girl's hands; everywhere they went, his eyes were sure to follow. Zito had to go first, having lost the bet. Macbeth had suffered a stream of curses, but had assured him he was going next. After all, Erin did say she thought the studs were sexy. But now, having watched this young girl work on Zito, not to mention the six-inch, twenty-two gauge needle, Macbeth started second-guessing himself. But he knew in the end he'd have to take his turn in the chair.

When the girl brought the needle out, Zito's forearms bunched. Macbeth thought for a second he was going to tear the arms right off the chair. Zito kept trying to say something, but couldn't be understood. His speech became slurred after the topical pain retardant was applied, and that was ten minutes ago; now, with his tongue stretched out of his mouth, forget it. She wasn't paying him any attention either. It looked like she was concentrating on the purple spot she'd made on his tongue. She did a quick peek under his tongue, then pushed the needle through from the bottom. It was done, just that quickly.

She tossed the pliers in the steel tray on the table next to the chair and grabbed the gold post; in a matter of seconds that too was in his mouth, and dropped through the top of the needle, into the hollow shaft. The needle came out and was tossed in the tray on top of the pliers. From the tabletop, she pinched a tiny gold ball between her fingers, bringing it into his mouth, too; and she quickly screwed it on the bottom of the post. It was long, but she'd explained that it had to be for the first couple of weeks, to allow for the tongue swelling.

The girl stripped a gauze pad from a stack on the table and dabbed at his tongue. There really wasn't much blood. Macbeth had expected a lot more, especially since they'd been drinking. She had Zito swish Listerine in his mouth for a minute, then spit. She peeled off her latex gloves, tossed them in the tray and looked up at Macbeth. "Your turn, big guy. Rinse with the Listerine, too."

Zito worked his jaw and leaned forward, massaging his face with his hands. Macbeth heard a faint click. Zito shifted his stare to him. Another click. He looked pale, and Macbeth figured he was clammy, too. Macbeth took a cupful of Listerine and gargled, spitting it back in the cup that he threw away.

"Tss iss scking werd," Zito said, clicking several times.

The girl scooped the tray off the table and stopped by the door, turning toward Zito. "Try and not hit the back of your teeth with your bar; it's bad for the enamel. Terrible for the gums, too."

She left and Zito stood. "Sckin tngues swoll."

Macbeth couldn't help but laugh.

"Wha?" Zito looked like he didn't get it.

Macbeth sat in the chair and jumped back up. "Seat's wet, man. You have an accident or something?"

Zito waved his hand, dismissing him. "Sck 'ou assole."

Macbeth sat back down laughing. The girl came back, carrying a new tray. She sat it on the table and began prepping the utensils. "Are you guys cops?"

Macbeth didn't answer at first, glancing at Zito, who was giving him the finger. "Yeah, we work in the Eighteenth District," Macbeth said.

"Where's that?"

"Chicago and LaSalle." He sat back and rested his head, trying to appear calmer than he really was. "We're on the tac team."

"What's a tac team?" She pulled on a pair of gloves and picked up her pen.

"We work in plainclothes and don't have to answer calls. Just concentrate on locking up bad guys." A clank from the tray and Macbeth figured she'd picked up the pliers.

She turned to him. "Open." Macbeth opened his mouth, thinking he could feel sweat bead on his brow. "You can do better than that," she said. He cranked his mouth as open as he could. Maybe this wasn't such a good idea after all? Erin had better appreciate this shit, he thought.

She caught his tongue with the pliers, then pulled. It tugged a little; it didn't really hurt, but it was uncomfortable. "Oh, almost forgot." She put the pen down and dug in her shirt pocket, coming up with a one-use packet of some kind of pain relief cream. She tore it open with her teeth, spitting the loose piece on the floor. "But I suppose a big, tough-looking guy like you doesn't even need this. You play football?"

"O. 'Ockey." It was hard to talk when someone was

yanking your tongue out of your mouth. He figured that since he was six-four and had been spending a lot of time in the gym, to her, he must look like a giant and a natural football player. Growing up in Minnesota, though, and Canada, had him on the ice before he could walk. He'd never played organized football.

"Oh, big, tough hockey player. You definitely don't need any of this, then." She winked at him and applied the cream to his tongue. She tossed the packet on the table, and picked up the pen. After another tug on the pliers, he felt the tip of the pen dot his tongue, followed by a kind of acidy, metal taste. "Let's give that ten minutes." She whipped off the gloves, picked the packet off the floor and left the room.

Macbeth heard a crash, then another, followed by the tinkling of glass on metal and concrete. "What the hell was that?" Macbeth sat up, then stood.

"O. O." Zito shoved Macbeth's shoulder back toward the seat. "Si' 'own. O wurry 'bou' 'at." Zito gave a dismissing wave at the door toward the street.

Macbeth settled back; Zito was probably right, nothing to worry about. The look on his partner's face made him laugh again. Some of his color had returned, but when he talked it looked like his cheeks were puffed out too far, maybe to protect his tongue or something like that. Macbeth laid his head back and closed his eyes. Soon enough he'd be talking like Zito, so he'd better get over it.

"Hey!" A female voice yelled, probably their little piercing-girl, from the front of the store. "Call the police. Some kids are breaking into a car."

Macbeth looked back to Zito, who was waggling his finger at him, like he was scolding a dog. Somewhere in the back of the store, someone picked up a phone. After a few seconds, Macbeth heard a male voice, probably another employee, tell the dispatcher about the break-in and give the address of the tattoo parlor. Then the male voice called out, "What do they look like?"

"I don't know, but they're dressed all in black."

Zito kept his head shaking like it was on a swivel. "S'ay 'ight 'ere, 'on't 'ouv." Macbeth raised his hands in defeat. Probably for the best; they'd been drinking, and the employees had a good handle on it anyway.

"What kind of car?" came the voice from the back.

"Black Taurus. Parked out front in the bus lane."

" 'Ey!" Zito yelled. " 'At's I 'ar!"

Macbeth jumped out of the chair and raced after Zito, who had bolted for the front of the store. They had to dodge a couple of people, who were in various stages of getting or giving tattoos, before they could get at the door. Macbeth could see the back end of Zito's Taurus and, sure as shit, a late-teen kid in a black hood was standing lookout.

The bells on the door jangled as Zito ripped the thick wood-and-glass door open, the tattoo parlor's name stenciled across the front in a splash of color and design. Macbeth was on his heels as they charged out onto the sidewalk. The lookout whipped around and shouted something in Spanish. He squared his shoulders to the two cops. Apparently he wasn't scared but, then again, he didn't know what or whom he was facing, either.

"Poe'eece!" Zito yelled. It took a lot of effort on Macbeth's part not to look sideways at his partner and double over laughing. He sounded absurd.

Apparently the kid thought so too; he stuffed one hand into his hoodie pocket, like he had a weapon. "What you say? You some kind of faggot or something?" He had a heavy Spanish accent.

Macbeth watched the kid's hands and reached for his own weapon back on his right hip. Next to him, Zito opened his coat, exposing his star on his belt and his own gun, a big, dark semi-auto. "O. Assole. Poe'eeeeeeeece."

The kid must've figured out what Zito was trying to say, or maybe he just saw the star on his belt and a light went off in his head, but he took off down the street with Zito behind him. Macbeth froze for a second, wanting to follow, but the guy in the car was backing out with what looked like Zito's tape deck in hand.

Macbeth let go of his holstered weapon and stepped up to the door. As the other guy, maybe twenty, bald, definitely Hispanic, stood up, Macbeth tagged him with a straight jab from his right fist. The guy fell hard, back against the car, then into the door, before hitting the ground. Macbeth grabbed him by the collar, prepared to give him another punch, but there wasn't any fight left in the guy. Macbeth quickly cuffed the guy's two hands through the now-broken window. "Don't go anywhere. You're officially under arrest." He stood and tried to get a fix on Zito, but he was out of sight, either down the street or in an alley.

As he started off after his partner, he saw the piercing-girl with her head out of the door. "Call the police and let them know there's two off-duty coppers out here." She ducked back in the store. He hoped she was making the call; otherwise, it could get a little dicey.

As he ran down the street, he tried keeping an eye on either side, looking for signs of Zito and the other bad guy's passage. Several gangways between homes were places they could have run, but he didn't see any open gates. Zito usually looked for the gates; he wasn't that good at hopping fences. Macbeth couldn't hear anything, but then would

Zito even be yelling anymore?

He stopped and listened, his breath coming out in billowing clouds of white. One of his rules of foot chases was that when you lost sight of your quarry: stop, look and listen. Another was to wait for the double-back. Macbeth started to back up, toward Zito's car. Where the hell was he?

Macbeth was already turning, when he recognized that he'd heard the scrape of someone's coat on a piece of wood, like on a porch or fence, as the wearer squeezed by. Next came the flap of feet on concrete. Someone was about to come sprinting out of one of the gangways on the north side of the street. Then, "Sop! Sop! Muddersckr!"

A black shadow darted out of a nearby gangway, doing the get-away run. Macbeth charged toward the figure. They met just as the guy tried to cross the street between parked cars. Macbeth lowered his shoulder and delivered the perfect check, sending the smaller man into a parked panel van. He bounced off and slid back across the concrete. He tried to get up and keep running, but Zito came into the picture and kicked what would have been a fifty-yard field goal, had the guy's spleen been a football. Whatever desire to flee came out, along with all of the air in his lungs and probably some of his dinner. Macbeth picked him up by the back of the coat and heaved him across another parked car, dragging his arms behind his back, cuffing him.

Zito bent over and put his hands on his knees. For a minute, Macbeth figured Zito was going to lose the night's festivities right there on North Avenue. What a waste that would be, he thought. But then he'd probably end up puking later anyway, so why not now, out here on the street, as opposed to home?

Macbeth began searching the coat pockets of their

arrestee, wondering if he'd actually had a gun. He came up with a knife, no surprise, and a CD, but no gun. He glanced at Zito and waved the CD. "This yours?" Zito stood. Macbeth figured, by the look on his face, that he couldn't see the cover, so he tossed it to him. Zito caught it and stared. It was *Dean Martin's Greatest Hits*, Zito's favorite. Zito shook the CD at the arrestee. " 'Ame a sog. 'Ame a sog, assole."

Macbeth pushed the prisoner back toward the store, as sirens blared in the distance. He shook his head, spun the prisoner to face him and stopped. "What my partner's so eloquently trying to say is that if you can sing one song off that CD, you can go free."

The guy stared at them, his breathing still hard and labored. He looked away, toward the store and car. "Man, you white boys is crazy."

Macbeth looked at the prisoner, then at Zito, whose mouth was starting to look like some kind of whacked-out chipmunk's. Macbeth felt a wicked grin tug at the corners of his mouth. "Ain't that a kick in the head."

"Sck 'ou. Ain' 'unny."

Chapter 2

Out

1900 Hours—Friday

Lonnie Huggins thought the cold air felt better on his face as a free man than as a prisoner. He waited, last in line, to walk through the final gate and freedom. He wasn't coming back; hell, no.

Most of the men released from the Pontiac State Pen with him had people waiting for them: wives, girlfriends or relatives of some kind. The real losers filed over to a raggedy-assed, white bus, with IDOC stenciled on its side in black. It would take them back to the city, back to the real world, to the 'hood. But Huggins didn't have to bother with that. He was going to travel in style. Once past the last guard, the gate slammed closed and, for the first time in fourteen months, he was on the right side of it. Huggins took a couple steps, then stopped. The other men went their ways, while he took in a deep breath; it came out a cloud in the cold. Felt good to be free.

A black Lincoln Navigator flashed its lights at him. He could make out someone behind the wheel, but didn't know who it was. Looked young, though. He ambled over, feeling his muscles dance. One thing about the joint, sure did a motherfucker good. He was solid; that's what happened after he'd been pumping iron and doing push-ups and sit-ups in his small-ass cell for fourteen months. Hours is what he kept count of, not reps.

Inside, he'd kept his mouth shut, and done a few things that needed doing. Now was payback time. Seeing as Cecil had sent down his personal ride with some young-ass driver meant Cee was seeing it Huggins' way too.

He popped open the door and got in, slamming the door behind him. The driver, a twenty-something black kid, was probably not from the Greens. Huggins didn't know him, but the kid stared straight ahead. Showing him respect. He liked that. Sometimes respect could keep a nigger alive.

The kid shifted the truck and they took off. Huggins twisted the rearview mirror, so he could watch the prison fade from sight. He didn't look away until all he could see was the glow from the lights. His head, cornrows pulling his scalp tight, dropped back against the headrest. Finally, he could relax. First time in damn near a year and a half. He kicked back, dropping his seat, Gangsta Style. No more having to watch his back no more; he could shit and shower in private, no guards watching him, no thugs trying to sink a shank in his ass.

The kid turned onto Interstate 55, his eyes never leaving the road. Huggins liked the respect, knew it was from the fear of his rep as the Mickey Cobra enforcer. There wasn't a Cobra in the city that hadn't been threatened with a visit from Lonnie.

"Cecil tell you anything to say to me?" Huggins asked.

"Cee say to come see him before you go anywhere else. He say it won't take long, and then you can go get you some."

Huggins nodded and smacked the kid's arm with the back of his hand. "Give me a square."

The kid reached into his coat and took out a pack of cigarettes. Shaking one loose, he held it out. Huggins took the whole pack. He stuffed the pack into his coat pocket and put the one cigarette in his mouth. Another smack on the kid's arm produced the lighter. He took that, too. Holding the flame to the tip of the cigarette, he inhaled. The smoke felt good; he let it out slowly.

"How about Latricia?" He pocketed the lighter. "She been stepping out on me?"

"Naw, she been cool."

Huggins nodded, taking in more smoke. Something about the kid bothered him, like he answered too fast or something; maybe Latricia been kicking it with him. "You sure about that?" he asked. He turned to watch the kid answer.

"I don't know nothing about anything like that. She been cool with me."

Satisfied, Huggins turned his face away and looked out the window. He saw his reflection in the glass against the cold darkness. Night didn't have shit on him.

He didn't have to stab no sissy booty tonight. Hell, no. Tonight he was going to get some real female ass. That was for sure.

Chapter 3

The Blessing

2300 Hours—Friday

Cecil Jones sat at the kitchen table in his woman's apartment on the fifteenth floor of 1150 North Sedgwick. Across from him, Huggins was making himself comfortable on the couch. Green leather. From Italy. Jones rubbed his belly and laughed as he looked at the dirty dishes. He didn't give a fuck. He'd gotten his, been fed first. Just like them lions do in Africa. Bet they don't give a fuck either what happens after they got theirs. Them lions got it made. All they do is eat, sleep and fuck. They even got their bitches doing the hunting. He laughed. That's how it should be. Fucking lions.

"Listen man." Jones thought Huggins had the scariest stare of anyone he'd ever met. Hard. Flat. Like he didn't care for nothing, like one of them sharks on TV just before they take a bite out of your ass. "I know you kept your mouth shut while you was in. I 'preciate that. I know you did some things needed doing. Did your nation proud. I 'preciate that." Jones saw Huggins' stare grow cold. "Most of all, you been loyal to me, more loyal than family. That's what I 'preciate most of all." He watched Huggins closely; not even so much as a blink. This was one crazy motherfucker.

28

"Ain't no problem, Cee." Huggins spread his arms along the back of the couch and pinched the leather like he was seeing if it was real.

Jones didn't usually allow one of his people to get so damn comfortable in his apartment, but Lonnie was different. Lonnie Huggins was a cold-blooded killer. He was the enforcer, the meanest motherfucker to ever take a life, far as he knew.

"Well, Lonnie, I wanna reward you." Jones smiled, knowing Higgins would catch a glimpse of his gold front tooth with the Cobra sign. "I'm going to give you a Cobra Nation Blessing."

"A'right." Huggins crossed his legs.

A'right? Jones had expected more than "a'right." Wasn't everyday he tell someone he was about to get four bricks of cocaine, free of charge. But this wasn't no ordinary cat.

"You also gonna do something for me, Lonnie."

"What you want me to do?" Huggins sat up, his elbows on his knees.

Jones leaned back, nodding. He glanced at the mirror on the wall, trying to get his eyes to look flat and threatening. He couldn't.

"I want to expand the Nation," Jones said. He paused to let that sink in. But the killer sitting on his couch just stared at him. "Those hooks"—Jones couldn't bring himself to say Vice Lords—"and GDs are making money hand over fist in Minnesota. I want my part. We can make money there. Lots of money." Jones thought he could see a little gleam of interest in Huggins' stare.

"What you want me to do about it?"

"I'm going to need somebody I can trust there . . . that's you, my brother." He watched closely and finally was rewarded. Huggins smiled; his eyes lit up like a crackhead at a pipe, except Lonnie's look was loaded with mean. It only lasted for a heartbeat before the stone-cold stare came back. Jones thought the glance of happy Lonnie might even be worse.

"I figure you get four keys from the Blessing," Jones said. "Then I might throw you another key or two at a discount, and BAMM—there it is. You in business. You be the man in Minneapolis. Answer only to me. We be almost equals, almost. You'd have your own niggers. You could bring a few with you and recruit the rest. Shit, you'd have your own enforcers, too, wouldn't have to dirty your hands no more. If things get bad, I send up some boys. POW, POW, and they come home. Poh-leece never catch us."

"When this gonna happen?" Lonnie settled back into the couch, stroking the leather like he might want one of his own.

Cecil watched him, but the cold, flat stare never changed. "I make a call. You pick up the Blessing, shit, tomorrow. Pick the boys. Shit, you be gone soon."

"Make that motherfuckin' call, Cee." Lonnie stood and stretched. "Now I'm gonna go see Latricia 'bout some pussy."

Chapter 4

Bad News

0945 Hours—Saturday

Latricia Gibbons stood naked in her bathroom, staring at her reflection in the broken mirror. Her breasts felt heavy on her chest, her jaw ached and her back was stiff. Despite the beating she'd taken last night, her lemon-drop hair coloring still looked fresh. She'd almost forgotten what it felt like to have a bloody nose after sex. Well, the bleeding hadn't started again while she was asleep. She had that much going for her. It was like she remembered. Lonnie hadn't changed much. Why did she think jail could do something to change him for the better? Never had so far. It could always be worse, though.

She stepped out of the bathroom clutching a towel to her chest with one hand while she wiggled one of her front teeth with the other. As she came down the hall, she could hear him eating, crunching cereal like he didn't have a care. He was at the table in the kitchen under the green phone. The walls were yellow, decorated with what was supposed to look like African art. One burner on the stove was lit, giving the place a gassy smell. A can of red pop was open on the table among stacks of dishes.

Lonnie looked bigger than she remembered. His time in

prison wasn't spent lying around. There was a new tattoo on his forearm, some Mickey Cobra bullshit, a crescent moon and a five-pointed star. She had always figured things would be the way they used to be before he went to jail. But she had been hearing rumors. She had suffered his love, but there had been money, a lot more than she got from the state. Some things could be forgotten for those kinds of presidents. Not forgiven, just forgotten.

"So, you fittin' to go back to work for Cee or what?" she asked. Lonnie looked up at her. She saw his stare and knew he expected her to shut up. But she had questions. "Things be like they was, right? You be working for Cecil again, stay here with me?"

He reached for the pop, brought it to his mouth and gulped it down. A red stream leaked down his chin.

"People be talking, Lonnie. They say Cecil doing something special for you. That you be leaving the Greens."

He slammed the can on the table. The dishes rattled and the empty can fell over. His eyes locked on hers and the hard stare turned colder, more threatening. She knew the look for what it meant, but something wouldn't let her give up. She tried to look back with as much disrespect as she could. His temper was on edge, but she knew she had to push it. She had heard rumors.

"You fittin' to take me with you?"

"People talk too much. I'm fittin' to shut your mouth." Lonnie stood and flipped the table over, sending the cereal, pop and a dozen other things scattering across the floor.

Latricia jumped back, the towel falling from her grasp. She reached for it, but then just tried to cover her nakedness. He stepped up and smashed her on the side of the head, knocking her into the wall.

"Ain't none of your motherfuckin' business what I'm

fittin' to do." A backhand across the face sent her staggering into the front room. She flipped over the couch, her leg whipping into a lamp, knocking it to the floor. It shattered, scattering pieces across the tiles.

He slammed her down and jumped on top. As he threw punch after punch, he yelled, "You want to know what I'm fittin' to do next? You want to know what I'm fittin' to do next?"

Latricia tried to cover up, but he was too strong. His punches found the places that hurt. Lonnie loved to hurt. It was like he lived to beat people down. She couldn't cry out or open her eyes. She tried to cover her face and stomach, but he kept pounding her.

Suddenly he stopped and got up, losing interest in her pain as quickly as he had wanted to inflict it. Latricia gagged and coughed.

"You ain't nothing but a tired, played-out hoe," Lonnie said as he walked into the hallway.

She tried to open her eyes. But only one worked and it felt like it was glued shut. Yet she could make out that he had walked down the hallway into her bedroom. She let her eye close, and for a short time there was no new pain.

"You still here? I'm talking to you." Lonnie's foot hit her in the back. She woke and bit her lip to stop the groan. She wasn't going to give him the satisfaction.

He stepped into the kitchen and picked the phone off the wall. She struggled to watch him as he retrieved a piece of paper out of his back pocket. Latricia saw the bulge in his waistband as his shirt came back down over his pants.

Lonnie's fingers were so thick, it was hard for him to hit only one number at a time on the telephone. He had to hang up twice before he got it right.

"Boo there?" Lonnie looked over at her. "This's Lonnie. I need to talk to him."

Latricia rolled over. She could hardly hear from the ringing in her ears, but she knew what she had seen, the black handle of a gun in his waistband. And she knew he'd hidden two in her closet before he went off to jail. She'd found them just a couple of months ago. Looking for some shoes she thought she'd saved. Didn't find the shoes but she'd found those damn guns. She wondered how many people they'd killed. Should have tossed them down the damn garbage chute when she'd had the chance. Yeah, right. Then Lonnie would have thrown a beating into her like nobody's business.

"Get ready, Boo. We fittin' to take a ride." Then, lowering his voice, "Lonnie, motherfucker! Who you think it is? You better be outside." He slammed the phone against the wall and left it hanging.

He came back to her and kneeled, grabbing a handful of bloody hair. "Bitch, you ain't going no fucking place." He let go. Her head dropped, hitting the floor with a wet thump. "Got it?" Despite the pain, she felt a wave of relief as she heard him go out the door.

Things could always be worse.

Chapter 5

Dropping a Dime

1000 Hours—Saturday

The phone started ringing and Macbeth hoped it was for him. He'd heard Sergeant Ryan's lecture on the need to be on time more than enough already. Save it for the guy who was late, Mike Zito. He was late again, and was late just about every day. Maybe it was Zito on the phone, taking the day off. He hadn't been in to work yet with his new piercing; if his tongue didn't slim down, he'd probably never come in.

Timmy Hagen, Macbeth's regular partner, reached for the phone. "Eighteenth District Tac." Hagen put a finger in his free ear, apparently because Ryan just kept on rolling on about tardiness. "You're going to have to speak up."

"Hold on." Hagen looked over to where Macbeth sat on the prisoner's bench. "For you." He held up the receiver. Macbeth got up and made his way past his teammates, several of whom gave him envious looks. He walked over to the desk, took the phone from Hagen and rolled out of the office.

"Hello."

There was silence. Then he noticed breathing, not quite heavy, almost wheezing. "Hello?" He took his sunglasses off, as if that would improve his hearing.

"Listen, Macbeth. This Latricia. I got sumthin' for you."

A couple of years ago, when Macbeth had first gotten to the Eighteenth District, he'd helped Latricia out of a jam. He'd locked up her boyfriend, Lonnie Huggins, when everyone knew the charges would never fly. But he'd been willing to do what he could. They'd developed a sort-of relationship after that, where they'd help each other out. He mostly helped her, on account of her kids, but eventually she came to trust him and sometimes gave him useful information. She knew a lot about what was happening in the world of the Mickey Cobras. But now, Latricia sounded hurt. Like she might have a broken nose, or something like that. He knew the sound. He'd had plenty of nose injuries, playing hockey. Was Lonnie out of jail already?

"Go ahead." Macbeth fished in the pockets of his coat. There wasn't anything to write on, but he came up with a pen. As Latricia began to talk, he reached into the office and grabbed an envelope from the incoming mail tray.

"Lonnie Huggins fittin' to get into his car. He got a pistol on him. He be riding with that boy people call Boo. They 'bout to get in the car now." It wasn't difficult to keep up with her; the words sounded like they came out hard and painful. He pictured her in the kitchen with her head hung over the sink, bleeding, with a towel pressed against her face. Yeah, Lonnie was a real piece of work. He wondered where the kids were, or who had they been pawned off on.

"What kind of car, Latricia?"

"Lonnie's car. You know, the one I been drivin'."

"Yeah, ragtop Beemer with the 'GCI bumper stickers." He couldn't believe that he'd had to ask.

"Uh huh. That the one a'right."

"What's Boo's real name?" He could think of at least

three Mickey Cobras that went by the nickname of Boo.

"I don't know, but he live on the sixth floor of 1150."

Macbeth could hear the exhaustion in Latricia's voice. He'd been trying since he first met her to get her and the kids into a shelter. He knew that she had chosen the life that constantly beat her down. But the kids hadn't, and that's really what bothered him most. Time and time again, she returned to Lonnie and the gang life, so what chance did those children have? They'd be lost before they even got to school.

"You hurt bad? Want an ambulance? Let me take you and the kids to a shel . . ." The line went dead. Macbeth turned back into the room and hung up. He stuck the envelope in his pocket. Looked like roll call was over—everyone was talking at once—and still no sign of Zito.

"Hey, Teddy. Is there a Cobra nicknamed Boo that lives on the sixth floor of 1150?" Macbeth shook his coat off and threw it on the table. He picked up his vest, slid it over his head, securing the side-straps down snug.

Theodore Ketchum was just light-complexioned enough that his freckles could be easily seen. He was in his late forties. He flipped through his infamous, small, spiral notebook while he sat by the office's only window. He and his partner, Franklin Jamal Hampton, had been on the Job for about twelve years, confined entirely to Cabrini Green. Ketchum stopped his search and put the notebook on his leg. "Antwan Simms. What's up?"

Macbeth's regular partner, Timmy Hagen, was on light duty since he'd had his shoulder pinned together. Zito, his current partner, was late. What else was new? Everybody else was either gone or tied up with something else. Timmy would go out in a second; he'd been complaining about being cooped up, but Ryan wouldn't hear of it. The sergeant went out as much as his paperwork allowed. They were lucky to have a supervisor like him. No one backed you up better on the street or on paper.

"Sarge, I just got a call about Lonnie Huggins. He's out and supposed to be driving around with a gun." Macbeth grabbed a set of keys off the vehicle board. He turned around to find Ryan looking at his watch. Ketchum was already in his coat and Hampton was reaching for his, after putting the notebook away.

"Go out with Teddy and Frank. I'll call when Mike gets in." Ryan sat back in his chair, reluctantly staring at the pile of paperwork on his desk.

"I'll get the radios," Hampton said.

Macbeth left the room quickly and took the stairs from the second floor two at a time. He threw his coat on as he ran from the building through the garage in back.

The old maroon Chevy was parked behind the District office in the diagonal slots on Superior Street. The doors were unlocked and the windows were covered with ice. When the engine caught, the heater came on full blast, blowing frigid air. Macbeth revved the engine and turned the heater off. A minute later, a short chirp of the siren got Ketchum and Hampton's attention as they came out of the garage door. It took another minute before he could see well enough to drive. His patience was growing thin.

He drove north on LaSalle as Hampton handed him a radio. He slipped the short-stem Motorola Sabre into a large pocket on his vest. He turned it on and took a left on Chicago Avenue.

"Your information good, Macbeth?" Ketchum asked from the backseat.

Macbeth looked in the rearview mirror at him and nodded. He knew Ketchum had a great system of informants in the Greens, probably the best of any copper he knew. He suspected Ketchum was pissed he hadn't gotten a call first. Ketchum acted like he was top dog in Cabrini, and he liked to show off, too.

"Yeah, Teddy, it's good. Let's just hope that we catch up to him." Macbeth turned north on Orleans and accelerated. "He's driving his silver Beemer." Macbeth could hear pages rustling behind him. Ketchum's book was never far from hand.

Ketchum said the plate number out loud, followed by an accurate description of the car, down to the two WGCI radio station bumper stickers.

"That's it." Macbeth turned west on Division. The concrete looked dry enough. He floored it. As they came in sight of the sixteen-story building at 1150 North Sedgwick, Macbeth quickly scanned for the Beemer. The parking lot was on the west side of the building, off the street. In a matter of seconds, it was apparent to all that there was no silver BMW to be found, and they sure hadn't passed it on the way there. Macbeth felt the rush of adrenaline diminish.

He hooked through the lot and drove onto the ice-encrusted sidewalk skirting the south side of the building, penetrating deeper and deeper into the housing projects. They combed Cabrini Green for half an hour with no luck.

The radio erupted with static and the unmistakable sound of Sergeant Ryan's voice. He told the dispatcher to send them into the district. Before Macbeth could get to his radio, Ketchum got on the air from the backseat. *Ten-four, on the way in. By the way, no sign of what we were looking for earlier.*

Macbeth caught a glance of Teddy's face in the rearview.

It was practically split in two. The Cheshire Cat didn't have shit on Teddy Ketchum. Macbeth figured Zito must've finally dragged his ass into work. He couldn't help but wonder how his tongue was doing.

Chapter 6

Patience

1400 Hours—Saturday

Macbeth shifted the unmarked Chevy into drive and crept along the north curb of Division. The easternmost edge of Cabrini was kitty-corner across the street, but Macbeth stopped by a garbage can made out of steel mesh. Zito, sitting next to him, lit a cigarette. The smoke was almost welcome, compared to the smell that lingered after their lunch. Sammy's dogs, and fries, and Zito had to have grilled onions. Macbeth rolled down his window. Better to freeze than gag.

Earlier, when Ketchum and Hampton had dropped off Macbeth, it had taken awhile to get Zito out of the office. Ryan wasn't happy with his arrival time and kept him in, letting him know just how pissed he was. Zito seemed to be making every effort to keep his mouth shut. Knowing Zito, that was a bit unusual. That meant the stud had to still be there.

Once Zito was released from his purgatory, they got in the car and Macbeth had raced back to 1150 North Sedgwick. They'd been on the thirteenth floor, knocking on doors. No luck, but then again, they hadn't been looking for any. Macbeth needed to talk to Latricia, had to know

41

she was all right. As cover, they knocked on all the doors on her side of the building, asking about a fight that never took place. Latricia's was the fourth door they pounded on. She hadn't answered the door, but she had looked out the peephole. She muttered something like she was okay, then had left the door. Macbeth was satisfied, for the time being.

Now they watched Division and Orleans. Macbeth played a hunch that Huggins would come by this intersection. Any other would bring him through rival gang turf, and that could be dangerous, even on a Saturday afternoon.

They hadn't spoken much before lunch. Zito apparently wasn't too happy with the way things had shaken out at the tattoo parlor. Macbeth expected as much, and he felt guilty for not getting his tongue done as he'd promised. But the sergeant from the Fourteenth District made it clear that one of them had to go into Fourteen and process their prisoners, and Zito was in no condition to do that. Macbeth didn't get home until after ten that morning.

"So 'Eddy weally said you didn' have shi' on da air, huh?" Zito laughed with a huff that was cut short. Macbeth didn't know if he was commenting on Ketchum's personality, trying to keep the smoke in his lungs a little longer or if his tongue still hurt. He found himself hoping that the tongue was hurting. Everyone on the team got along, but sometimes Ketchum's attitude did grate on people's nerves. He was a good copper, though.

Macbeth balled up the waxed paper and stuffed it into the grease-stained bag. A can of Diet Pepsi that had already gone flat was on the dash. Fucking Sammy. Probably expired. He was a cheap bastard, buying expired pop out of the back of the delivery truck. Macbeth took the can and drained it. He had to get rid of the aftertaste left by the dogs. Wouldn't last, though. In another half hour, he'd be burping and have to experience the whole meal over again. Zito loved the food, and ate here as often as he could talk Macbeth into it. At least the price was right. Sammy might be cheap, but he wasn't stupid.

Zito dropped his cigarette into his pop can, then grabbed Macbeth's ball of garbage before he hopped out of the car. He made a jump shot with the bag, but missed with the can. He had to bend over to pick it up. His coat rode up over his gun, then his belt.

Zito stretched after he slam-dunked the can. His black nylon Army surplus jacket was open and had a reversible orange lining. He had on jeans, insulated boots and no hat. His ears were red. His jacket barely covered his 9 mm Beretta 92F, two extra mags and cuffs. He'd been in the military—well, the Air Force, actually. He hadn't spent one night in a trench or foxhole, never had been issued a rifle, not at least permanently. He'd been an air traffic controller but, with few college credits, found himself directing traffic of a different kind upon his discharge. He was still in good shape, but his stomach pouched over the top of his jeans.

Macbeth shifted in his seat and adjusted his Carhart. It was unzipped, but somehow had bunched into a knot behind his back. He reached around and found that it wasn't his coat, but his cuffs. They had slipped up his belt and were digging into his kidney. Macbeth figured he'd start wearing his handcuffs in front of his gun, the way they were teaching the recruits now. It made sense, really. He'd only been out of the academy for eight years, but it seemed a lot longer when he heard the recruits talking. They made him feel old, and he was only twenty-nine.

Macbeth bet that Huggins had left the Greens earlier, and had gotten on the expressway. Otherwise, they would have found him. He had to show up. Macbeth believed

Latricia. For all of her faults, she was usually right on the money when Lonnie beat her. Macbeth wanted something good to come out of her pain. Maybe if Huggins got sent up again, she'd take her kids and leave the projects for good. He knew he was being naïve, but he was hopeful for the kids. As it stood, they didn't stand a chance.

A car turned onto Division.

Bingo, asshole at twelve o'clock. "Mike!" Macbeth reached for the gear shift.

Zito hurried back to the car and hopped in. "Thee 'em?"

"At the light." Macbeth ripped the lever into drive and gunned it. Zito pointed at the convertible BMW. There were several heads in it. Macbeth nodded. "Can't let them get too close to the jets."

" 'Ut him off!" Zito's hand hovered by the door release. " 'Ut him off!" The light changed; the cars waiting with Huggins started to roll. Macbeth blew the red light and swung into the intersection, jamming on his brakes. His car skidded, stopping inches from the BMW. Macbeth bailed out of his door a split second after Zito. Guns drawn, the officers approached.

Macbeth knew they had the right car. Sure as shit, Lonnie Huggins' stare bored into him. He didn't even look surprised, but, as he got closer, Macbeth could see what little emotion was on Huggins' face slip away. To be replaced by what had to be rage. He knew he was caught. Nowhere to run.

Lonnie Huggins stared at one cop, then the other. His right hand gripped the .380 by his leg. He knew these two. The tall one with dark hair had sent him to prison on some bullshit. The short one had been there, too. But it was the tall one that had lied on him. Macbeth. Nobody did that to

Lonnie Huggins and got away with it. But Huggins knew the .380 wasn't big enough to get these two right now. He needed something bigger for that. Couldn't drive. Fucking cars all around. Couldn't run. Not with four bricks in the car. He was fucked.

"Thee 'ands!" Zito yelled, stepping to the driver's side of the BMW.

"Now!" Macbeth forced himself to keep an eye on all three of the occupants. He didn't think he knew the other two, but if they were with Lonnie, they were dangerous.

Huggins' right hand was out of sight in his lap. The passengers slowly brought their arms up over their heads. Hands empty. They seemed calm, like they'd been here before. Huggins eased his hand out slow, sneaky-like.

"Gun!" Macbeth took the slack out of the trigger. A little more pressure and . . . But Lonnie dropped the pistol to the floor.

Shit. He'd been so close, too. Macbeth followed Huggins' hands as he raised them over his head. Empty. Huggins had to be pissed. Caught like a rat.

They took the two passengers out first. They were clean. Macbeth didn't recognize either of them. They'd get their names later. Once they had the two secured, they brought Lonnie out. Macbeth searched him with Zito covering. Macbeth recovered a different gun from his pants pocket, a small .25 semi-auto. Macbeth slid the little gun into his vest pocket, then cranked Lonnie into a painful arm bar. He didn't so much as grunt. He might be an asshole, but he was tough. With Huggins cuffed, Macbeth recovered what ended up being a Lorcin .380 from the floor of the front seat.

Zito called for an assist car. When a Housing North car

45

arrived, they pulled everything into the lot of a failed pizza delivery store. Apparently you couldn't deliver pizza in the shadows of Cabrini Green. They searched the BMW. Nothing. Macbeth completed contact cards on the two passengers, Antwan Simms and Dedrick Dease, and after their computer checks came back clear, they were let go.

"Eighteen sixty-four David," Macbeth said into the radio. *"Give me a mobile with eighteen sixty-four. Sergeant Ryan."*

The dispatcher raised Ryan. It sounded like he was still at his desk, on paperwork. Hagen was probably cranking him up about being stuck inside. Macbeth didn't know who to feel more sorry for.

"Sarge, this is sixty-four David. We're on our way into Eighteen with the offender we were looking for earlier."

"Ten-four. Any weapons?"

Macbeth could feel the beginning of a smile tug at the corners of his mouth. He keyed the radio, *"Two."* He released the switch. "Kiss my ass, Teddy."

Chapter 7

The Preliminary Hearing

0930 Hours—Monday

It was a Monday morning in Branch 42, a satellite felony courtroom at Belmont and Western, part of the Circuit Court of Cook County. It was crowded, but it always was, particularly on a Monday. It stank, too. The heater was going full bore. The place smelled of stale sweat and . . . funk, and this in the dead of winter, too.

Judge Margarette Coleman-Brown slid her reading glasses to the end of her nose. She wanted to take a deep breath, but she didn't dare. Not when it reeked like it did. Instead, she sat back in her chair. How she hated the beginning of the week.

She had recognized that her sour moods were no longer contained to just Monday mornings. Her disposition began to darken as the afternoon waned on Sunday. It wasn't fair to her family; they were suffering from her crabbiness. She had begun to doubt whether a felony trial room was worth the price, but doing bond hearings and prelims was a necessary step to get there. Yeah, life would be good then. There weren't many black female trial jurists. She didn't see how they could pass her again. The next seat had to be hers. It had better come soon, though.

She sighed and wondered if a fan might not help with the odor. But stirred-up funk was still just that. It occurred to her that the bench sat up high in the room. Was funk hot air? Or did the hot air rise and bring the odor with it? She could get lower in the room, but then she'd be closer to the source. This wasn't getting her call handled. She gave a nod to her clerk. "Let's get the in-custodies out of the way next."

The clerk flipped the last in-custody file open. "Mister Sheriff, bring out Alonzo Huggins." The holding cell door clanged open and two deputies escorted a black man out. He was wearing a Department of Correction tan jumpsuit with the sleeves ripped off to expose arms that were thick with prison muscle. His hair was pulled tight in cornrows. She hated that style. It looked stupid and was associated too strongly with the whole "thug life" motif. If that wasn't enough, the man wore on his face an expression of utter contempt. She couldn't tell if it was meant for her personally or just for the whole legal system in general.

"Are you Alonzo Huggins?" she asked, as the man was brought in front of her. Jailhouse tattoos ran up and down his arms. He made her uncomfortable. And that was hard to do. "You will either say yes or no."

"Yeah." Huggins flexed his hands. The sheriff's deputies must've felt the same way about him. There were two, where one usually sufficed.

"Do you live at 1150 North Sedgwick, apartment 1301?" This day couldn't be over quick enough for her. She had to admit, though, she was glad this asshole wasn't going anywhere. He looked like a real piece of work.

"Yeah."

"Do you have an attorney, Mr. Huggins?"

"Yeah."

48

"Who's your attorney?" She had to admit to being a little surprised. What self-respecting member of the bar would want this guy as a client? Then again, were there any self-respecting attorneys to begin with?

"Mr. Sherman Gold."

She raised an eyebrow. Ah, that's who. Gold was in it for the money. No. Not just the money. He liked the glory, too. The action too, or, as she was sure he would say, the challenge. Huggins must have quite a bit to have Gold for his counsel. "Is Mr. Gold going to be here today?"

"He outta town."

"Public Defender appointed for the purpose of the preliminary hearing," she said to the court reporter. She had briefly entertained the thought of giving Huggins a date. She'd just as soon not see him anymore today. It was bad enough, as it was.

"That's bullsh . . . I want my lawyer!" Huggins raised his voice. He turned to the Public Defender's bench. Steven Reifman, the courtroom's PD, sat at the table. He was a skinny, nearly-bald white man in a brown, wrinkled suit two sizes too big for him. He looked like what she expected Bob Cratchet to look like. Overworked and underpaid. But, he was still a good, competent attorney.

"Mr. Huggins, you're not getting a continuance. Public Defender appointed. Take him in the back, Mr. Sheriff."

She sighed, feeling worn out. Maybe Traffic Court would be a better alternative?

Steven Reifman took his stack of court files from the clerk and sat down at the Public Defender's table. There were a lot of cases, as usual. He was handling the call without a partner, as usual. At least his day wasn't as bad as the one it seemed the judge was having. Then again, most of her Mondays were crappy.

He quickly looked through the folders. Since he'd worked in the office for twelve years, he'd come to know what to look for. This group of defendants was typical, except for Alonzo Huggins. Maybe it was going to be an interesting call, after all. He put the Huggins file on the top and stood.

He walked behind the bench to the detention area. The sheriff just nodded at him as he passed. As he got close to the holding cell, Huggins stood. He'd been sitting on the metal bench: big, mean-looking, muscular, with a face that would freeze the heart of the bravest rabbi, particularly his eyes. Alonzo Huggins had absolutely frightening eyes. Like death whacked-out on crack.

"Mr. Huggins?"

"Yeah."

"I'm the PD appointed to represent you today. My name is Steven Reifman. I'm going to be your attorney." He opened the file but couldn't bring himself to look into those eyes staring at him through the lock-up bars. He waited for some kind of indication that Huggins had heard him. There was none. So he had to look up. Shit. "I said I'm representing you."

"What charges?"

"Two counts Unlawful Use of a Weapon."

"What 'bout my car?"

"Well, let's see." Reifman scanned the case report. "It seems, Mr. Huggins, that your car was towed and impounded. It's the law now that if you get caught with a gun, they can confiscate your vehicle."

Reifman compared the case and arrest reports for discrepancies. None. Huggins had been caught the day after release from prison with not one, but two, handguns.

Reifman became aware of Huggins standing within feet of him, staring. He felt the skin on his forehead start to burn. He knew Huggins could reach through the bars and snap his neck.

"Who tricked on me?"

"Excuse me?" Reifman took a step back.

"Who gave me up?"

"I can't tell from these reports." Reifman looked up, but stared at the bridge of Huggins' nose to avoid eye contact.

"Give me some paper and something to write with. I got to get a message to my boys."

"Mr. Huggins, really." Reifman grew brave. He lifted the files in front of his chest, as if they would protect him from the cold chill that gripped his heart. "I can't give you anything to write with while you're in the bullpen and, even if I did, I would have to read it first. If it contained any criminal content, I'd have to disclose that to the State's Attorney. I'll not be a party to a criminal conspiracy."

The clank of the lock-up door echoed throughout the holding area. Reifman took another step back and looked over his shoulder. The man entering the detention area was white, in his middle to late forties, and almost glowed with a golden hue. No salon tan. He had long salt-and-pepper hair pulled back in a ponytail and was dressed in a tailored Italian suit. Reifman stole a glance at Huggins. The monster was smiling; one gold tooth showed.

"Good morning, Lonnie," the man said, approaching. "I'm Sherman Gold, Mr. Huggins' private counsel. Nice to meet you." He held out his well-tanned hand, decked out in gold and diamond rings.

Reifman was surprised. But recovered well enough to hand Gold the Huggins' court file, instead of his hand. Better to be done with this one, anyway. A little too interesting, thank you very much.

Sherman Gold opened the file and read. Finished, he turned to make sure no one was within earshot.

"Not good, Lonnie," he whispered. "Out Friday, pinched Saturday."

"I got to get my car back."

"We're going to have to beat the case first. Might. Might get it back." Even Gold felt uncomfortable giving Lonnie Huggins bad news. "There's a different standard at the impound hearing. It's only a preponderance of the evidence, not beyond a doubt anymore. On the face of it, I'd say that you're screwed."

"Man, fuck all that. I got to get my motherfuckin' car!"

Gold fancied he could feel the heat from Huggins. He'd caught a last-minute flight from his Palm Springs home, cutting short his winter getaway, just to represent this client. He was well aware of the compensation he had received from representing the Mickey Cobras, but the money carried risk. Taking it was dancing with the devil; the fire was always there, so you could get burned by the slightest misstep.

"What happens if we lose the case?" Huggins asked.

"Well, you'll go to prison on the violation, and they'll try you for the gun case." He looked up at his client, definitely the worst of the worst.

"No, what be happenin' to my car?"

"Sold at an auction, more than likely." Gold watched as Huggins grabbed the bars. The muscles in his arms bunched and swelled, but the bars held.

"You got to tell my boys something for me," Huggins said. "We got to be gettin' that car back. Shit still be in the motherfucker. Tell 'em I be calling Boo's."

Gold nodded and turned to walk back out to the court-room. "I'll tell them," he said. "I just don't see them being able to do anything about it. Not right now."

"Hold the fuck up," said Huggins. "Who gave me up?"

"Says here," Gold said as he read from the case report, "that a concerned but unknown citizen flagged down the officers, after seeing you get into your car with the gun sticking out of your pants."

Huggins smirked, shaking his head. "Now, ain't that some motherfuckin' bullshit."

The hearing took place ten minutes later. There was a finding of Probable Cause and a filing of the Violation of Parole. Gold wasn't surprised in the least. He'd better plan for a jury. His client would be doomed at a bench trial.

He put on his cashmere coat, draped a scarf over his shoulders, packed up his briefcase and picked up his wool cap off the bench. As he walked out through the courtroom, he nodded at the woman with the swollen face and yellow hair. He remembered her from Huggins' last court case; she must be his girlfriend. The title apparently carried some penalties. Gold had a hard time looking at her left eye, which was swollen shut.

There were two young teenagers with her. They must be the young men Huggins spoke of. Gold couldn't help but wonder what kind of criminal backgrounds they must possess. Job security, no doubt.

The entourage followed him from the courtroom to a secluded corner. The young men stepped in front of the woman. They didn't identify themselves, nor were they asked to. The young man on the left crossed his arms and stared at him. The one on the right chewed at his thumbnail and looked at Gold with the eyes of a tired, old man.

"Boo?" asked Gold. The man on the right nodded, still chewing on his nail.

"Mr. Huggins asked me to deliver a message to you." Gold thought for a second. How could he say this without saying it? He was a lawyer; it should be easy. Yet, it had to be within their ability to understand. It'd have to be practically spelled out and that, of course, was a good way to get into trouble. "He wanted me to tell you that he's concerned about some . . . property he left in his car. He's hoping that you'll be able to get it back for him. He'll call you at Boo's apartment."

Boo stopped gnawing his fingernail long enough to shoot a glance at the other man. He nodded back. Boo dropped his hand. As he spoke, he looked away, talking into the corner of the lobby. "So, Lonnie only be charged with them guns, not no drugs, right?"

Gold nodded his head. You just couldn't be subtle these days. The sun of Palm Springs seemed like an eternity ago. He looked out of the window and watched the snow fall. Traffic was going to be terrible on his way back to his office, and his calendar was empty for the next two weeks. Wonderful.

Latricia Gibbons' swollen mouth twisted into a grin after Boo and Dease had walked by. A trickle of blood ran into her mouth from her split lip. The attorney began to bundle up. He told her that he was doing everything he could for Lonnie. Things was looking up. Shit, things could still be worse; he could get Lonnie out.

Chapter 8

A Call to Boo

1330 Hours—Three Weeks Later—Tuesday

Huggins watched from across the table as his attorney closed his briefcase. Gold put on his coat and threw a scarf around his neck. Gold never looked at him, after he had finished talking. He rapped on the window. Huggins looked down at his tan jail clothes. This shit wasn't right.

The deputy came back to the room after Gold had been escorted out. He opened the door and held it. Huggins didn't need to be told he was expected to leave. He stood, chewing the corner of his lip. There was a small piece of paper on the table. A date, address and time were written in Gold's handwriting. Huggins picked it up.

"I be needin' to make a phone call," he said to the deputy.

The deputy followed him over to the pay phones on the wall. Four were being used by prisoners and the fifth had a broken sign on it.

After a couple of minutes, a phone was free, which was more than could be said for Huggins.

Donna Collins was a mother of four who lived in a two-bedroom apartment on the sixth floor of 1150 North Sedgwick with three of her children. The second oldest, Jermaine Taylor, stayed with her mother in Mississippi. She'd sent him there a year and a half ago, so that he wouldn't hang around his older brother, Antwan. She knew that Boo—that's what everyone called him—was no good. She also knew there was nothing she could do about it. The kid scared her half to death. All she could do was see that none of the other children fell in with him. The others were too young to come under his influence. She hoped Boo would be gone or dead before she had to send them away, too. It tore at her heart to be away from Jermaine, but it was the only way she could save him. He had begun to idolize his drug-dealing big brother.

The phone rang.

"Hello," she said, half asleep.

"This is a collect call to Boo from Lonnie Huggins. Press one if you accept the call," said the recorded voice.

"Yes." She pressed one and called for Boo.

Before opening his bedroom door, Boo turned off the VCR and pulled on his baggy boxer shorts. His mother and the twins stayed in the other bedroom. He walked into the kitchen and took the phone from his mother.

"What's up?" Boo said into the phone.

"Motherfucker, lost my motherfuckin' car," Huggins said in a low voice. "Listen . . . you fittin' to go to a poh-leece auction?"

"A'right," Boo said, as he brought his thumbnail to his mouth and started to chew.

"Get some money from Cee and go get my mother-fuckin' car."

"A'right."

"Shit still in the motherfucker." Boo recognized

56

Lonnie's mood and knew what he could be like when he was really mad, like he sounded now.

"A'right." Boo tasted the salty flavor of his own blood.

"I be taking care of you when I get out. You understand?" Huggins was quiet, as if he wanted Boo to think about being taken care of. "I be taking you with me when I move up."

"A'right."

"Write this shit down. And don't be on no CPT either." There was silence. Like he'd be on Colored Peoples' Time with some serious shit like this going down? What'd Lonnie take him for? Boo took his thumb out of his mouth long enough to get a pencil. Then he took his mother's work schedule off the counter.

"A'right."

Chapter 9

Notification

1700 Hours—Wednesday

On the sixtieth floor of the John Hancock Building, Robert Russell Starr, Jr. answered his phone. "Hello, Bob Starr." He was the son of supermarket mogul, Robert Russell Starr, Sr. and Vice-President of Starr Markets. It had been a long day. Lately, they were. Starr had been in the business for fifteen years now. The supermarket business was, he always joked, eat or be eaten.

Starr's executive assistant, Rachel Westing, sat in the chair across from him. Her eyes left his and looked over his shoulder out the window onto the Chicago skyline.

"Yeah, Mr. Starr," a voice said on the phone. "My name is Jimmy Lewicki. I work down at the City Auto Pound." The background noise was filled with ringing phones, men shouting and the echo of clanging metal. Lewicki spoke with a heavy south side accent.

"How can I help you, Mr. Lewicki?" Starr stared at Rachel's face as she continued to look past him.

"Well, sir, I have been led to believe, so to speak, that you was interested in getting a real nice car."

"As a matter of fact, I'm in the market. Pardon the pun."

"Well, I talked to a guy, name of Max, last week." Lewicki paused to swallow. "He says that he was looking. I tried to get back to him earlier today, but I got his wife. She says to me that it's you who was looking. So I call you. I hope you don't mind?"

"No, not at all. Max works for me on occasion."

"Well, this Max says you're looking for something nice, but reasonably priced."

"That's correct."

"Well, see, I run the auction down here at Thirty-Ninth. Just so happens that we got a car in this afternoon that you might be interested in. It gets auctioned off tomorrow. It's a real looker and will go quick. Know what I mean?"

"I think I do." Starr tried to recall his calendar in the morning. Fairly loaded, but nothing that couldn't get pushed back a bit. "What time does the auction begin?"

"Well, people get in at eight. Auction don't start 'til ten. We give people a couple hours to look over the goods."

"I see."

"But . . . ahh, well . . . maybe you could get here early, look this baby over. Maybe drive it outta here before we even open."

"How early?"

"I get here at six."

"Okay." Starr leaned back in his chair and stretched his legs under his desk.

"Well, it would be better if you were gone by six forty-five, latest," said Lewicki. "That's if you want the car, after you see it."

"Ummmm," Starr said. "What model are we talking about here, Mr. Lewicki?"

"BMW, 325i convertible. Two years old, low miles, very nice."

"I guess I'll see you at six. Will a company check suffice?"

"Ahhh, well, I was hoping for cash."

"Oh, I'll bring some of that, too."

"Well, thank you, Mr. Starr. See you at six."

Starr placed the handset into the receiver and crossed his hands over his head.

"What's that all about, Bob?" Rachel was looking at him again. She had the most gorgeous eyes. Big, brown, sexy. Total bedroom eyes.

He stood and walked around his desk as she turned to face him. He stopped and considered her. Reaching down, he offered her his hand. Her grip was warm and firm, like so much else she had to offer. He pulled her up to him. "I might've found you a company car."

She smiled. What beautiful straight, white teeth she had. Her parents must've spent a fortune on them, like he and his wife were spending on their daughter's orthodontics. Without any further speech, he leaned down and began to kiss her. Her mouth opened and her tongue pushed past his. He dropped his hands to her breasts, warm and firm, all right. He caught the glint off his wedding ring in the office window. He had a moment of panic, thinking it was some kind of camera light, or something. No problem. He led Rachel from the desk to the couch. It was out of sight of the window. As he settled down, he pulled Rachel on top of him. That felt better. She began unbuckling his belt. Funny, how he felt worse about the thought of getting caught than the guilt of the act itself.

Chapter 10

The Early Bird

0410 Hours—Thursday

Robert Starr left his home in Winnetka early the next day and was parked in his reserved spot by five a.m. He went into his office for thirty minutes before catching a cab on Michigan Avenue, outside the John Hancock building. The ride to the city garage was conducted in silence. A light snow had begun to fall, making the streetlights and traffic signals seem soft and dreamlike, but as the cab drove deeper into the South Loop, the landscape looked anything but soft.

The cab pulled in front of a massive red-brick city warehouse ten minutes early. Starr stayed in it until a minute before six, when he saw several workmen enter the building.

He stepped through the door and looked around the large interior. To his right was a wooden counter topped with several phones. Two men stood behind it. One man was drinking coffee out of a steaming cup. The other was drinking a Coke. Starr walked up to the counter.

"James Lewicki?"

"Yup," said the man with the Coke. "That'd be me. You must be Mr. Starr. Nice to meet you." Lewicki extended his hand. Starr noticed Lewicki's weak grip and moist palms, despite the cool temperature. The man with the coffee walked away, leaving them alone.

"The pleasure's mine."

"Well, the car's over here." Lewicki stepped from around the counter and led him toward the back. "It's in great shape. Only two years old. Doesn't have five thousand miles on it." They entered a rear bay and stepped into a side garage separate from the larger warehouse floor. The convertible sat under fluorescent lights. The Beemer was silver with a black top. Starr walked around it and noticed two WGCI bumper stickers on the rear bumper.

"Those mag wheels are worth twenty-five hunert, easy," Lewicki said, pointing to the rear right wheel. "Of course, if you don't want 'em, I could take 'em and cut some off the price."

"Not necessary, Mr. Lewicki. I like them myself." He thought it would make the car appeal to Rachel, who was so much younger than he.

"Only problem, Mr. Starr, is that this car must a been owned by some shine drug dealer 'cause it smells of pimp oil like you wouldn't believe." Lewicki made a face. "Should come out if you have it professionally cleaned, though."

"I'm sure it will."

"So, you like it?"

"Yes, I do. This will do nicely." He removed the company checkbook from his suit coat inner pocket. "How much do I make the check out for?"

"I gotta get eight Gs for it, Mr. Starr." Lewicki wiped his sweaty palms on his blue workpants. "I'm gonna put it down as the first sale at ten o'clock. Nobody'll know that you was here this early."

"Sounds good to me." Starr made the check out to the

City of Chicago. He handed it to Lewicki, who stuck it in his shirt pocket while looking around, as if he were worried about getting caught. Starr removed his wallet and took out five crisp one-hundred-dollar bills. "This is for you, Jimmy. It's been a pleasure doing business."

"If you don't mind, I gotta get you to fill out this card. Everybody does here. I'll be sure to time-stamp it after ten or so. Make it look all legit." Lewicki handed him a four-by-six index card. "Just name, home address, shit like that." Starr filled it out and handed it back. Lewicki took the card and gave him the keys. "You can pull out the back, hang a right in the alley and another right on Thirty-Ninth. The light will be Michigan. I guess you'll know your way from there."

Starr was about to get into the car, when a question occurred to him. He called out to Lewicki, who was about to raise the garage door. "You guys searched this car good, right?"

"Oh, yeah," Lewicki said as the door lurched up.

"Good," Starr said.

Blowing snow swirled into the garage, to melt on the oily floor.

Chapter 11

Too Late

0800 Hours—Thursday

Dease parked the Blazer a block east of the city garage on Prairie. Boo sat next to him. The wind had picked up. Snow blew inside the truck when they got out. They were dressed in black starter jackets with red five-point stars on the front and back.

They half-jogged to the door, got in and found that the auction was crowded. There were people all over, kicking tires and looking under hoods. They walked all around, but couldn't find Lonnie's car. They split up and looked again.

"Man, fuck this shit," Dease said later. "Lonnie's shit ain't here."

"Supposed to be, man," Boo said. "He's gonna be one pissed-off motherfucker, we don't come up with that car."

"He's gonna have to be pissed-off, then," Dease said.

"It's my ass." Boo had checked out the employees on his last lap around the warehouse. He figured there were a couple possibilities. He looked for them now. Now that he was worried.

There he was, the best prospect. A black teenager about Boo's age was filling a bucket with water. As Boo walked over, he looked up.

"What's up?" said the kid. His baseball cap was cocked to one side.

"I'm looking for a car."

"Plenty of them around."

"No. I'm looking for a special one." Boo looked around like he was about to let the kid in on a big secret. "Silver, drop-top BMW with three-spoke chrome mags."

"You too late. That drove off this morning, man." The young man picked the bucket up and set it on a dolly. Sudsy water slopped onto the floor. " 'Bout six-thirty."

"Motherfucker!" Boo couldn't believe it. He wanted to hit something. "Motherfuck this shit!"

"Stay cool, my brother," the young man said. "Car that special to you?"

Boo shut up. Hear this guy out, he told himself.

"Maybe I can find out where it got itself to." The young man looked around himself, now. "That be worth something to you?"

Boo calmed down. Cool. A'right. It ain't over yet. Fat lady ain't even warmed up yet.

He nodded.

"Give me thirty minutes." The young man looked around again. "I need to get paid, though." Boo went into his pocket and brought out a money roll for him to see. "Cool."

"I be outside in my ride. We on the corner of Thirty-Ninth and Prairie."

"Cool." The kid said, pushing his dolly into the crowd.

Thirty-five minutes later, Boo saw him standing on the corner, looking around. Boo cracked the window and waved. As the kid approached, Boo opened the window all the way; the cold air shot in.

The kid handed Boo a folded piece of paper, which he opened and read. "Man, where the fuck's Winnetka?"

"Fuck if I know, but that's where he live."

"Don't be fucking me."

"I got it off the paperwork. That's the for-real shit."

Boo went into his coat pocket and slipped him a fifty. "We a'right?"

"We cool, man."

Two hours later, Boo stood in the kitchen of his mother's apartment with his right arm across his chest. His left elbow rested on it, with his thumb stuck into his mouth. He wasn't looking forward to this call. Lonnie told him he would call at noon. He knew Lonnie was going to freak. At least Boo knew where the car was. He jumped when the phone rang.

Donna Collins knew her son was in trouble. She didn't need to be told. Not wanting to hear anything of it, she got up and went into the bedroom. Cradling the twins to her chest, she rocked on the bed, not for their comfort but for her own. She could still hear her son. A son she didn't know anymore.

"But, but, Lonnie," Boo said. "But, Lonnie, I know where the motherfucker be at. I know, man." There was silence. It seemed like he could feel the violence creep across the line. He held the phone from his ear. His thumb was wrapped in the front of his shirt, staining it with blood. Boo pulled his thumb back out and brought it to his mouth.

"Go get that motherfuckin' car, Boo," Lonnie said. "I don't care what you go to do. Get my fuckin' shit!"

Boo picked at his thumbnail with his teeth. The line had gone dead. He knew that he had to get the car and the coke back or he'd be as dead as the phone line.

Chapter 12

Lunch

1100 Hours—Thursday

Starr drove his Lexus GS300. It had snowed all morning, but now the snow had stopped. Rachel sat beside him in her winter coat, but she had those gorgeous, shapely, young legs sticking out. He was getting an erection just looking at them.

He had dropped off the BMW at a carwash. Once back at the office, he'd called and made sure that it would be ready after lunch. The carwash owner was expecting him to drop off his car for a wash and wax, too. After lunch they'd pick up both cars. The Lexus rolled quietly westbound on Ontario Street. He saw the long line waiting to get into the carwash.

He couldn't help but smile as he pulled in front of the first car. An attendant ran out and opened the door for Rachel. Starr got out and handed him the keys. They walked to the Middle Eastern restaurant next door. When the hostess found them a private table in the corner, Starr ordered a bottle of wine.

"It's awfully nice of you to give me a company car," Rachel said. She had dressed for the occasion: beautiful red dress, sexy, with just a hint of slutty.

"It's my pleasure." He handed her a wine glass. "You're very valuable to Starr Markets." He toasted her. "Here's to you." He caught her staring over the glass at him. "I don't want you thinking of the car as some sort of payoff, though," he said. "You've deserved it for a long time, even before we became involved."

"Thank you," she said as she took a sip of wine and nodded. He wasn't sure whether she was complimenting the wine selection or acknowledging his little speech. "I don't consider it a payment," she said. "If that's what it is, I wouldn't accept it. I'm not a prostitute, you know. I happen to think I do deserve it. I've done more for this company than say . . . Catherine or Monica, and they both have company cars."

He had to agree. And she was much better in bed than either of those marketing associates. And he should know. He looked at her. God, she was hot. He knew it would make him look like an ass, but he couldn't help himself.

"Now, about this weekend," he said.

She put a ripe cherry tomato into her mouth. "Yes."

"Well?"

"I'm just about ready. I've got one more thing to get, yet." She smiled at him. "A little something special to wear."

"I like the sound of that." He knew his blood pressure was on the rise as he felt his groin grow warm.

"How're you getting away for a whole weekend?"

"You let me worry about that," he said. "Bring something warm. It's going to be cold in Door County."

"Oh, I don't think we'll be outside all that much. Do you?"

His eyes drifted down to her tits that were barely contained in her top. "Well . . . Actually, no."

Rachel sat in the driver's seat of the BMW on Erie Street at the light. She couldn't believe that this was her car now. Bob had told her not to mention it to anyone yet. Where had he gotten it? It did have some miles on it and two WGCI bumper stickers: not her radio station, that was for sure. She didn't care anymore. Her parents would be so proud. She began to think about telling her mom and dad. After all, they didn't know anyone from work. They lived up in Green Bay, Wisconsin. What harm could there be in telling them?

She continued east when the light changed. Her plans were to go back to the Hancock Building, park and shop. She had taken the afternoon off and was going back to work only long enough to validate her parking receipt.

Chapter 13

When Snakes Comes Calling

1340 Hours—Thursday

Boo sat in the front seat chewing his thumbnail as Dease drove. They were headed toward the place called Winnetka off the Edens Expressway. Boo was the leader, as it was his ass on the line. Dease looked over.

"Ain't you 'bout ate that thing down to nothin'?" asked Dease.

"Nah," said Boo, still uneasy about being the point man. He wasn't crazy about the responsibilities and he sure as hell didn't like the penalties either. It was a little better now. They had a plan.

They'd found Old Willie in his apartment in 1157 North Cleveland, another Cobra building in Cabrini. Old Willie had driven a cab and usually worked the south and west sides of the city, but he knew where Winnetka was.

He showed them on a map where to go and even wrote it down for them. He went over it with Boo and Dease, while the other two, Melvin Early and Anthony Raspberry, sat watching TV.

Before they got on the expressway, they had stopped in a

parking lot where Anthony Raspberry, who they all called Pookie, stole a license plate from a snow-covered car. He'd quickly put the plate on the rear of the Blazer and threw the other plate in the back. Pookie squeezed into the backseat with Melvin.

They'd been on the road since one, fighting heavy traffic, getting madder and madder sitting on the highway. They were about to turn around, thinking they'd missed their turnoff, when they saw a sign for Willow Road. Dease eased up and took a right.

At Green Bay Road, they turned right again and slowed. The street signs were smaller and harder to read. Not as many streetlights, like in the city. Dease passed Cedar, the street they wanted. He drove back around the block. Boo couldn't believe his eyes. The houses were huge, just like in the movies.

On Cedar, they drove even slower. The streets weren't plowed and the addresses were hard to find. Then, there it was.

"Somebody's home," Boo said. "They sidewalk is shoveled."

"Yup," Pookie said, wedging himself between the front seats. "Man, these motherfuckers got some serious money!"

"Boy!" Early said. He kept wiping a small, round spot on the window to see through. "Boy!"

"Four niggas just can't walk up to the door in this motherfucker," Boo said, looking over at Dease, who nodded. They parked three blocks away from the house at a small corner park that was crammed with new swings and monkey bars. Boo noticed how much nicer the playground was than their lots in the Greens, even though he had outgrown them a lifetime ago.

"You right 'bout that shit."

"Go back 'round by them stores. I got me an idea." Boo thrust his hips up off the seat and dug into his pants pocket. He pulled out a wad of cash.

Rosemary Starr was on the phone when the doorbell rang. She wasn't expecting anyone. Who would want to go out in this crummy weather anyway? She shuddered as the doorbell rang again.

"Mom, somebody's at the door. I gotta go," she said into the phone. "Bob's got some business trip this weekend. If the weather improves, I'll bring the kids over to visit you and Daddy, I promise." The doorbell rang again. She didn't want to keep them waiting. "I'll call tomorrow if it's still snowing, I promise. Bye-bye."

She hung up and looked over at the teapot. It wasn't boiling over yet, or even threatening. It could wait. She walked to the front door, wondering, "Oh, I hope they're not too cold." She pulled the door open as the bell rang for a fourth time.

Dease stood on the front porch, looking at the peephole intently through the flowers in his hands. It was the first time he'd held—what'd they call it, a floral arrangement? Yeah. It was the first time he could remember smelling one, too. And here he was standing in some rich-ass white neighborhood with a bunch of flowers. Standing on a porch waiting to bust in on some white folks. He held the receipt in his other hand.

Boo had picked him because he had the lightest complexion of them all. He'd said that Dease being lighter would keep the white people from being too afraid when they answered the door. Boo had warned him to keep track of everything he touched with his bare hands. What did Boo

73

think he was, stupid or something? Well, he'd touched the bell four fucking times now.

The door opened and he stood there looking at a woman. He saw money in her clothes, in her jewelry, in her manner and in her things that he could see over her shoulder. Her face was covered in makeup. Her hair was blonde and shoulder-length.

Rosemary saw the bouquet of flowers held by a nice-looking young African-American who must be cold. "I'm sorry. Step in a moment. Let me put these in some water," she said, taking the arrangement. "Then I'll get you a tip."

She walked into the kitchen. Why would Bob send flowers? He hadn't sent flowers since Bobby was born eight years ago.

Dease left the door cracked and followed her through the house into the kitchen. She laid the flowers out by the sink and knelt on the floor. He looked around quickly, didn't see anyone else. She started digging in a cabinet under the sink. "Man, this is one nice house you got, lady."

He knew the house was huge and there could be more people home. But he couldn't let a chance like this pass either. He crossed the kitchen in three steps and pulled her to the floor on her back. His hand came down hard on her mouth and he stared into her wide eyes. "Don't be screaming, lady. I don't want to hurt you." He said it in a whisper loaded with violence.

He was bending over her with a finger in her face, when Early came running into the room. Early looked over. "We a'right?" Dease asked.

"Don't know. Boo and Pookie checking the house."

An hour later, the Blazer was parked next door in the

driveway. The wife had told Boo that the owners were gone for the winter. Dease and Boo sat in the master bedroom with the woman. They'd found some duct tape in the basement and used it to tape up her arms, hands and feet. It was looped around her head, covering her eyes. She'd stopped screaming, so they peeled the tape from her mouth. Now she was crying and begging, not for herself, but for her kids who were coming home from school soon.

Boo was happy they had the right house, but the woman didn't know nothing about no car. They all had their gloves on, and everything Dease had touched earlier had been wiped down. Pookie and Early were on the first floor in the back, playing X-box.

Boo kept running his hand through the woman's hair. What wasn't taped down.

Dease walked over and stared at the top of her head. He pointed at the hair closer to the woman's skull where it was darker. "See, man." He looked up at Boo. "See. This bitch's hair be brown like everyone else. She just color it."

"No," Boo said. "It's soft. I never felt hair so soft." The woman's whole body shook under his touch. She shook so hard that the bed squeaked. "Please, pleeeease," she cried.

The school bus dropped off the two Starr children at the corner. Jenny put her gloves on, while Bobby threw a snowball as the bus pulled away. Their friends were in the back window, sticking their tongues out. Jenny walked ahead through the deepest snow on the parkway, kicking snow this way and that. Bobby ran up and gave her a shove. She didn't fall. She had good balance. Must come from the dance lessons her mom made her take.

They walked quietly down the block toward home. Jenny got a little excited when she saw a car in the driveway of the

Bendas' house. It died when Bobby told her that it wasn't theirs. Besides, he said, their driveway wasn't even shoveled.

He led the way into the house. They took off their boots at the door. He dropped his coat where he stood, while Jenny hung hers in the closet. She looked at her little brother's boots and coat. She picked up the coat and hung it next to hers, so Mom wouldn't get mad. She took the two pairs of boots and put them over on the rug, out of the way and out of sight. Bobby must've run off to the family room and the X-box.

She went into the kitchen and poured herself a glass of Kool-Aid. She was beginning to wonder about her mom, when a black man came around the corner smiling. She began to scream when someone grabbed her from behind.

Boo removed his gloves and ran his hand through the woman's hair again. The other hand was at his mouth, his teeth tearing at his thumbnail. His dick was stiff.

Dease was over by the window, playing with a Little League bat. Who knew what thoughts ran through that boy's mind? "Man, you ever gonna quit running you hand through the o' girl's hair?" Dease asked. He'd just returned from smoking some blunt—weed wrapped in cigar paper— with Pookie in the basement. "This shit's gettin' fuckin' old."

As soon as Bob Starr opened the door into the kitchen, he knew something wasn't right. The house was too quiet. Rose's Land Rover was still in the garage. Where were the kids? They usually came running when he got home. He was early, though. He was trying to surprise them. Spend a little time with the family before breaking away with the dolly for the weekend.

"Hello," he said. Maybe Rose had sent the children to a friend's house? He walked into the front room and stood at the bottom of the stairs. He could smell something. Unusual. Almost sweet. He couldn't quite place it at first. Then he did. Grass. Rose? Smoking grass?

He heard talking. Faint at first, but it grew. Muffled voices. Adult voices. Coming from his bedroom. So, Rose smoked grass and had a boyfriend. That must be his car next door. Right here in his own fucking house. Under the roof he provided. In his bed.

He took the stairs two at a time. No fucking way. This wasn't going to be some ordinary scene. He had just the thing to make this a memorable experience. How dare she take another man into his house. In his bed. At least he had the decency to take his broads to hotels.

He opened a closet and reached up on the top shelf. His fingers closed on the Browning twelve-gauge and he pulled it out. It was loaded, but the firing chamber was empty. He turned toward the bedroom with the gun in both hands. Its weight was reassuring. He could handle this if he went on the offensive. He wasn't going to kill them, but sure was going to scare the shit out of them. No patsy here. Hell, no. Not Bob Starr.

He crept up to his bedroom door, deciding on the direct approach. Leaning back, he kicked with all his strength. The door flew around, crashed into the wall and stuck. He brought the shotgun up and stepped in. He froze.

A young black man stood beside his bed. Rosemary lay next to him. He had her by the hair. Bob heard her sobs. He saw the duct tape. He saw how her hair was matted in the tape. He saw the tape around her wrists. The shotgun hung forgotten.

Dease jumped when the door crashed open, but reacted just as fast. He swung the bat like a motherfucker who grew up fighting in the jets. The bat hit the white man in the stomach. His shotgun flew across the floor as he bent over and fell.

Dease kicked him. The man rolled onto his side. Dease hit him in the back, high up on his ribs. There was a crack. Then again lower, over his kidney. There was no fight left in this motherfucker. Got me a nice shotgun, too.

Rosemary Starr stood in the shower with hot, scalding water running down her body. It was over—she'd survived. And her children, her children were okay, physically. How long had she been in here? She leaned back against the wall and slowly sank to the floor.

She curled her legs in front of her. Her body shook. What was she going to do? They'd taken Bob. They said if she called the police they'd kill him, and then come back for her and the kids. What was she to do? There was a soft knock on the bathroom door.

"Mommy, are you okay?"

Chapter 14

Decoy

1830 Hours—Thursday

" 'Hy do I haa to be da vicim?" Zito asked. He wasn't enthusiastic about the plan, but at least his tongue was almost back to normal.

"Mike," Ronnie Ryan said. "Trixie doesn't have the experience, not to mention she's female. Timmy's light duty and Macbeth, well . . ."

"Yah, I kno'. Stacey's huge."

"You're the same size as Timmy."

"Ge da sck ou'!" Zito said. "I'm 'aller an 'immy."

"Barnhill's too well-known," Ryan continued, as if he hadn't said anything. "Ketchum and Hampton are black and don't fit the profile."

"Yah, I kno'. I jus' never 'id dis afore." He hated it when Ryan was right, which was damn near all the time. The guy had, like, a photographic brain or something. The only time Ryan was out of sorts was when he was hung over; then he was usually still right, just an asshole about it.

"You'll do fine," Ryan said.

Zito was wearing ankle boots with very tight jeans tucked into them. He had on a sweatshirt with a lined jeans jacket that was two or three sizes too big, because he had bor-

79

rowed it from Macbeth. A baseball cap was pulled so low, his ears were pushed out.

The temperature had risen to some extent, making it possible to run the street robbery decoy. The district had been getting killed by quick stick-ups and pickpockets. Lieutenant Rosetti had told Ryan to run a sting when the weather broke. So here they were, and Mike had to be the bait. Was this how a worm felt?

"Now, Mike." Ryan handed Zito a pair of thick, black eyeglasses. "You need to look like a victim. You can't be eye-fucking people."

"Come on, Ronnie. I sai' I never 'id dis afore. Didn' say I was supid."

"Just keep your head down. We'll be next to you in the van, and a couple cars will be only seconds away." Zito thought he could detect a slight grin on Ryan's mug. He didn't even want to see Macbeth's evil-looking smile.

"Do I go' ou wear dese?" Zito looked through the non-prescription lens. "I a'ready 'ook 'ike a bi' 'ork."

Ryan felt Macbeth slip the van into park, after he had pulled up to their spot. They were parked at LaSalle and Illinois. Macbeth got out and walked away. He turned the corner and was gone.

Ryan was still trying to get comfortable by the side window of the van when Zito came staggering into the bus stop. Ryan had a perfect view as Zito, the drunk, leaned back against a brick wall.

"Listen up," Ryan said into his radio. "Mike's in place."

There was a splash inside the van. "Fuck me," Hagen said in the rear.

"What?" Ryan wanted to roll his eyes. Why had he

agreed to bring Hagen along? He should've left him in the office, typing reports.

"Fucking spilled Coke down my boot."

"Quit moving around," Ryan said, as Timmy kept shifting around in the back. He was making noise and making the van shake.

"Fuck! Fuck! Fuck! Fuck! Fuck!"

"Come on, Timmy. Knock it off." They were going to be spotted before they even got things started. Hell of a way to start the night.

"Motherfucker!"

"*Macbeth's in,*" Petty said on the radio a block away.

"*Ten-four,*" Ryan responded. "Timmy, I want your eyes on Mike. Period. You watch nothing but Mike. I'll watch everything else."

Hagen moved to a different window. His boot squished. He apparently didn't like what he saw, so he moved again. His boot squished again.

"Timmy," Ryan said. "You keep rocking this van and making noise, people are going to start wondering what we're doing in here."

A half hour later, Zito was still leaning against the brick wall, looking at his boots.

"Ronnie," Hagen said.

"Yeah." Ryan stifled a yawn.

"Mike's supposed to be a street robbery decoy. Right?"

"Yeah."

"With the wallet, right?"

"Yeah." Ryan was still looking at the street, but was wondering what Hagen was driving at.

"But he's had his ass, with the wallet, pressed up against the wall this whole time."

"Mike . . ."

"Not to mention he's eye-fucked every potential asshole that's come along."

"Fuck me."

"Too goddamned cold," Zito said to himself. "Fucking snow. Fucking Ryan and this street robbery bullshit." Zito continued to mutter to no one, as he stepped out of the tavern where he had been warming up. He figured the team should be in place by now. The wind hit him in the face. "Shit." Zito turned his shoulder.

"Fucking Timmy and his brittle bones." Zito tugged on his pants. He was so pressed into them, it felt like they were going to roll down his legs. "Hockey secret, bullshit." Zito reached inside his pants and tugged on the pantyhose that were supposed to keep him warm. Macbeth had to be laughing at him. Probably was lying about his hockey player secret bullshit. He'd never heard of hockey players wearing pantyhose to keep warm. Fuck Macbeth, too. At least there had been some small improvement in the attention he was getting from the girls.

Zito turned into the alley where he was supposed to set up. Ryan and Timmy were in the van, waiting for him. The wallet was in position. The tip was supposed to be sticking out of his back pocket, with some bills exposed. His pants were tight, so the wallet would be secure and hard to get out.

Halfway down the alley, the cold took hold of him and he stopped to take a leak between some dumpsters. The cold always did that to him. He almost didn't make it, had to tear a hole in the panty hose. After he finished, he checked the wallet. It was good. He staggered from between the dumpsters and moved toward the street. When he wobbled out of the alley, he made his way to a wall by the van.

Zito and Ryan had decided he should play the sick drunk routine this time. They figured his back to the street was the best solution to his cop's instinct of challenging everyone who approached. Ryan had been pissed earlier. Zito hadn't seen him that mad in years. Zito knew he'd fucked up, but this was Timmy's kind of thing, not his. And it was Hagen's fault he was out there in the first place. Timmy would be buying rounds all night, if he had anything to say about it.

Zito leaned into the wall and coughed. He made some retching sounds, shrugged his shoulders and spit. He felt stupid, but knew pretty soon the cold would change that to the feeling of being frozen.

Ryan tensed.

"That's pass number four," Ryan said. He brought his radio up. *"Stand by,"* he whispered. *"Male black. Green fatigue coat. Blue pants. He's eyeballed Mike four times."*

The man rounded the far corner.

"How's Mike?" Ryan asked.

"He's gotta be cold," Hagen said. "But he's hanging in there. It's been forty minutes."

After five minutes, the man came back around the corner. He stopped and looked up and down both streets.

"Here we go," Ryan said.

The man started walking toward Zito.

"Stand by," Ryan said into the radio. *"Same subject's approaching Mike."*

The man stopped ten feet from Zito and looked around again. This was it.

"Come on, motherfucker," Zito said to himself. "Come on. Do it. Before I freeze, you asshole!"

Zito could hear the footsteps. What the fuck! He stopped again. The man took a couple more steps. He was close now. Damn near next to him. Another step. Zito could see his work boots splashed with paint. "Yeah, come on. Game time!"

"Stand by," Ryan said again.

"What's he doing?" Hagen asked.

"Leaning," Ryan said. "He's got both hands in his coat pockets." Ryan had his radio to his mouth. "I think he's saying something to Mike."

"What's he saying?"

Zito waited and waited. Finally, he looked up, mustering the stupidest "drunk smile" he could.

"Officer," the man said, pointing back at Zito's ass. "Your wallet's sticking out of your pocket."

Chapter 15

God Help Me

2300 Hours—Thursday

Robert Starr couldn't focus his eyes. He could feel nothing but pain, pain that radiated through his broken body. He knew they were going to kill him. He was pretty sure that they hadn't killed his wife and kids, and God, poor Rose. He couldn't begin to imagine what they had done to Rose.

Where was he? He heard them mention a couple streets that he knew were on the south side. From what he could tell, they'd been on the road for a while. He didn't know for how long.

All they wanted was the damn car. The beemer. He'd admitted to buying it. Offered to get it back for them. No problem. He promised not to go to the police. Anything they wanted. They could have all his money.

It was starting to hurt too much to stay alive any longer. He looked forward to death and no more pain. He was going to miss his kids, though. He hoped that they'd be able to cope with the memories of today.

At first, he'd offered to return the car to them. He said that it was just as he had gotten it. They wouldn't settle for anything short of its exact location. Right fucking now, they'd said. He told them. He told them where Rachel lived and where she parked. He'd begged for his life. He had children to watch grow up.

They stood nearby and discussed how to make him go away. He could only hear bits and pieces. His own screams rang in his ears, screams that had been muted by the rags and tape over his mouth. "God help me," he prayed.

It was after eleven p.m. and Rachel knew the lights would be off on the sixtieth floor of the Hancock Building. The Office of Vice President Robert Starr, Jr. would be dark and lonely, lit only by the soft glow of the skyline filtered through the coated windows. It would be quiet. Different from the last night they'd stayed late.

Rachel knew the silence would be shattered by the ringing of the phone. It rang four times before the answering machine clicked on. There was no message, just an electronic beep to let the caller know to leave a message. Rachel knew Bob hated voicemail and answering machines. He didn't trust them.

"Hello, Robert. This is Rachel," she said from the phone booth at Houlihans. "I hope you don't mind, but I need tomorrow off. I'm leaving tonight to see Mom and Dad. I'll just meet you in Door County. I know where to go, and ahhh . . . I picked up something you'll like. See you."

Chapter 16

The Photographs

0020 Hours—Friday

"Eighteen sixty-four David, emergency!"

Timmy Hagen spun from the computer screen and reached for the radio lying on the desk.

"Eighteen sixty-four, you've got the air," the dispatcher said.

"Eighteen sixty-four David," Zito said. *"Partner's chasing a male black! Blue coat. Blue jeans. He's got a gun!"*

"From where, sixty-four David?"

"On 534 Scott! Westbound!"

Hagen turned up his radio and could hear the squeal of tires in the background of Zito's transmission. If Zito was doing the talking and driving, that meant Macbeth was doing the running.

"In custody, squad," Macbeth said.

Hagen could hear a little fatigue in Macbeth's voice. Or was it frustration?

"Where are you?" the dispatcher asked.

"Behind 1230 Larrabee." Macbeth was breathing heavy, but you could easily understand him. *"Slow it down."*

As the dispatcher told the responding units to slow down or disregard, Hagen returned to his data entry. Five minutes later, the phone rang. "Tac. Hagen."

"Timmy," Macbeth said. "We've got to take this asshole to the hospital."

"You get the gun?"

"Yeah. A .25. He hurt himself flipping a fence."

"Sure he did, Stacey."

"No, really," Macbeth said. "He fell on his face, jumping the fence."

"Yeah, okay. Whatever."

"Hey, Mike." Macbeth wasn't talking into the phone. "Timmy doesn't believe that this asshole fell going over the fence."

Hagen couldn't hear Zito's response.

"Where're you gonna take him?" Hagen asked.

"Grant. He knocked out a couple teeth and I think he busted his nose."

"Okay." Hagen began to laugh. "I'll tell Ryan."

"No, really . . ."

Hagen hung up and dialed Ryan's pager number. He went back to his data entry. The intercom buzzed a few minutes later.

"Tac. Hagen."

"Ryan in?" Hagen recognized the watch commander's voice.

"No, Cap. He's on the street," Hagen said. "But I got a page out to him."

"I'll get him." The captain hung up. Seconds later Captain Finny was on the radio getting a mobile with Sergeant Ryan. He told Ryan to come into his office immediately.

Hagen called down to the desk and asked what was going on. The desk officer didn't know exactly, but ten minutes earlier they had said that a black woman, about forty, had come in and demanded to see the watch commander. She was pissed off about a couple of plainclothes coppers in Cabrini Green. They assumed she had some kind of beef with them. Hagen paged Macbeth.

"Timmy," Macbeth said, when he called back a minute later. "What's up?"

"You guys have a problem earlier?"

"No," Macbeth said. "Just this dickhead. Why?"

"Anybody around when you took care of business?"

"Timmy." That frustrated sound had returned to Macbeth's voice. "I told you. He fell, flipping the fence."

"Any witnesses?"

"I don't fucking know. What's going on?"

"There's a black chick downstairs in Finny's office. Desk says she came in to beef against a couple tac guys in Cabrini."

"Yeah, so?"

"Well?" Why wasn't he getting it?

"Timmy," Macbeth said. "We're all good here. Nothing to worry about. Okay?"

"Sure." The intercom buzzed twice, as if the person on the other end was impatient. "Gotta go. See ya." Hagen connected with the intercom. "Tac. Hagen."

"Timmy," Ryan said. "I need you to come down here. Bring a radio and a set of keys with you."

Hagen grabbed his coat, radio and a set of car keys before heading to the watch commander's office. He knocked on the door. Ryan opened the door, saw it was him and stepped into the hallway.

Ryan pulled his hand from his coat pocket and handed Hagen a roll of film. "Go get this developed. I want you to go to some one-hour joint and wait for it. Okay?"

"Must be important."

"Don't worry about it," Ryan said. Hagen thought he

seemed distracted. "Take it easy, you're on light duty. Remember?"

Hagen nodded as he left to find the car.

What the fuck did Macbeth do now? He didn't think Macbeth and Mike would be beating someone in the middle of the projects long enough for someone to get their camera and take a bunch of shots. Hell, they usually were pretty damn fair about it. Once someone gave up, that was it. She must've already been taking pictures when Macbeth caught him, or something. Good thing it wasn't a video camera. She might've gone right to the highest-paying television station.

He was halfway to the drugstore when he pulled over. He couldn't let these pictures get developed. Hagen sighed as he slipped his knife from his pocket and began to work at the edge of the film canister. It finally came loose. He pulled the end cap off and tugged the film out. He stretched it all the way out to be sure he exposed it all, before he used his pen to roll it back up. The film slid back into the canister and then he popped the cap back on.

Hagen waited for the film to get developed. It didn't take an hour. The old Korean man running the machine just shook his head as he packaged the prints.

"You no take pictures good." The man shook a feeble finger at him. "Need practice."

"No shit," Hagen said, trying to sound disappointed. "My boss's gonna kill me."

He was gonna make Macbeth and Zito pay for this shit. This was a heavy-duty favor and they didn't even know about it yet. Man, was Ryan going to be pissed.

When Hagen got back to the district, Ryan wasn't in the watch commander's office. He found him in the tac office, typing on a report.

"Sarge." Hagen held up the print envelope. "Here you go. They didn't turn out too good."

Ryan took the envelope and opened it up. He shuffled through the prints and shook his head. "Goddamnit."

"What?" Hagen thought he should be happy. No evidence of anything. He wondered what gave.

Ryan let out a loud breath. "I gotta take them all over again."

"What're you talking about?"

Ryan dropped the pictures on his desk. "I took pictures of the drapes in my front room, so I could match a piece of carpet to them."

Chapter 17

The Mess

0010 Hours—Friday

Boo joined Dease, Pookie and Early in the basement of an abandoned house on the south side. They stood over the white motherfucker, who was laid out in layers of garbage bags and tape. He was alive, for now. They'd told him they were gonna let him go, but Boo knew the motherfucker didn't believe them, especially when they wrapped his ass in those plastic bags. It made things easier, though. Boo was surprised how cooperative he was. Must've accepted it. Boo knew he'd never go out like this. They'd have to take him away kicking and screaming. This white motherfucker was a pussy bitch, nothing but whimpering and crying. Maybe growing up in the projects was worth something, after all.

"We ain't putting him in my truck?" asked Dease.

"He too big to be putting in the truck, a'right," Early said.

"Nah, we can use my auntie's van," Boo said. "It got that door on the side, and I know how we gonna do it." He looked around the basement. "We got to get rid of this motherfucker before the poh-leece catch our ass, though."

Twenty minutes later, Boo and the boys were rolling down the street in the van. It was snowing. The soon-to-be-dead-guy was lying on the floor by the sliding door, crying. They fired up a blunt and passed it around. They laughed. Just another trip.

Five minutes later, Pookie looked out the back window. "Man, is that the poh-leece?"

"Fuck you, man!" Dease said, driving. He started to look in all his mirrors, like he thought the police were creeping up on him from all sides. He was the only one with a driver's license. It was suspended, but he had one. "That poh-leece shit ain't funny."

"I ain't fuckin' around," Pookie said.

"Melvin, look," Boo said from the front seat. "Pookie just too high from all the blunt he smoked today." Early joined Pookie at the back window. Pookie was pointing behind them, but Early shook his head. Boo felt better.

"Can't tell. Could be."

The man whimpered on the floor. Early came back to the middle seat and kicked the man on the ground. "Man, shut up!"

"Get on the highway," Boo said to Dease. Boo knew his plan could be changed a little bit. No problem.

"A'right." Dease turned right at the next corner. They drove along the boulevard through the snow, until the sign appeared for the Dan Ryan Expressway. Boo told Dease to take the first ramp. The suspicious car was gone, but they'd been smoking weed all day. They started seeing poh-leece in every car.

They headed toward Indiana with all the snow. Early started to freak, wanting to pull over and bail out. That was what gave Boo the final idea. Why not here? The snow had things so people couldn't see good. He took the Taurus revolver, loaded with hollow-points, from his coat pocket.

He looked in the back, then flipped the gun, holding it

by the barrel, to Early. He twitched it a couple of times to get Early to take it.

Early just stared at the gun and then looked at him. "Why I got to do it?"

" 'Cause you the only motherfucker here that ain't done shit," Boo said, making perfect sense to himself. "We got to know you in. Can't be worried 'bout you going to the poh-leece."

Early reached out with a shaky hand and took the gun by its fat handle. Boo knew he'd shot at people before plenty of times in the Greens. But Boo didn't think he had ever actually hit anyone. Maybe nobody had, but this guy was just about dead anyways.

"Get over, Dedrick," he said, never taking his eyes off Early. "By the shoulder. Come on, man. We ain't got all motherfuckin' night." Then to Melvin, "Ain't no big thing."

Early shrugged and held the gun out. The barrel was inches from the white man's head.

"No," Boo said. "Push him up against the door."

Early shoved the man against the door. Sitting on the side of the bench seat, Early pressed his foot up against the man's back to hold him still. He shoved the gun into the back of his head. The loose plastic bag hid the end of the barrel.

Early pulled the trigger. The explosion shook the van. He brought the gun back down, pressed it into the bag and pulled the trigger again. The van swerved. The second bullet blew the white motherfucker's head up. Blood splattered up and back from the body. The side window behind Early got blasted with bright red blood, and with white slop. The shit was all over Pookie, too. Then Boo felt something wet and hot on his hand. When he looked, he found that he had pieces of the guy's head up and down himself, dripping, sliding toward the floor.

"Get the fuck over on the shoulder!" Boo shouted. He had to slap Dease and point. Glops of blood flew on the dash. Boo reached over the seat and cracked open the sliding door. Cold air and snow blew in.

At first, Pookie and Early just watched. Finally, Early must've figured out what he wanted them to do. He climbed over to the door and pulled it open, letting in a new rush of snow. When the door was open wide enough, he sat back and began to kick hard at the body. It slid only partway out. He pushed with both feet, slipping in the blood.

As the body slowly slipped out the door, Boo started thinking about how they were going to find a white bitch named Rachel who was driving around in Lonnie's car with four kilos of his shit.

Chapter 18

A Bumper?

0035 Hours—Friday

"Goddamnit!" Wendell Chaney fought the sloppy steering of his Ford Escort. His wife Sharron, sat next to him. "Shit!" He tried to regain control of his car. They'd fishtailed after hitting something in the road. Traffic on the southbound Dan Ryan swerved around him in the heavy snow. It was a miracle that no one had spun out and caused a major accident.

His headlights shone dimly in the snowstorm. He steered his car into the right lane as snow flew everywhere. If it hadn't been for the expressway's overhead lights, he'd have been in deep trouble. The windshield wipers were working, if that's what you called it. They did little more than move the crud from one side to the other.

"Wendell," Sharron said. "You know you shouldn't use the Lord's name in vain." She adjusted her thick glasses.

He looked at her in disbelief.

"You got to be kidding me," he said. "We just get clobbered, our car's fender is smashed in and you riding me about my mouth." He didn't say any more, though. She was a woman of strong will, if nothing else, and he knew better than to argue with her, particularly in matters of faith and religion.

"That's no excuse, Wendell." And another thing, she was persistent to a fault.

He squinted through his windshield. There it was, a large red van. He accelerated as much as he dared; the car shook more than usual. "Baby, write down the plate of that van," he said. "I think he ran over whatever we did."

Sharron dug into her purse and got out pen and paper. She pushed her glasses up off the tip of her nose and leaned closer to the windshield. Wendell knew the crud was far worse on her side, and he expected her to tell him about it at any moment.

"I can't," Sharron said.

"What?" Here it comes, where she tells him exactly how many times she told him to fix the wipers.

"I can't see the plate."

"How about an orange sticker in the window?" Maybe whoever had just bought the van and had one of them new registration stickers or something.

"Maybe . . . I can't see anything," she said. "It's just so hard . . . you know you got to get these wipers fixed. I thought I told you."

He tried from his angle but he couldn't see any plate either. For that matter, he couldn't make out any bumper. Could it have been a bumper they rolled over? Sure felt like there was a lot of damage. Seemed a bumper would have felt different, but still . . .

The front end of his car shook. It probably didn't help that he was driving so fast. They didn't have the kind of money they would need for major bodywork.

"Let me get around front." Chaney changed lanes and floored it. "See if they got a front plate." It took a couple of seconds for the little car to go faster. The Escort slowly passed the van. Sharron looked hard out the window and wrote on her paper. Hard out the window and then wrote on her paper again. She did that three times or so. Then the van eased up the exit ramp at Eighty-Seventh Street.

Chaney didn't have enough time to make it over. He shifted back in the right lane so he would be able to get off at the next exit, Ninety-Fifth Street. "Did you get it, Sharron?"

"Uh-huh. I think so." She held her paper up to what little light came through the windows.

Chaney got off on Ninety-Fifth Street. At first he sat on the frontage road and looked north, hoping the van might come south yet, but it didn't. He pulled into an Amoco Station and got out to look at his front fender. "Damn!" The fender was caved in so badly that the tire rubbed against the torn edges. The grill was smashed in and the headlight was crushed.

Sharron rolled the window down a crack. "What did I tell you about your mouth?"

"I know, but this is really messed up." He wasn't a violent man, but he found that he really wanted to kick something. Guess this was one of those times the preacher was always talking about. Having to do with one's character.

"We'll just have to make a report." Everything seemed so easy to Sharron. But she didn't know exactly how their finances were at the moment. They surely couldn't afford no big body job, and they couldn't afford no new car neither.

"Baby, we only got liability insurance." He shook his head as the wind blew snow into his face. "Maybe I can track down the van and get them to pay. It was their bumper we ran over, anyway."

"Let your friends track that van down." Sharron pushed

her foggy glasses back up onto her nose. "You going to get yourself in trouble playing police. You just a security guard."

Just a security guard, he thought, as he came over to the window and reached in for the slip of paper she had written the license number on. She held on to it for a second, before letting go. Then she rolled up the window and he saw her reach for the heater switch. He walked over to a bank of pay phones, fishing for change in his pants pocket. He punched a number into the phone and turned his back to the storm. "Hello, is Terry in?" he asked loudly over the expressway noise.

"Farmer."

"Terry? This is Wendell Chaney. How're you doing?" Damn wind was trying to steal what little warmth he had.

"Hey, Wendell. What's up?" Farmer sounded relaxed, how only a man who was warm and comfortable could sound. Chaney could picture him sitting behind the desk at the Public Housing Police Desk, probably having something to eat or chatting with some females.

"Listen. I was hoping you could do me a favor." Chaney had to shift to keep the wind at his back. "I kinda got in an accident."

"You okay? You got the wife and kids with you?"

"Yeah. I just got Sharron with me. The kids are with her folks. But we're fine. My car ain't, though."

"What happened?"

"I think a bumper fell off of this van on the Ryan and smashed in my fender."

"You'd better make out an accident report. If it happened on the Ryan, you'll have to call the State Police."

"My insurance isn't going to help me out. I was hoping to get hold of the owner and have them give me the money, without making a report." Before reaching into his coat pocket for a pen, he wiped the snow off the ledge of the pay phone.

"That's where I come in, I take it?"

"Yeah. That's where you come in. I promise I'll never tell where I got it." Chaney gave him the plate information. "I can wait," he said pushing another quarter into the coin slot. Getting the address was the easy part. Getting the money would be a whole other matter.

A minute later, he had the information. Terry made him promise again he wouldn't tell where he got it.

"Terry, can I call you tomorrow if I have a problem?" He didn't want to come out and ask Farmer to go with him. He thought maybe he could do it on his own; he just wanted to know he could call if he needed too.

"I'm gonna be outta town."

"Oh, where you going?" Suddenly the wind felt that much colder.

"Vegas. You need me to set you up with someone from here?"

"I hear it's nice down there this time of year. Nah, I know another guy I can call if there's a problem. And listen, I really appreciate this. I owe you one." Hell, he could handle it. Couldn't he?

Chapter 19

First Stop on the Way to Work

2100 Hours—Saturday

The next night Chaney left for work early. He wasn't due at the seniors' complex until eleven p.m. He'd told his wife that he had to go in to see his police friend who was going to handle the accident for them. She'd been relieved. He knew that his working as a security guard made her nervous. She was always telling him that he wasn't a cop, and to quit acting like one. It was better that she not worry about him. Plus that saved him her lectures. She always lectured him when she worried. At least that's what she said.

He let the little car warm up for a couple minutes. His duty belt was in the trunk, but he had his uniform on under his coat, a white shirt with the eight-pointed Chicago Security star pinned over his left breast pocket and navy blue pants. With his coat on, Chaney was often mistaken for an off-duty Chicago police sergeant, much to his amusement. Sharron probably didn't like it much, though.

The snow had let up since last night, but the side streets were still bad. Chaney drove slowly. At low speeds, the front end didn't shake much. Once on the main streets, he picked up speed. So did the shimmy in the front end.

City snowplows had been doing their job and it looked like they were going to be at it a while longer, if the weathermen were to be believed. They were calling for more snow.

He drove north on State Street to avoid the expressway. He turned west on Garfield Boulevard. It was a large four-lane street with a tree-covered median. He turned right onto Bishop, a one-way street, and slowed down. He drove slowly, knowing he was getting close.

He nearly came to a stop after crossing Fifty-Fourth Street. Bishop was lined with single-family homes. The street was hard traveling; deep grooves and ruts in the packed snow threw his car back and forth. Both sides of the street were lined with snow-covered cars, making it a tight fit. The streetlights were on, but it was still hard to see through the windshield; he should've taken the time to clean it. He was going to have to get those wipers fixed soon. He rolled down his window and kept an eye on the even-numbered houses on the west side of the street. There it was, 5326, a dark little bungalow. The only light was in the back. Oh, well. Here goes nothing. Chaney parked in an open spot halfway down the block.

The sidewalk hadn't been shoveled, but it had been heavily traveled, making walking easier than driving. Chaney found the front walk packed with snow, but a path had been worn through it. Three steps led to a small, concrete porch covered in ice. He climbed the porch carefully and tried the doorbell. Nothing. He knocked and waited. Nothing. He knocked again louder. He reached over the railing and rapped on the window.

He thought he heard something. He shifted his body so he wasn't directly in front of the door. He'd seen the police do that when they worked together. The porch was small, making it hard to not stand in front. What room there was, was on ice.

Liberty Collins thought she heard someone pounding on her door. She hit the mute button on her TV remote and kept watching "M*A*S*H." There it was again. Yep, someone was at her door. With a bit of effort, she got up off the bed and walked to the window. She looked out to see a man standing on her porch. He looked like a cop. Pulling her robe closed, she went to the door. He knocked on the window like he was family or something.

"What you want?"

"My name is Wendell Chaney. If you're Liberty Collins, I need to talk with you about your van."

The door opened a little and Chaney could see an eye staring at him like a black marble set in white. "What about my van?"

"Listen ma'am, it's awful cold out here." Chaney opened his coat to show her his uniform shirt and badge. "You think we could talk inside, please?"

"You a poh-leece?"

"No, ma'am. I'm a security officer." He let his coat stay open a little.

"Okay." She unlatched the door and opened it. She stood in the doorway for a second, blocking it with her fat. "You don't look like no killer, no ways."

He knocked the snow off his patent leather shoes before going in. He stood in the doorway, not wanting to track in any water. There was no rug to wipe his feet. She walked toward the back of the house through a hallway crowded with junk. He wondered how she fit without knocking anything over. He shrugged and followed.

"So, what 'bout my van?" She kept going down the hall.

"Are you Ms. Collins?"

"Yeah, that's me."

"Well, ma'am. Last night I was driving on the Ryan behind your van when your bumper fell off and damaged my car," he said. She didn't say anything but walked into the kitchen. He was a little concerned. He didn't know if anyone else was in the house, but he followed her anyway. He looked around; the room was lit by an exposed cluster of bulbs on the ceiling. Flames flickered from the burners on the stovetop and the oven door was open, too. It gave the room a peculiar smell. A couple of roaches scurried from crevice to crevice. His stomach flipped. He might save some money by not eating tonight.

"I don't know nothing 'bout that," she said, taking a glass from beside the sink. She looked into it. Her mouth twisted and she put it down, taking another. Her mouth returned to the frown she'd answered the door with, as she poured herself a glass of water. She didn't offer him any. "I ain't seen my van for days."

"Do you own a red van?"

"Yep. Sure do."

"Do you mind if I use your phone?"

"Ain't long distance, is it?"

"No, ma'am," he said, removing a business card from his wallet. He crossed over to the phone on the wall and picked it up. The crusted earwax and dirt on the earpiece made his stomach flip again. He dialed the number on the card and held the receiver away from his ear, as if something might jump on him.

He punched in some numbers on the phone and hung up. "You said you haven't seen your van for a while?"

"That's right. That's what I said."

"Were you driving it last night?"

"Nope."

"Is it here now? Can I look at it?"

"Nope."

"Listen, ma'am. I'm not looking for no trouble," he said. "I just want to get some money to fix my car."

"I don't know 'bout shit."

He bit his lip to keep from raising his voice, knowing that would make the situation worse. He tried to think how the police would handle it. No, he couldn't do that. The officers he knew would be yelling and screaming and threatening to take her to jail. He couldn't do that. That never worked for him.

"Ma'am. I got a wife and two kids. We don't have the money to fix the car, and it has to be fixed."

"I got bills, too," she said crossing her arms over her chest.

"I'm sure you do." Chaney waited.

"If that Boo wrecked my van, I'll beat his black ass. That motherfucker be sorry when I get hold of him."

"Excuse me?"

"I loaned my van to my nephew. He still got it."

"I guess I need to talk to your nephew, then." Maybe he was getting somewhere.

"You sure do." She crossed the kitchen to the phone. She opened a drawer below it and pulled out an address book held together with a rubber band. He thought the book looked older than he was. She wrote down an address and phone number for him. Boo was at a friend's house.

Chapter 20

The Second Stop

2200 Hours—Saturday

The big house on Sangamon Street was easier to find than the one on Bishop. It was just south of Garfield, on the east side, by an alley running parallel to the Boulevard. It was a tall frame house that looked to be leaning a touch north, like it was trying to get away from the abandoned wreck next to it. There were no lights on the porch, but there were lights on inside.

Chaney climbed the wooden stairs of the rickety front porch. The roof creaked under the weight of the snow. Water dripped onto his head as he knocked. He heard sounds of running feet. A black boy about seven years old opened the door; he looked excited, as if he were expecting someone.

"Hi," Chaney said, bending a bit to get to the kid's level. "I'm looking for Boo. Is he here?"

"Momma!" the boy yelled. He stared at Chaney. "Is you a poh-leece?"

"No," Chaney said.

An attractive young black woman came to the door and pulled Pee Wee around and behind her. She looked hard at Chaney, kind of cocking her head, too. But she didn't say anything.

"Hi, ma'am. My name is Wendell Chaney. I'm looking for Boo." He figured he better tell her how he came here expecting to find Boo. "Liberty Collins told me I might find him here."

"You the poh-leece?" She still hadn't opened the door, hadn't even reached for it.

"No ma'am. I'm a security guard on my way to work." She seemed wary, but he was wondering if Boo was even there.

"Boo's here. What do you want?"

"I need to talk to him." Chaney pulled his hands from his coat pockets and held them out. Kind of like a peace sign or something.

"About what?" She sure was asking a lot of questions.

"About the van he's driving is all." At this rate, he was going to be late for work.

"Come on in. I'll get him. He upstairs with my brother."

Chaney stepped in. The young boy sat on the couch and stared.

"My name is Wendell." Chaney held out his hand. The boy came over and pumped his hand. The kid sat back down and stared. Like he was expecting Chaney to start doing tricks.

"My name is James, but people call me Pee Wee."

"Nice to meet you, Pee Wee. Do you have a phone?"

"Yep." The kid didn't point it out or nothing.

"I've got to call work. You think your mama would mind?"

Pee Wee finally pointed to a phone on a table on the other side of the room.

"Thank you." Chaney took his wallet out, looking for the card. "What's the phone number here, Pee Wee?" Pee Wee recited it proudly; it sounded like he'd been practicing.

Chaney made his call and hung up.

He stood when the girl came bouncing down the stairs a minute later. She told him that they'd be down in a minute, then disappeared toward the rear of the house. She took Pee Wee's hand and dragged him with her down the hall. Chaney was alone and was glad he had used the phone when he did. Did she say "they'd" be down? He didn't suppose that he could get away with just talking to Boo alone. Shit. Maybe he'd been a little rash, after all.

Another minute passed before he heard footsteps on the stairs. He looked at his watch. It wasn't even ten fifteen. If this went quick, he would have plenty of time to get to work before eleven. If . . .

Two young men in their late teens or early twenties stepped off the stairs. Both were black, about five-ten or five-eleven. The one on the right was bigger, muscle-wise. The other, on the left, chewed on his thumb and it looked like he'd really been digging in it. Yet, somehow he still looked smarter than the other guy. Both had the eyes of men who had seen and done violence to the point that they didn't care anymore. Chaney didn't have to see the tattoos to know they were gangbangers. He could tell by their eyes. He'd worked at enough project complexes to know that these two were hard-core trouble. And here he was, standing in their living room. Suddenly his wife's warnings didn't sound so silly any more.

The one chewing his thumbnail introduced himself as Boo. The other one mumbled that his name was Pookie. Boo went back upstairs to get the van keys. Chaney wasn't happy when Boo returned, wearing his coat. He knew he shouldn't have come here. His gun was in the trunk of his car, not doing him any good. Coming here had been a big mistake. He should've gone to the police in the first place, but that wasn't going to get his car fixed. These guys did sound like they were concerned and all, but still . . .

Pookie led them out the back. The cold air stung Chaney's face. He'd gotten used to the inside temperature but now began to shiver, really shiver, like he couldn't control himself. Or was he just scared? He didn't see any van. He didn't see a garage either, except the one belonging to the abandoned building next door. And that was where they were headed.

Once inside the garage, Boo walked Chaney around the rear of the van. The bumper was still there, with no license plate. They walked to the front. It had a bumper too. Boo noticed the front license plate was still on. Motherfucking Melvin!

Oh shit! Chaney thought. He wheeled around just in time to see Boo reach into his waistband and pull out a large revolver. Boo pointed it as Chaney stared at the muzzle of the gun. Goddamnit!! His wife's nagging words came to mind: "Leave it to the police."

Chaney only saw the board for a flash, as it struck him upside his head. He only knew the pain shot through with red streaks for a split second before the ground smacked his face.

Chapter 21

Overtime

2230 Hours—Saturday

The referee blew his whistle and waved his hands furiously in the air as he skated into the knot of players. They kept digging and pushing for the puck before breaking up. The white team, the cops, skated to their bench. The firemen, in red, being close to their side, hopped off the ice, too.

The game was tied, going into overtime. Two-all. Macbeth skated to the bench and sat down. He was tired. The fire department had some big guys. They had a lot more time to work out, too. There was still a lot of animosity running between the two departments from the firemen's strike in the early eighties, though none of tonight's players had even been on the job back then.

Someone pounded on the glass, yelling his name. Macbeth turned and saw Erin McAuliffe, his girlfriend. She was five-foot-seven and weighed one hundred and thirty pounds. This he knew. Well. She had on a green turtleneck under a dark blue Notre Dame sweatshirt, one of his, in fact. Her jeans framed her butt perfectly, and her dark, curly hair was held off her face in a ponytail. He waved. She kept yelling. He held up his hands and shrugged.

"What?"

She shoved his pager against the window, but he couldn't make out the numbers. He stood and climbed up on the coach's bench.

"What's up?"

She gave him the pager. "You got a couple pages. The last one has a nine-one-one on it." He didn't recognize the numbers. He handed the pager back.

"Would you call them and find out what they want?"

"I suppose."

"Thanks. I'm a little tied up."

"Very funny, Stacey." Erin turned and walked up the aisle. As he watched her ass, he suddenly didn't feel quite so tired.

When Macbeth stepped out of the locker room, he saw Erin leaning against the pop machine, looking at her hiking boots. His brown T-shirt was tucked into his old jeans, and the hockey gear bag was slung over his shoulder. He held a Diet Coke can, more wet than cold, to the right side of his face. She shook her head as he approached. His left eye was open.

"How many this time?" she asked. He set the bag at her feet. She stretched up on her toes and kissed his good cheek. She pointed at his nose, which was red and swollen at the bridge. "That broken again?" She shook her head and lowered her voice, like she was talking to herself. "Why do you even play this silly game, anyway?"

He fished into his pants pocket with his free hand for some change. "You want a soda?"

"No."

He pushed the coins into the machine with one hand, made a selection. The machine shuddered, dropping another diet can into the bin.

"I think I opened an old scar," he said. He reached down and took the can, switching the new can to his eye. He opened the old can one-handed and took a giant gulp. It tasted good.

"Ouch!" She pointed at the two butterfly bandages.

"Looks worse than it is," he said. "My nose doesn't feel broke, either." He took another drink. "And, if you must know, it's for the chicks."

"What?"

"I play the game for the chicks," he said, smiling. "And to win."

"You got one evil-looking smile, you know," she said, putting on her coat.

"No shit," he said, before finishing the soda. He wiped his mouth. "Hey, McAuliffe, who paged me?"

"Oh, I forgot," she said. "The second number, the one with the nine-one-one, nobody answered. The other one, some lady answered and said she didn't page nobody."

"White lady or black?"

"Black, I think. Why?"

"Just wondering." He walked over to a phone sitting on the arena information counter. His .45 was exposed on his belt, along with his star. The attendant turned the phone toward him.

"Who're you calling?" Erin asked. He cradled the receiver against his shoulder and dialed one-handed as she zipped up.

"The office." He opened his second can and took another long drink. "Timmy. Stace. Listen, do you think Ryan would mind if I took the rest of the night?" He shook his head. "No, I'm not going to the damn hospital. Well . . . yeah, but I think the butterflies'll hold." He sat the can down and motioned for Erin to come over to him. "We won." He reached for the pager. "Can I? No, not you, Timmy." He took the pager from Erin.

Macbeth gave Hagen the two numbers, knowing he'd have time to figure out who called. Hagen knew the routine by now. Macbeth always had to know who paged him. Before he hung up, Macbeth told him they might meet up at The Boss Bar later.

Macbeth slipped his old police leather on. He bought it when he was in the academy, from a guy who was retiring. He'd worn it ever since, but Captain Finny had finally told him earlier this winter he had to get rid of it and get a new one. This one was just too beat-up.

He walked back to Erin. "How about a beer?"

"I thought you'd never ask."

Chapter 22

Late-Night Visitors

2245 Hours—Saturday

"I ain't paged nobody," Liberty Collins said into the kitchen phone before hanging up, and she wouldn't be paging no white girl neither. She walked over to the refrigerator and opened the door. She stood there and put her fists on her hips. Shit, nothing to eat. Shutting the door hard, she turned and went back into her bedroom.

She'd just sat back down in front of the TV when someone started pounding on her front door again. "Dag," she said. By the time she was standing in the front window, looking out at her nephew and his friend, she was out of breath. She thought about pretending to be asleep, but knowing Boo as she did, she figured he'd just keep knocking until she got up. Boo could be hard-headed. Reluctantly, she went over to the door and opened it. The cold air rushed into her warm house.

The young men opened the screen door and walked into the hallway without wiping their feet or knocking the snow off their shoes. She shut the door behind them. "What's up?"

"Why the fuck you be sending that dude over for?" he said, getting in her face.

" 'Cause I thought he might be telling the truth. Maybe you messed up my van."

"That's fucked-up." He paced in the foyer.

"Did you wreck my van?"

"Fuck, no!" he shouted, stopping and turning toward her.

Pookie stood off to the side, not saying a word.

"So, what's the problem then?" she asked. "He wasn't no poh-leece."

"Problem is, that dude seen some shit he wasn't supposed to be seeing. Now we got another problem 'cause of you."

"You used my van for some illegal shit?"

"Don't be sweating 'bout what I used your van for. Ain't like I didn't buy the motherfucker to begin with," he said. "I'm taking care of the shit, a'right."

"Don't sound like you're taking care of nothing."

Boo was walking back and forth in the entryway. "Watch your mouth, bitch. You putting all our shit in danger 'cause of your big, motherfuckin' mouth." Boo turned to her. "You ain't so important. Family is family, but business comes first."

It finally sunk into Liberty that she was in trouble. She'd only seen Boo this mad one time before, when he beat another kid half to death with a baseball bat. She hoped that being his auntie would save her from that. "I had no idea, Boo. How I suppose to know?"

"I ain't got to tell you shit!"

"I'm not saying you have to. Only how I to know?"

He pushed past her and walked into the kitchen. She and Pookie followed, as he opened the refrigerator door. Just some chicken getting old and a few vegetables little past their time. Her beer was gone, at least until she got paid.

But with Boo being pissed off like he was, that might be awhile.

"Damn, I thought a fat bitch like you would have somethin' to eat." Liberty bit her lip. She knew better than to say anything. He began opening cabinets. "Shit, and I be hungry, too." After a few minutes, he gave up his search.

Pookie opened the door to the basement and turned the light on. He walked down the stairs. When he came back up, Liberty and Boo were still in the kitchen, but they weren't talking. She was staring at the dirty floor with her ass resting against the counter. She could see Boo out of the corner of her eye. He was up against the counter, too. He was staring at her while chewing on his thumbnail.

"You just gonna have to leave out for a bit," he said.

"What you mean?"

"You gonna have to go someplace," he said. "You can't be staying here, waitin' for the poh-leece."

"I wouldn't tell the poh-leece shit."

"What if the poh-leece have a look downstairs? Shit could get you locked up for a long time."

"Poh-leece ain't gonna look downstairs, Boo."

"You want to bet the rest of your life that they ain't?" He kept staring at her. She shook her head ever so slightly, knowing he was right. "A'right then."

She shook her head more. She knew taking the money would get her in trouble. Here it was. What the fuck did Boo use the van for? She knew she should've said no to the cash. But she'd never had money. She never had any kids. She now knew why her sister, Donna, was scared of this kid. Donna had always been smarter. Oh, well. That's the way it'll be sometimes. She guessed she'd better start packing.

"Where you figure you can go?" Boo asked.

"We got some peoples in M'ssissippi I haven't see in a while."

"We got to shut down here for . . . 'bout two weeks, I figure."

"Okay," she said.

"Wait 'til this shit blows over." He reached into his pocket and removed a roll of cash. Stripping off several fifty-dollar bills, he threw them on the kitchen table. "This should get you there and back. You pay the rest." Boo pushed the roll back into his pocket. He looked at her hard, like he was really seeing her.

"A'right," she said.

Boo's pager squawked. He took it off his belt and looked at it. "We fittin' to pick you up in the morning, take you to the bus station." Boo waved the pager in the air. "That's Melvin."

"That motherfucker!" Pookie spoke for the first time since they had entered the house. He had a wild look in his eyes. "That motherfucker brought this shit on."

"Chill, my brother." Boo brought his thumb to his mouth. "I think we gonna be a'right."

Chapter 23

Where's My Husband?

Sharron Chaney tossed in her bed. The only noise in the house was coming from the baby monitor at her bedside. It carried the heavy breathing of her youngest daughter, Kimberly, who was fast asleep in the only other bedroom. Keisha's breathing could be heard in the background. Keisha was five and enjoyed helping with her little sister. The two girls had a special bond.

The phone next to the baby monitor rang. Sharron answered. When it rang again, she awoke and reached for the phone. "Hel . . . lo."

"May I speak with Wendell, please?" The voice was one she knew she could've placed had she been fully awake.

"Ah . . . he's not at home. May I help you?"

"Sorry to wake you, Mrs. Chaney. This is Don Freeman down at Chicago Security."

She mumbled, "Uh-huh."

"Mrs. Chaney, Wendell hasn't gotten to work yet. Do you know if he's coming in this evening?"

"Yeah," she said, coming awake. "He left early tonight, too. He should've been there a long time ago." Her heart raced. Wendell hadn't missed a day of work in years. He al-

118

ways worked overtime for extra money by picking up shifts other officers were going to miss, but he never gave them a chance at his.

"Does he have a pager?"

She heard the question but couldn't make herself answer. Her mind filled with the different possibilities of what could've happened to her husband, none of them good. She'd told him last year, when he got involved with those police officers from Cabrini, that it was too dangerous. He was all excited about doing "police work," he had said. But they had a small daughter and another on the way back then, and she had reminded him that he owed it to them to stay safe. He hadn't listened. He kept on working with the police and ended up testifying against those drug dealers in Cabrini Green. They weren't happy about it, either. They all got a lot of years in prison. It was the threats he'd received as a result of the trial that had gotten him transferred to the seniors' complex. But that complex wasn't far from Cabrini. It wasn't safe, and she'd told him that. She'd told him to quit. There were plenty of security jobs. But he'd said he had to stay put with this company if he wanted to make shift supervisor, then account manager.

She'd been scared for months that the gang would retaliate. The police said that would never happen, but how did they know? She had Kimberly prematurely, and blamed it on the stress. Wendell didn't agree, but what did he know?

"Mrs. Chaney, does he have a pager? He may have just broken down somewhere."

"He doesn't have a pager." She knew the worst had happened. "If he was broke down, he would've called you or me. He has never, ever been late for work without calling." She heard her own voice crack. Oh, God. What was she going to do?

"I'm sure there is nothing to worry about. He'll probably walk in here any minute. Call me if you hear from him and I'll do the same. Okay?"

"Okay." She hung up the phone. Her thoughts raced down the dark, shadowy paths of violence that the gangs brought to innocent people. She knew Wendell shouldn't have helped the police, and she had told him so. The police were nothing but trouble for decent folks.

Chapter 24

Overconfident

1000 Hours—Sunday

"Hi, baby," Latricia said, as she took the seat across from Huggins in the visiting area. A line of tables split the room. Plastic chairs of different colors lined each side. Guards stood by the doors, some inside the room, some outside. There weren't many prisoners.

The place had a funny smell. Like, Latricia didn't know, maybe like fear. Not the kind that twisted your guts, but the kind when you weren't looking forward to something. Like she wasn't looking forward to what she'd come to say to Lonnie. But he had to see it her way now. If he didn't, he would before she left.

"What you want?" His voice was low and dangerous.

"I want to talk to you, Lonnie." Maybe she was just smelling her own self and not the place or everyone else, like she thought. She sure had other places she'd rather be, but he owed her. He wasn't going to leave her behind when something good happened to him. That wasn't fair.

"I ain't got shit to say to you . . . bitch."

"I think you do." Some of her confidence was slipping away as she faced his cold, hard stare. His eyes seemed like they saw right through her, like she didn't exist. It never seemed she did exist to him, but that didn't stop his beating her, hitting her. "I figured you might change your mind."

" 'Bout what?" The way Lonnie said it didn't sound much like he cared what she had to say.

" 'Bout me going with you when you get out."

"Man, fuck that. What is you, stupid or something?" He looked away from her like she was dismissed.

"Don't you want to see your kids?"

He leaned forward, "Quit dancing, bitch. You got something to say, be saying it." He lowered his voice like he always did when he wanted to get his point across. So many niggers thought shouting at people got attention. Lonnie, he knew the opposite was true. There wasn't nothing more frightening than Lonnie Huggins whispering, and Latricia agreed.

His hoarse whisper shocked her; maybe this wasn't such a good idea. Her neck prickled but she spoke anyway. "Well, I was thinking you should be taking me with you."

"You be 'bout one stupid bitch then."

"No. I ain't." It was now or never. Her stomach was a tight knot of hard muscle. What she was about to say might change his mind, but at what cost? "Lonnie . . ." She paused for a moment. He didn't say a word. She couldn't even hear him breathe. Maybe he didn't. This was crazy; she must be out of her mind. "Well, baby . . . I would hate to see the poh-leece find all that dope you be having hid up in that car a yours." There. She'd said it. It was all on the table now. Her stomach flipped and knotted tighter as she waited for him to speak.

He didn't say anything. He just stared at her. Stared at her with those hard, dead, bloodshot eyes. She, at first, thought he hadn't heard. She wanted to say it again but couldn't find the strength.

"Lonnie?" she said tentatively. He still didn't answer. "Lonnie?" He sat in silence. His stare never left her eyes. No sign at all.

"You couldn't do it," he finally said. It seemed minutes had passed. Was that good?

"Oh, yes. I could."

"You couldn't do it," he said again, as if he was trying to convince himself. "You wouldn't do it."

"I know I shouldn't be telling you this, but I just want to go with you, baby. I love you. I can't stand to be away from you again." Her confidence recovered slightly, but her stomach remained tight and painful. He had to believe her . . . had to agree. . . . Why wouldn't he believe her?

"You don't love me." He spat. "You love the money and shit."

"No, no, Lonnie." Her voice went from something that held power to a pleading whine. "That ain't true."

"Fuck you, bitch," he said. "I said it before, I say it again. You ain't nothing but a tired, played-out hoe." He looked away.

Her fantasy world crashed around her. All she had left to hold onto was the painful knot in her stomach.

Huggins watched the color drain from her face. Her medium complexion lightened as he watched. He smirked, knowing she was suffering because of him. Do her good. Who was she, thinking she could come in here and tell him shit?

"Fuck you, bitch." It felt good to know he could still hurt her, even though he was locked up behind these bars. He couldn't reach over and slap her, but he knew what she was feeling now was as powerful as any slap he'd ever given her.

After a minute, color began to return to her face. A dark blush crept up her neck. There were tears in her eyes, but they didn't fall.

They wouldn't fall, if Latricia Gibbons had anything to do with it. She gritted her teeth. Her stomach convulsed and then relaxed. She was all of a sudden flooded with emotion. Not the emotion of rejection or denial or fear, but of anger and revenge. She'd suffered at the hands of this man. She had given herself to him time after time. He had taken and taken. Now she saw it for what it was, and she was ashamed of what she had become. It was pitiful. It was disgusting. It was his fault, and she had to strike back. Somehow. There must be some way to hurt him.

There was, and she knew how. Fuck the consequences. He was locked up. And she could keep him locked up for a good, long time.

"Fuck me?" she said in a quiet whisper. "No, fuck you, you no-good, rotten, low-down dog. I'm fittin' to call the poh-leece, a'right."

He laughed. "You ain't going to call no poh-leece. You think you can scare me? You sure is one dumb bitch."

"You think so, motherfucker?" She whispered so hard she sprayed the table between them with spit. "Well, you sitting here, ain't you, motherfucker? How you think the poh-leece got you? I sent 'em. I'm the one that sicced 'em on you. I dropped a dime on your dumb, black ass. I put you in the shithouse, motherfucker. What's you be thinking of that shit, now?"

He sat there with a blank look on his face. He leaned back in his chair, his hands falling into his lap.

"That's right, motherfucker. Not only that, but I'm the one that called up Macbeth and gave you up the time before this. What you think 'bout that, baby? Who you think called the poh-leece the time before that? That's right. Me, motherfucker. I'm fittin' to keep you up in this jail for the rest of your goddamned life!" She stood so fast that her plastic chair flew backward behind her and hit the wall. She turned from the table and began to walk out. She got about ten feet before she turned around to look at him one final time.

"Fuck me? No. No. No. I don't think so. Fuck you, bitch!"

She turned and saw the guard walking toward her. She'd seen brawls in the visiting area before. The guard slowed when she turned back to leave.

Huggins slowly turned and watched her dimpled butt disappear through the door. He sat without moving until the guard patted him on his shoulder. What the fuck? He couldn't believe it. That bitch! He thought about it. Yeah, he guessed she could've done all she said she'd done. That fucking bitch! All this time . . . He looked up at the guard. "I need to make a phone call."

Latricia Gibbons walked out of the Cook County Jail with her head held high. She felt great, better than she had in years. But as she got on the bus, she started to have doubts about whether she would actually call the police this time. Finally, she'd seen Lonnie acknowledge her as someone. She mattered all of a sudden. After all, she wanted to go with him, get out of the Greens. Maybe if she gave him time to think about it, he'd change his mind and let her go. Shit, things definitely were looking up. She saw the bus heading northbound on California Avenue. After all, things could be a lot worse.

Chapter 25

A Call to Boo

1100 Hours—Sunday

Donna Collins thought it was safe to answer her phone even though her son, Boo, was in his room asleep. She was much happier when he was out. "Hello?"

"This is a collect call to Boo . . ." Donna let the recording go on in hopes that it would somehow disconnect. It didn't. She pressed one and waited.

"Hello, Boo?" The voice was deep and masculine. She recognized Lonnie Huggins immediately. He was the monster that had stolen her son's heart and there wasn't a thing she could do about it, except keep the other children out of the way.

"No, this is his mother. He's asleep," she said, hoping she wouldn't be expected to wake him, but like everything else associated with Boo, she didn't get her wish.

"I got to talk to him now." The tone in his voice said it wasn't a request. Some things never change.

"I'll get him." She put the phone down on the countertop and walked through the front room. She knocked on Boo's door. There was no sound. She knocked harder. No way was she going in. "Boo, Lonnie's on the phone." She knocked again.

126

Seconds later, the door opened and Boo walked out, dressed only in baggy block boxer shorts, no shirt. He walked past her into the kitchen, picked up the phone with one hand and brought the thumb of his other hand to his mouth.

"Yeah." Boo was groggy, but he was awake enough to wish he was dreaming.

"Wake up, motherfucker."

"A'right. A'right. I'm up," he said. His mom walked away. "We need to talk, Lonnie."

"No shit. What you call this?"

"No, man. We got a problem." Boo bit hard into the skin on his thumb. He didn't feel any pain.

"What kind of problem?"

"Well, first off, I know where your car's at. I ain't got my hands on it yet, though. Should have it any day now." He wanted to soften the bad news with a little good. Boo waited for his reaction but heard only silence on the line. He continued, "But, see . . . someone seen what we had to do with someone. Know what I'm saying?"

"Latricia?"

"No." All of a sudden it occurred to Boo that the old days were a hell of a lot better, slinging rocks, running from the poh-leece but none of this kind of shit.

"Poh-leece know?"

"Uh-uh, no way. But now I got to be doing something with him, you know?"

"As long as the poh-leece ain't involved, fuck it. Do what you got to do."

"A'right."

"That's it?" asked Huggins.

"Yep. That and I should get your car back this week.

127

Maybe tonight, even." He wanted Lonnie to know to what lengths he'd had to go. "We been havin' to go out to Lombar . . ."

"Fuck all that, man!" Huggins whispered to him.

Boo stopped and held his breath.

"Get to that shit later," Huggins said. "There's something got to be taken care of right motherfuckin' now."

"A'right."

"Latricia knows 'bout the shit in the car. She say she fittin' to go to the poh-leece."

"Aw, fuck." This shit was getting out of control.

"We can't be having that bitch going to the poh-leece," said Huggins. "No way. That bitch got to be shut up for sure."

"An accident?"

The line was silent for a moment. "No. Macbeth got to know she be talking too much."

"A'right."

Chapter 26

More Calls

Pookie's momma answered the phone at the Raspberry house, and told Boo her son was out but would be back in a minute. Boo then called Melvin Early and Dease and told them to come to his mother's. After he hung up, he walked back to her bedroom and, without knocking, opened the door and walked in. His mother looked up as she finished changing one of the twins' diapers.

"You need to leave for awhile," he said and walked out. In the kitchen, he got a can of orange pop out of the refrigerator.

Ten minutes later, Melvin Early was knocking at the door. Early had a dark complexion that seemed darker with the bright red skullcap and bright green face mask he was wearing. His left eye was puffy and red. One corner of his mouth was swollen from a small cut.

"Fucking colder than shit out there. The hawk be out strong, man." Early took off his coat.

Boo's mother walked out of the hallway, pushing the bigger twin in front of her as she carried the smaller one.

"How long?" she asked.

"Give us 'bout an hour or so," Boo said around the

129

thumb in his mouth.

She hiked up everything in her arms, along with the smaller twin, and left the apartment. The bigger twin, bundled against the cold, waddled after her. The cold wind off the sixth-floor ramp blew hard through the open door. Boo slammed it closed. Yep, the hawk was certainly out.

"Dedrick say he be right over," Early said. "So, what's up?"

"Wait 'til he get here."

"A'right."

Five minutes later, Dease stood in the front room with them, still wearing his winter coat. Boo had told him not to take it off when he came in the door. Now Boo was talking to Pookie on a cell phone. Pookie was still at his house.

"I sending you, Dedrick," Boo said. "You all got to do that security dude. Wait 'til tonight, a'right?"

"A'right," Pookie said.

"I fittin' to tell Dedrick everything, so listen to what he say. Then you all got to get up here in the van. Bring whatever you get outta the security's car, too."

"A'right."

Boo hung up and looked at Melvin and Dease. Boo walked over to the TV and turned it on. You could never be too sure about nosy neighbors.

"Latricia told Lonnie that she was fittin' to go to the poh-leece 'bout the car," he whispered.

"Motherfucker," said Early.

"She on the bus right now. Bitch ain't got no car no more." Boo had this all thought out, but it was getting hard to keep track of everything. He thought he'd be able to pull this off as long as no one got scared or caught red-handed. "Dedrick, after we get our hands on Latricia, you got to go down to Pookie's and help him with the guard. A'right?"

"That's cool."

"Take everything he got on him and in his car that we could be using. Then after it get dark, burn the car. Take him someplace different, away apart, and shoot his black ass. Don't be bagging him up, though. Just strip him naked. I don't want nobody to know who he be. Use the van again, but don't be fuckin' it up. And put some plates on it. I don't care where you get them from, neither."

"That's cool. How we fittin' to do Latricia?"

"Lonnie want something special with her," Boo said. He thought for a moment. "We got to grab her when she get off the bus, before she can call the poh-leece."

Chapter 27

The Bus Ride

1115 Hours—Sunday

The bus lurched away from the curb into traffic on California. There had been no shelter at the bus stop across from the jail. The howling wind must've cut into the other people waiting with Latricia; they danced from one foot to another, trying to stay warm. But Latricia hardly noticed the cold or the bite of the wind. She didn't really notice much of anything, since she was glowing with the thrill of her first win against Lonnie. Her mind kept going back to the blank, stupid look on his face. She'd kicked his ass!

After paying and getting her transfer, Latricia took a seat near the rear of the bus. She stared out the window, barely acknowledging the city as it passed. It was prettier under a layer of snow, something she usually noticed this time of year. The people on the bus changed as it went north. The Mexicans got off and more blacks got on; by the time it crossed Ogden Avenue, everybody was black. A half hour and a bunch of stops later, she got off at Grand and Western. What next, she mulled?

It took awhile before the Grand Avenue bus came along. The seats were all taken and she had to stand in the rear door well, holding on to the chrome vertical pole. Her ribs hurt too much for her to grab the overhead rail.

She knew she could call Macbeth when she got home and that would be that. There wasn't a doubt in her mind that she could turn Lonnie in. But, hadn't she just won? Didn't that change things? Never in her life had she seen the look she put on his face. What did it mean? Was there a chance Lonnie would change his mind? Was what she saw on his face fear? She'd never seen him afraid before.

She shifted her weight against the acceleration and deceleration of the bus without thinking. Halsted finally came, and she almost missed it. She stepped off the bottom stair and stomped through a pile of snow. Maybe she should give Lonnie one more chance.

She waited another long spell in the metal and Plexiglas shelter at the six corners of Halsted, Grand and Milwaukee. It was filthy, covered in graffiti and old, tattered posters hawking either a concert or new recording. The telephone pole to the right of the shelter was wrapped completely with election signs, some from years ago. The graffiti was different-colored spray paint, with some marker thrown in. Most of it was just kids tagging, but gang graffiti was mixed in there, too. Latricia hardly noticed any of it, she couldn't figure what to do next. She knew what she wanted to do, give him one more chance, but . . .

When the next bus pulled up, she dragged herself up the stairs. Her fingers were so stiff she could barely get the change from her pocket for the ride and transfer. She'd pretty much settled that she owed Lonnie at least one more chance. What could it possibly hurt to wait one day?

As the bus reached Division Street, she was thinking about how to get a sitter for her kids. Her mother had to work tomorrow and wouldn't be free like today. There were other people, but they'd cost money. If she had the car, she could run them out to her sister on the west side, but there was no car, not anymore.

Latricia got off at Division running. The eastbound bus was pulling up and she was afraid that the driver might not wait and pull off. She still had her transfer in her hand when she climbed the bus stairs. Her breath came out in clouds, but she didn't care, she'd won. She'd seen it in Lonnie's eyes. It couldn't be anything else. Now that she'd had some time to think about it, she was sure that he would change his mind. Everyone said Lonnie was getting promoted; that had to mean more money, a lot more money. She got off at Cleveland Avenue, one block west of her building. Everything was falling in place.

Things could be a lot worse.

Chapter 28

Waiting

1145 Hours—Sunday

Parked in the back of the lot at 1150 North Sedgwick, Dease settled in the driver seat of his Blazer, and pulled his coat tighter. The wind shook his ride as it blew across the hood; people outside bent against it and the snow, holding their winter coats tight. Dease was bundled up and had the heater on full blast, but was still freezing his ass off. Niggers in parkas like his could stand outside in the cold and sling rocks for hours, but now he had a chill. Was he just cold, or was he being a pussy?

He mostly watched the street north of the parking lot where Latricia would be coming from after she got off the bus. Boo had a plan. Dease had come to respect the planning of his home boy. So far, Boo had kept them out of trouble with the police and Lonnie.

Dease had only moved to Cabrini Green from the south side about a year ago. Where he was from, the Cobras ruled the streets and nobody messed with them. But he'd been locked up and spent some time in juvie with some cats from Cabrini. When he got out, he moved to the projects and he'd been quickly accepted into the Cabrini Cobras. He'd even been elevated. That was what happened when you worked around Cecil Jones. Jones rewarded hard work, like when Lonnie had been given his Cobra Blessing. A blessing Dease had seen.

Dease heard about Lonnie when he lived out south. Every Cobra did. He was the threat. The Killer. When someone stepped out of line, they'd be told, "You want Lonnie on your ass?" That was usually enough to get just about anybody in line. If not, Lonnie was called. First time was a violation: a beating. The next could be another, more vicious beating, but it could be a killing. Dease respected that kind of rep and wanted the same kind of respect.

But for now, he sat in his Blazer and watched, content to follow Boo's lead. He knew this would help him along. You didn't just develop the kind of rep Lonnie had overnight. Dease knew he would be ready when his chance came.

Boo had him in the parking lot because he was the only one with a car. Early was supposed to be waiting on the ground-floor stairwell, while Boo was on the thirteenth-floor stairwell. Waiting. Dease's signal was the key.

Melvin Early shifted from one foot to the other. It wasn't cold on the ground floor, but it wasn't warm either, not by a long shot. The lobby had fucked-up doors, broken windows and a lot of holes where the wind got through. The security guards had a little room where they ran a heater. They left the Cobras alone and the Cobras did the same, for the most part. Sometimes they had to straighten a guard or two out, but not too much anymore. At one time, it got ugly. But now, things were straight. Early tugged on his hat, so that it rode over the top edge of his facemask. "Where is that fat bitch?" he said under his breath.

Boo huddled in the thirteenth-floor stairwell. He didn't

want to stand out on the ramp and be seen by other residents. So, he stood in the darkness. It helped to block the wind, too. He kept one ear toward the ramp door; he couldn't afford to miss the signal. The weight of the gun tugged at his waistline; it felt good, like some kind of security. He was the man, after all, and pretty soon he was going to prove it.

Chapter 29

Surprise

1200 Hours—Sunday

When Latricia Gibbons got off the bus, the wind didn't take her by surprise. She'd been in and out of it enough to know it was waiting for her, waiting to steal her breath. But in weather like this, it felt more like robbery than theft. She climbed over a snowdrift that was too frozen to go through and began walking on the sidewalk toward home. She tilted her head down against the wind with her hat pulled low. The cold nipped at her skin, threatening to freeze her cheeks.

She couldn't stop. She had to push her victory away and focus on the weather's assault. Her joints creaked with the cold and she had to scale another drift at the edge of the parking lot. Almost home.

A car horn sounded as she trudged through the parking lot. Someone in the back of the lot beeped the horn twice in long, high notes. People did that every day. They didn't have no intercoms in the jets, just the universal Cabrini doorbell.

The ramp leading into the building was covered with ice, so she went slowly. She made the door without falling and had to fight the wind to get it open. Once in, she let the door slam closed; it was as if the wind had chased her in.

A man stood by the elevator with the up button lit up, wearing a red hat and a green face mask. His jacket looked familiar, but really it was the colors, black and red. Cobra colors. She couldn't see his face: a Cobra, no doubt. He sure wouldn't be in this building if he wasn't a Cobra. Might be one of the guys that worked for Lonnie.

"These things working?" she asked as she walked up past the security booth.

"Yep." The man coughed and turned away from her. She still couldn't place him. What did it matter anyway? She turned her thoughts back to the problem of a baby-sitter. Maybe she could use her crazy sister; it wasn't like it would be all day. If she were taking her medicine, it would be all right.

Time passed without comment from either one of them. The elevator arrived a couple minutes later and they both got on. As the door began to close, a woman called out. Latricia held the door for an older woman from the third floor, who struggled with two plastic bags of groceries. The guards didn't offer to help her with the bags. Worthless. You couldn't count on them bastards, unless you paid them or fucked them and even then they weren't worth shit.

Latricia pressed the button for the old lady, then hit hers; the man waited, then hit one for two floors below Latricia's. The elevator was slow and stopped at every floor. The wind howled at the top of the shaft and the man had to force the elevator doors to close after the woman with the groceries got off.

Finally, the eleventh floor arrived. The man got off without saying a word or even looking at her. That wasn't unusual; people didn't much make eye contact in the projects.

When the elevator doors opened on the thirteenth floor, Latricia took a deep breath before she stepped out. It didn't help as the wind ripped it out of her throat. She gasped, gulped another breath down, and walked toward her apartment.

The key struck the plate around the lock when she tried to push it in the hole. Her hands shook from the cold; it felt like someone was slicing her fingers with razors. She'd have to go to the liquor store and buy some gloves from the Arab. It was just too goddamned cold.

Latricia turned to close the door and came nose-to-barrel with the muzzle of a gun. The hand holding it was invisible to her, as if this thing in her face was suspended magically in front of her. The gaping black hole moved forward and pushed against the swollen bridge of her nose. It didn't hurt, but she took a step back to get away from the surprisingly warm metal. It pushed her again, forcing her back into her apartment. It kept coming. She backed up farther.

"A'right," a man's voice said. Her eyes left the muzzle and looked into a pair of hard eyes. The gunman had black pupils that swam in white pools against his dark skin under a navy face mask. The man with the red hat and green face mask stepped in and closed her door. Oh, God, she thought, things have just got worse.

Chapter 30

Let the Prima Donnas Do It

1230 Hours—Sunday

Sharron Chaney answered the door with her youngest held tightly against her chest. She hadn't slept since the phone call and had practically watched the dark bags form under her own eyes. She was desperately waiting for another call, either from her husband or Mr. Freeman. Neither had called and her fears grew worse by the minute.

She had gone to her church in the morning, before it opened. The custodian had let her and the girls in. Then he'd called the reverend at home, to let him know there was some kind of emergency. The reverend arrived in ten minutes. He guided his flock with a compassionate hand; each member of the church was like his extended family, and there was nothing he wouldn't do for them.

Reverend Middleton had stood in his church office in his pajamas with his woolen overcoat still about his shoulders. Sharron knew him from her church attendance, but Wendell worked odd hours and missed church a lot. But the reverend would know Wendell well enough to know that he hadn't just walked out on his family. Wendell worked hard and was a man who took his responsibilities seriously.

Reverend Middleton had spent some time calming her down. Then he told her to go home and get some rest. In the morning, if she hadn't heard anything, she should call the police and make a report.

Sharron had gone home and lay on the couch, but the kids had slept all night and wanted nothing to do with sleep in the morning. She got little rest and had no one to call to watch them for her. Finally, she could stand it no longer and called the police.

Now she stood looking at the police officer at her door. His police coat was open, exposing a tie that was six inches too short and stained with who knew how many meals. He was sweating, even though it was cold outside. His holster, looking more abused than his tie, was about to dump his gun on her porch. He had a metal report box under one arm and his belly hung well over his gun belt, but she could forgive him all that. He was a savior. He was going to find Wendell. Or, at least, start the process to find him.

She invited him in and didn't mention the hour wait. She'd spent the better part of an hour looking out the window, chewing her lip, wringing her hands and doing anything else that she could think of to keep the horrible things out of her mind that she just knew were happening to Wendell. She put Kimberly in the playpen and led the police officer into the kitchen, asking if she could get him something to drink.

Roy Dietz sat down at Mrs. Chaney's kitchen table and pulled out a Missing Report from his report box. He clipped it to the front and took out a pen. It was all for show. He had no intention of writing a report, if he could help it. Particularly since it was almost time to go home.

The kitchen chair creaked as he shifted his weight. "All right, who seems to be missing?"

"My husband, Wendell Chaney," she said.

He looked up at her. This was going to be as easy as it gets. "Did you say your husband?"

"Yes, I did." She had her hands in her lap, twisted around one another. For a moment, he thought maybe she was disabled. Then he remembered how she opened the door. No, this broad was really worried. She'd just have to worry a little more, until the next shift was on.

"When was the last time you saw him?" He knew the tactic he was going to take. Worked every time.

"Last night around nine p.m., when he left for work." She wiped away a tear.

"Well, ma'am, I hate to be the one to tell you this, but you're going to have to wait a full twenty-four hours before you can file a report," he lied in a serious tone. His spirits lifted. It probably was bullshit anyway. He'd bet that she'd driven the poor bastard crazy with all her worrying, and now he was shacked up with some dolly. He'd seen it a thousand times. He put the pen back in his pocket and re-placed the report in the box. "It isn't uncommon for hus-bands to disappear for a day or two. We don't want to make a report out, if it's not bona fide."

She stood there with a blank look on her face, like she all of a sudden didn't understand English. She didn't say a word the whole time he walked back to the front door. But when he grabbed the knob, the dam burst. She pleaded with him to make an exception. She told him her husband had been working with some officers in Cabrini Green and must need help or he would've called.

He told her that only happened in the movies. That her husband was probably just blowing off some steam somewhere. If she was that worried, she should call the officers that he had worked with in Cabrini. Let them prima donna motherfuckers make the report.

Chapter 31

Going to the Store

1300 Hours—Sunday

Pookie zipped his coat to the very top, pulled thick gloves on and wrapped his face with his little brother's scarf. It was cold outside. When he looked out the back window of the porch, he saw little swirls of snowflakes blowing around the yard.

"Anthony, you got to be shutting this door all the way," his sister said as she started to close the heavy wooden door that led into the kitchen from the back porch. "What do you need from the store anyway?"

"I just be needing something," he said, walking slowly down the stairs. He couldn't see his feet, so he pushed his coat in around his stomach and craned his neck forward. Now he could see. The door into the backyard was cracked open, and a small drift of snow had formed. He kicked at the drift and stepped outside. No one else was out as he walked north across the alley through a gangway and onto the sidewalk. He turned and began walking to the Shell Station three blocks away on Halsted. It had a mini-mart.

Once there, he bought a bottle of Pepsi and cigarettes. Then he was back in the weather under the thick, gray clouds, trudging westbound on the sidewalk. Not many people were out driving around. Practically no one was walking. He turned on Peoria, a block before his street. He walked past the mouth of the alley down the street until he was four or five houses from the corner. He cut through a gangway again. This time it brought him into his own alley, several houses south of his. No one from his house would be able to see him.

He walked around the garage and saw no new footprints in the snow. Then, feeling in his pocket for the key, he went over to the basement door of the abandoned house. There were no tracks through the drifts. He took the key out and quickly opened the lock. He pushed the door in, stepped over a drift and closed the door quickly. He was out of the wind, but it was still cold. He walked through the basement toward the front of the house. Halfway down, he felt for the string that hung from the bulb in the ceiling. A tug flooded the room with light.

He turned and looked back at the door: no wet foot-prints, only his own. He turned back around and pushed through a blanket that he and Boo had nailed up over the doorway. It was supposed to keep the light in the next room from being seen, but you could see plenty of light from under and around it when the light was on.

The security guard was huddled in a corner, still alive. He was dressed in his coat and had a blanket wrapped around him. He was tied up, blindfolded and gagged, all with duct tape. The tape showed signs of struggling. But it still looked tight. He wouldn't get away. After all, Pookie had some experience with taping people up. He considered it a special talent.

Chapter 32

Victory Lost

1600 Hours—Sunday

Dease started his Blazer and then got out with his scraper. He walked over to a wrecked car in the lot of 1150 North Sedgwick; it had been dropped by a Transit Authority tow truck. The car, a Toyota Camry, had been in an accident a couple weeks ago and had been blocking the intersection. The front was smashed and the driver's door had been pried open by the fire department. Now, thanks to the Cobras, it was missing two rear tires.

Dease brushed the Camry off. The ice under the snow was thick and took some effort to scrape off. Ten minutes later, he was driving the Blazer south on Orleans Street on his way to the expressway and the south side.

Yeah, he thought, this'll do.

Latricia sat on her broken couch. The men had pulled a skullcap over her head and eyes and taped it down tight. She couldn't see and could barely hear. She had been like this for what seemed like hours and she could smell her sour sweat through the cap. Since they hadn't killed her yet, she thought she might have a chance.

She was almost asleep when she heard the ring of a cell

phone. One of the men answered, but must have left the room. She couldn't hear him anymore. He was gone for awhile; then she thought she heard him come back. Someone pressed what had to be the phone against her head.

"I can't hear nothing," she said. Someone ripped the taped cap off her ear and slapped the phone against it.

"What you be thinking now, bitch?" said Lonnie in a coarse whisper on the phone. "Fuck me, huh? I don't fuckin' think so. And don't be thinking some fat, stupid hack gonna be listening to this call neither. They do what I tell them around here."

She sat forward, leaning into the phone. "Oh, baby! I was just mad. I didn't mean none of them things I said."

"You said you was going to the poh-leece."

"I be telling you that shit just to get you to let me go with you," she pleaded. "Really, baby. Please."

"Fuck you. You said you put me in here. You said you been puttin' my ass in the motherfucker all along," he said. She could hear the phone creak, as if he were squeezing it to death. "Now we gonna see who be doing what to who, bitch."

"Lonnie, I'll do anything. Please. I was just lying. I didn't really trick on you. Please. Please." She knew he could be ruthless and hated people begging, but she didn't know what else to do.

"Fuck you."

"Baby, I'm the mother of your kids. Please. Please." That was followed by silence. Her hopes rose a little. He must be thinking.

"You be willing to sign a confession that any dope in that car be yours? That I be havin' nothin' to do with it?"

"Anything. You just be telling me what to say, Lonnie."

She felt tears welling up in her eyes. "I don't wanna die."

"A'right," he said. "My boys are fittin' to take you to my lawyer's office. He drawing up a paper. You better sign the motherfucker, or they'll do your ass for sure."

"Okay, okay. I do it." The phone was removed from her ear and she cried until her whole body shook. This morning's victory was long gone. Now, there was only staying alive. Whoever took the phone must've moved into another room; she couldn't hear any more conversation. Her ears were filled with her own cries and sobs. She had been so close, too. Now he'd never take her with him.

But she would be alive. And things could always get better.

Chapter 33

Eye on the Decoy

2100 Hours—Sunday

The air inside the car was making Macbeth gag. He hated cigarette smoke. He scooted across the backseat, Trixie's wiry hair barely visible over the front headrest. Barnhill, her partner and front passenger, didn't move when Macbeth popped open the back door.

"Where're you going?" Trixie asked as she looked in the rearview mirror, an unlit cigarette bobbing in her mouth.

"Out." Macbeth held her gaze.

"Why?" She flicked a match and lit the cigarette.

"Trix," Macbeth said. "That's your fourth smoke in fifteen minutes. I need some fresh air."

"Ryan won't like you being out of the car."

"He'll understand when I tell him I couldn't see out the windows."

"I thought a big stud like you could handle a little smoke."

"Ain't nothing little about how much you smoke."

"Zito smokes."

"Yeah." Macbeth pushed the door open with his foot. "But he keeps his window rolled down, too."

"Fuck that." Trixie puffed on the cigarette, making the

end glow red. "It's too cold." She let out a thick, gray cloud. "Suit yourself, but I ain't waiting when I get the signal."

"Trix." Macbeth stood, turned and leaned into the open door. "I'll beat you there."

"Not likely." She took another drag. "Car's faster." She blew smoke out her nose.

"Don't think so."

"Bet?"

Macbeth shook his head. "You're going to have to look, pull into traffic and make the corner. I'm just going to run across the street. You don't stand a chance." Barnhill turned in his seat and glared at him.

"Put your money where your mouth is." She reached for her purse. "You're crazy if you think you can run faster than I can drive."

"Trix," Barnhill said. His disapproval was apparent in his voice.

"Shut up, Henry," she said.

Macbeth closed the door.

Ryan watched the trio on the street before him, as the scene continued to play itself out.

"Did she wipe his mouth again?" Ryan asked Hagen, who was kneeling at the side window of the surveillance van.

"What's she using? Kleenex?" Hagen was staring through a crack in the curtains.

"Looks like it. It's been balled up in her hand since they walked up. She keeps dabbing her eyes, too." Ryan couldn't get a better view for fear of attracting attention.

"Yeah, what's the name of that Greek broad?"

"What?" asked Ryan.

"Macbeth'd know." Hagen shifted on his knees. "The one whose tears affected people when they touched them."

Ryan knew he had to get Hagen back on the street. Soon, too; he was obviously starting to lose his mind, particularly if he was showing signs of missing the discussions Stacey liked to have about Greek mythology. "Watch Mike, would you? She keeps talking to the dude she walked up with. I think they're gonna do it."

Ryan brought his radio up to his mouth and whispered the description of the woman who'd been playing nursemaid to Zito's sick drunk robbery decoy and her apparent male partner. "Standby."

It took another five minutes before the man told the woman loud enough for Ryan to hear in the van, "Nuff of this. Get the ma-fucker's shit and let's go."

She felt along Zito's back and tugged his wallet free. She reached around his front. For a second, Ryan thought Zito was going to get a "thank-you-very-much reach-around." Then her hand dug into his pants pocket. When she pulled it out, change clinked on the sidewalk.

"Go. Go. Go," Ryan said. "Grab both of them."

Ketchum and Hampton pulled up first, but that was after Macbeth had put both offenders on the wall. Trixie and Barnhill pulled up with a screech of tires. Ketchum led Zito, still playing the stumbling drunk, around the corner.

Ryan parked the surveillance van a block from the district station and walked back into the building through the garage. As he climbed the stairs to the second floor, he heard a lot of laughing. That in itself wasn't unusual, except they had enough work that there shouldn't be time for bullshitting, not yet, at least. He came around the corner and there was Zito bent over a garbage can, throwing up.

Macbeth, whose nasty grin looked particularly evil, stood behind him, holding his belt.

Hagen leaned against the doorjamb, holding his side, tears streaming down his red face, trying to talk over the need to breathe. "First his tongue. Now this."

The office door opened and Trixie stormed out. "You guys are a bunch of assholes." As she stomped off, she dug in her purse. "Henry. You coming?" She didn't wait for Barnhill's reply.

Hagen doubled over; it looked like he might pass out, he was laughing so hard.

"Timmy, you okay?" Ryan asked.

" 'Immy?" Zito stood, wiping his mouth. "W'at da sck abou' me? I'm da one pooking my gu's ou'."

"Mike," Ryan turned to face Zito, "you were preoccupied. But since you seem to be through, are you okay?"

"Don't worry about him," said Hagen between gulps of air. "He's a method actor."

Ketchum came out of the office wiping his eyes, followed by Barnhill. "Sarge, go on in."

Ryan looked at his guys one at a time. Something was definitely up. Zito obviously was getting his balls busted. He stepped into the office; everything looked normal. Hampton was at a desk doing an arrest report. The two prisoners were fastened to the wall. One man. One woman. There was that Kleenex again, the one she had been using on Zito, as she dabbed at her eye. She looked at Ryan.

Oh, shit, he thought. There was no eye, just an empty, scarred socket with some kind of yellowish discharge. Ryan didn't know whether he should laugh or blow his dinner.

Chapter 34

Stripped Naked

2130 Hours—Sunday

Dease arrived at the Raspberry house in the afternoon. He and Pookie pulled the security guard's car into the alley. They went through it and found a gun, a stainless steel Ruger .357 magnum. Pookie put the whole gun belt, including the holster, gun, handcuffs, keys and nightstick, into a cloth bag. There wasn't anything else worth keeping from the car, except the license plates.

They checked the abandoned building basement and garage again. There hadn't been any prowlers. Pookie led the way back into his house, where they settled in front of the TV to watch some basketball. They had some time to kill.

By nine o'clock that evening, snow had begun to fall. It started light but quickly turned into large flakes, falling fast and thick. Pookie looked out the window. "What you think?"

Dease crossed to the window and saw the snow but, more importantly, he saw the darkness. Perfect. "Cool. Ain't no motherfuckers gonna be out in this shit."

They put on their coats and hats. Pookie brought along the security guard's stuff. Pookie had his game face on as he led them out of the house and into the garage. Dease opened the van and removed the shotgun. Pookie took the magnum out of the bag and hefted it in his hand, admiring the way the light played off the shiny barrel. "A'right," Pookie said as he shut the van door.

Wendell Chaney heard the basement door open and two sets of feet. The light cord clinked. Chaney's head felt like it was on fire; part of it throbbed, while other parts were shooting hot streaks of pain. He could smell vomit in his nose and taste the acidy remains. He knew it had to be caked down his front, but he couldn't remember if or when he had thrown up. He had been in and out of consciousness and had no idea how long he had been out, or up, for that matter. He shivered, more from fear than from the cold.

Chaney heard a saw, then the sound of a board hitting the floor. If that wasn't bad enough for his head, it started again, except this time it was metal getting cut. Each stroke of the saw brought new pain. It lasted a long time. Chaney heard someone cursing, sawing, cursing, sawing; then, the air rang with the sound of metal dropping and rolling on the floor. The noise just about split his head open. There was conversation. Then he felt a draft, but felt a stare more strongly.

Dease held up the shotgun. The barrel was short, with the stock cut off just under the handgrip. The whole thing was less than a foot and a half long. The gun felt good in his hands, giving him instant power and respect. Wasn't a motherfucker in the world going to fuck with him as long as he had this. He looked past Pookie, who stood in the doorway; the security guard looked cold and scared.

Pookie walked over and grabbed the guard's hair, pulling him up on his shaky legs; the blanket covering him fell off.

Pookie let go and shoved him toward the door with the front of his pistol. Dease stepped aside and let them through.

Twenty minutes later, the van was moving slowly north down Halsted with the security guard's plates on the front and back. The van slid slightly in the falling snow. Dease was driving. He had reluctantly stuck the shotgun in the sleeping bag way in the back. The guard lay on the floor behind him, taped up tight.

Pookie had told Dease where to go. They'd dump the car first. Then they'd dump the security guard. Just like Boo had said to do it. Pookie followed, driving the security guard's car, with the magnum tucked in his pants.

Chaney shivered, knowing he was in trouble. They had stripped him naked except for the duct tape on his head, hands, arms, legs and ankles. The cold metal floor sent freezing jolts through his body. Chaney knew he was about to die. He had heard them planning to burn his clothes and identification with his car. He prayed silently, not for mercy, but for his wife and children . . . that they would be looked out for.

Dease had Pookie go around him into an alley. The security guard's car sped up, turned and plowed into a vacant lot. Pookie backed up and drove deeper and deeper into the snow pile. On the third try, all the wheels were in the lot. Pookie got out and left the door open. He reached into the backseat and took out a five-gallon gasoline can. It was full. He sloshed gas inside the car and, when the can was empty, he threw that into the car, too.

Dease got out of the van and walked over to the Escort. He had known a guy once who started a bunch of fires. The guy got caught because when he set his last fire, his arms had burst into flame. He was arrested at the hospital. The guy told Dease later, when they shared a cell in county jail, he had gotten gasoline on himself, and his arms started to burn when he lit the match.

Dease pulled a book of matches from his coat pocket. He struck one and lit the book. He threw the book into the car and it exploded. Dease fell backward and rolled. He came up and looked himself over. That guy never told him about no goddamned explosion. He wasn't on fire, but his eyebrows were singed. He ran back to the van and drove off.

Dease and Pookie drove south on Halsted Street. Dease gassed it through the stoplight at Garfield Boulevard. Hardly any cars were out, even fewer people walking. The street had been plowed and driving was pretty easy. Dease slowed down, but his heart wanted to jump out of his chest. Tonight was the night his reputation would begin.

Pookie told him where to turn to get to the spot he was looking for. They stopped at Fifty-Eighth and Shields, beside a vacant lot. Pookie nodded. Yeah, this was it. Dease pulled away from the curb and onto the railroad property. The road, dirt in the summertime but grooved snow and ice now, pitched up toward the tracks above the street. Dease stopped along the road, out of sight. He turned around; Pookie was sitting in the back with his feet resting on the guard.

"I get to do it, right?" Dease asked.

"Only got the five shells for the gauge. I'll do it with the magnum," Pookie said, holding up the gun. "We got plenty of bullets."

Dease didn't say anything. He turned to look out the front window. There was no one on the railroad property. Game time, motherfucker.

It occurred to Chaney as he lay on the floor of the van that he was about to be killed with his own weapon. For some reason that seemed immensely unfair. He was determined not to let these men see him cry or beg, so he asked God for the strength to be silent.

He felt the tape being cut from his legs. Whoever was doing it wasn't very handy with a knife. How could he escape? Make a quick move, or fall and roll, or just play dead? Suddenly, ice cold air rushed over him. The side door was open.

Rough hands grabbed him from behind and hoisted him up. He was dragged out of the van and dropped on his face and shoulder. He struggled to get up and run, but his legs wouldn't work. They'd been taped up too long and too tight. He got on his knees, then got one foot under him. He panicked and slipped in the snow. He expected his head to explode at any moment.

The first bullet struck him in the back. He never heard the shot, but felt something hot rip through his back and stomach. He twisted but didn't fall. He got his other foot under him and stood. The second bullet hit him in the shoulder; somehow it bounced and tore down his arm. He took a step. His bare foot came down hard on the ragged edge of something, probably a broken bottle frozen into the mud. His foot gave out and he pitched forward on to the snow-covered mud, hard as concrete. The third shot slammed into his skull as he fell.

Pookie walked over to the guard. The motherfucker was still breathing, but barely. Steam rose from the blood that was flowing slowly out of several wounds. Pookie brought the gun up from his side and shot the guard in the back, in the ribs. It looked like it blew out the side of his chest.

"Come on, man. We got to get outta here!" Dease said. "Come on. This is some fucked-up shit here."

Pookie turned away from the guard and hopped in the van. He closed the door, looking back. The blood leaking into the snow looked black. Pookie checked himself out; he didn't think he had any blood on him, not like Melvin the other night. Not this time.

That was fuckin' easy. Pookie looked over at Dease, who was backing the van down the road. The van bounced through the ruts in the snow. A minute later, they were eastbound on Garfield Boulevard, heading toward the Dan Ryan Expressway, back toward Cabrini Green.

The snow was falling heavier now. Wendell Chaney groaned and tried to sit up. His body wouldn't respond. He opened an eye and was struck by a big snowflake. He blinked and stared up at the sky. The falling snow grew thin, then into a dot, and, finally, that too disappeared.

Static crackled in Rachel's ear as she listened to the recording of his voice. After the beep, she started. "Hi . . . ah, Robert. This is Rache. I waited for you. I hope everything's okay. I didn't hear anything. God, is it beautiful up here. I know you're not at the office right now. It's after eleven-thirty. I'll call you in the morning. I'm snowed in outside Green Bay and it's still falling pretty heavy. I'll come straight to the office tomorrow. If you get this message tonight, I'm at the Roadside Motel on Highway 41. Okay, take care. I really hope everything's all right. Bye . . ."

Chapter 35

Things Just Got Worse

2300 Hours—Sunday

Boo stood in the front room of Latricia's apartment with Dease, Pookie and Early. They had on their winter coats, all black and red, with their watch caps pulled down low. Early had his facemask on and Boo wore his knit mask. Pookie and Dease wrapped scarves around their faces.

Boo went into the hallway and motioned for Dease to follow. "This bitch knows me," Boo said in a hoarse whisper. "I want you to do the talking, a'right?"

"A'right. That's cool."

Boo went on to give Dease his instructions, while Early and Pookie dressed Latricia in her winter coat. They left her hands taped together in front, draped her coat over her shoulders, and buttoned it up. They put her empty sleeves in her pockets and removed the tape from her hat, but left her eyes covered.

Boo followed Dease over to her. "We fittin' to take you to the lawyer's office downtown, a'right," said Dease.

"Okay."

"You staying tied up though, 'til we be there," Dease said to her. "If you try anything, we right behind you with these." Boo brought the Taurus up to her covered face and

160

pressed it against her cheek. She pulled away. "We'll shoot your ass in a heartbeat, if you pull any shit."

"I ain't gonna do nothing, I promise." She turned toward the gun. "Please, don't hurt me."

"When we step into the lobby, we gonna let you see 'til we get outside. Don't be turning around or nothing, a'right?"

"Okay." Her mouth stayed open, quivering.

Latricia knew the door had been opened when she felt the cold air blow hard and freeze the tears on her cheeks. The cold found its way into her coat and stung her taped-up hands. She was shoved out of the apartment toward the elevator.

She was pretty sure she could recognize them if given the chance. That was why they didn't want her looking back. That little rat, Boo, had to be one of them. He was Lonnie's boy. She wanted to believe they were going to the lawyer's office, and maybe they were, since they didn't want her seeing them. She knew she couldn't try anything. With those worthless security guards, it'd only get her killed. Maybe the police might be in the lobby. Then she would scream her lungs out. She wanted to believe they were going to the lawyer's office. They didn't want her to see them.

After some talking, she heard one of them get sent down the stairs to the lobby; so much for the police helping. The elevator arrived. This late, on a night like this, the chance of someone else calling for an elevator was small.

The elevator ride took a minute but it felt like ten as it shuddered down the shaft. It was knocked about by the strong wind. Latricia had never noticed the smell in the elevator like she did now. It smelled of piss and garbage. She could feel the Cobras in the elevator with her. She knew one-on-one, she could hold her own, even against these young, project-vicious men. But that wasn't the way these new-bred gangsters operated. There was security in numbers. No fair fights. The weak joined together to defeat the strong. And these were some really weak motherfuckers.

She heard the bell ring; it couldn't be the ground floor. The bell never worked on the ground floor. Someone behind her reached up and tugged the hat out of her eyes. The door opened on the third floor. She saw the man with the red hat and face mask waiting for the elevator. He motioned them off with a small nod of his head. Two flights of stairs and ten steps later, they were outside on the ice-covered ramp that led to the parking lot.

Before her hat was pulled down again, Latricia saw that it was still snowing. Someone took her by each arm, leading her to the parking lot. Her feet slipped on the icy grooves in the lot. She felt snowflakes land on her chin. They pulled her to a stop and one of them spoke. "We don't got no lock for the chain."

She pulled away from the men holding her. What the fuck did they need a chain for? She was already taped up tighter than shit.

"Where the fuck you think you going, bitch!"

She struggled until she felt hard steel pressed against her side. "Keep it up."

She stopped.

"Use these," someone said.

"A'right."

An object clinked in the night. Moments later, she heard the sound of a chain being run over something metal and then the sounds of handcuffs closing.

Latricia was shoved from behind. She stumbled before

being dragged back upright. A car door was opened with a loud pop, like it was fucked-up. Maybe they were going for a ride downtown after all. She was turned and shoved again. Someone grabbed her head and pushed her down and forward. She landed on a car seat that was stiff from the cold. She kicked and pushed until she was sitting up. It still could get a lot worse.

Latricia could feel the presence of someone. It was like she could feel his heat. Whoever it was wasn't saying anything. She heard his coat crinkle in the cold air.

Boo stood next to the open window of the abandoned car and looked around at the buildings. No one seemed to be looking out their window. That was good. He gave Dease the sign to go start the van. They'd need to make a quick getaway. The van was right next to the lot on Sedgwick.

Latricia sat quietly. Boo remembered what Lonnie had told him, that she had to know what was coming. That wouldn't be a problem; he just had to make sure everything was good. He knew the bitch would be screaming her fool head off.

The driver's door was kept closed by a steel chain, held tight by the security guard's handcuffs. Boo yanked on the cuffs. He still didn't trust Early, not after the license plate thing. He looked up to see Pookie putting the gas-soaked rag down the gasoline nozzle. He reached into his waistband and grabbed hold of the loaded gun.

"She gotta be knowing the shit's coming. I want to know how she look when you tell her she gonna die," Lonnie had said.

"We going now?" she asked, almost sounding brave. "To the lawyer's office?"

"Yeah, we is. But you ain't," Boo said. She turned toward him. "See, Lonnie don't be believing your lying ass. He figures you did it once, you be doing it again." She started crying, crying hard. Boo pulled the gun out. She had to know what was about to happen.

"Lonnie say I was to shut you up for good." Boo reached into the window and tore the mask from her face. "Oh, and he said to tell you, you is one stupid bitch."

He stepped back from the open window, brought the gun up and shot her six times. He didn't take time to aim, just brought the gun down from its kickback after each shot. It had a hard jerk. The first two shots went through her arms she brought up to protect herself. The next four hit her in the chest and belly.

Latricia rolled onto the seat. She didn't feel anything. She knew she was hurt bad but hoped the ambulance in the nearby firehouse would come quickly. She knew people in the Greens that had lived after being shot. Hell, they said Big Rob took nine and lived, so why couldn't she? It couldn't get any worse, could it?

Boo turned and ran past Pookie, who lit the rag. Once it started burning, Pookie followed Boo to the van and they pulled off quickly. The van was turning on Orleans when the gas tank blew up. The fireball could be seen over the pizza delivery store.

Boo was two blocks away when he heard the first wail of the fire engines stationed in Cabrini.

"Fuck! Did you see that!" said Pookie.

"Goddamn!" said Dease, who was driving.

Boo had memorized the trip to their next stop, Lombard. He stared out the back window of the van with his thumb in his mouth. He knew he would be seeing her face for awhile. "Who got the phone?" Boo looked over at Dease, who pulled the cell phone from his coat pocket.

Chapter 36

A Hot Call

0135 Hours—Monday

Sergeant Ronnie Ryan looked up from his desk in the Eighteenth District Tactical Office when Zito walked in. "What happened?" Ryan asked.

"We followed that cocksucker for an hour." Zito took off his coat. "The asshole must've looked at every car on the north end of the district. He would park, get out and walk. He was always looking in cars, rubbernecking the whole time."

Macbeth came in from taking the one-eyed robber down to the wagon that was going to take her to the female lock-up in Area Three. He went over to the computer desk, where Timmy Hagen was busy logging past arrests into a computer program. Hagen was still on light duty and would be for at least another month. "You're not missing anything out there," Macbeth said.

"I'd rather be freezing my balls off than doing this bullshit," Hagen said, looking up. "I'm going cross-eyed, man."

"He didn't hit anything?" Ryan asked Zito.

"Nah, we gave him to the Michigan Avenue guys. They'll follow him all night 'til he fucks up," Zito said. "I thought maybe we'd all go to The Boss for some beers."

Ryan looked at his watch; it was after one thirty in the morning. They were due to get off at two. "Not a bad idea," he said. He had spent the day catching up on paperwork. It was an aspect of being a sergeant he didn't much like. A beer would taste very nice right about now. "I think we can do that. What do you think, Timmy? Wanna stop?"

Hagen stopped typing and looked around the monitor at him. He smiled. "Definitely. Macbeth?"

"Works for me." Macbeth set his vest on the table by the bench.

"Teddy, Frank and Hank still out?" Ryan asked.

"Yeah," Macbeth said over his shoulder, as Zito dialed a phone. "Hank called and said something about one last pass."

"Wonderful," Ryan said sarcastically. He knew that when the phrase "one last pass" was invoked, it meant there was a chance of a late arrest or some other overtime-generating action.

"*Eighteen sixty-four Adam, emergency!*" Teddy Ketchum's voice was relatively calm on the radio, but Ryan recognized excitement tempered by urgency.

"*Unit with the emergency, go ahead,*" said a female dispatcher. Zito hung up.

Macbeth grabbed his vest off the table and threw it over his head.

"*We got shots fired. From 1157 Cleveland or 1150 Sedgwick!*"

Zito was a step behind Macbeth going out the door. They ran for the stairs.

Ryan got up and picked up his coat from the back of the seat. He grabbed his radio from the desk. Hagen pushed away from the desk and got out of his chair. "Shots fired" calls, even those called in by officers on the street, weren't uncommon in Cabrini Green.

"Where do you think you're going?" Ryan asked.

"Come on, Ronnie," Hagen said. "I gotta get outta here."

Ryan looked closely at Hagen and recognized himself. He knew he had to get out of the office and away from the paperwork, too. He'd only spent the last shift here, not the last few weeks like Tim. "Okay, but don't get hurt. And that's a fucking order."

Hagen smiled and stripped his winter coat off a hanger on the coat rack by the door. As they walked down the stairs, they could hear the sound of a car roar down the street. A siren blared. Had to be Macbeth and Zito.

"Eighteen sixty-four Adam, emergency!" said Ketchum over the radio. The excitement was rising in his voice as he continued, without waiting for the dispatcher's response. *"We got an explosion and lots of smoke from around the front of 1150 Sedgwick. You'd better roll fire!"*

"Ten-four, eighteen sixty-four Adam," said the dispatcher in a calm, disinterested tone. *"We'll get fire rolling."*

Ryan and Hagen exchanged looks after Ketchum's last transmission. Something was definitely up. "Tim, I'm sorry." He put a hand on Hagen's good shoulder. "I need you to stay here to make notifications." Ryan quickened his pace, which carried him out into the parking lot and into the falling snow.

"EIGHTEEN SIXTY-FOUR ADAM! GET FIRE HERE NOW! WE GOT A PERSON TRAPPED IN A BURNING CAR!" Ketchum shouted into the radio held in front of his mouth. He stood away from the burning Toyota Camry in the parking lot of 1150 North Sedgwick. The car was en-

gulfed in flames, but he could see a body in the backseat. One that Barnhill was still trying to get to.

Ketchum watched as Barnhill let Hampton pull him away from the burning car. They left it for the firemen. Before the firemen could get any water on the car, it exploded, lifting it off the ground.

Then, water blasted it from a hose off the pump truck. Firemen wrestled with a frozen fire hydrant cap. Nearby, a second hose was laid out on the ice-covered ground.

Ketchum looked toward Sedgwick. When Macbeth and Zito pulled up, their maroon squad car slid to a stop dangerously close to the fire truck. No one noticed but him. They jumped out of the car to join him, Barnhill and Hampton on the sidelines and watch the firemen work.

They were silent for several minutes. No one expected the passenger to be alive. The whole interior of the car was charred, the metal bare. All the windows were gone, as well as most of the upholstery. The outside of the car was blackened around the openings, but the color was still discernible. A chain and handcuffs were visible on the driver's side of the car.

Ketchum turned to Macbeth. "There was nothing we could do."

Macbeth nodded. He knew what Ketchum was probably thinking; there must've been some way he could've prevented this. If only they had been in this lot instead of another, or something like that. Macbeth shook his head. "I know."

Ryan walked up as the firemen finished with their hoses and began with their pry bars. They raised the hood of the car and blasted the engine with water to prevent the fire from rekindling later. They popped the trunk and did the same. Ryan turned to Zito. "Get the tape from my trunk."

He tossed Zito his car keys.

"Sarge," Ketchum said, coming over to Ryan's elbow. "Did you see the chain and handcuffs?"

"Yeah," Ryan said. He didn't look away from the burnt husk of a car and its sole, grisly occupant. "I did."

Chapter 37

Walking the Dog

0145 Hours—Monday

Old Rufus Beasley turned onto the railroad property, following his old hound dog up the ice-covered dirt road at Fifty-Eighth and Shields. He was walking as slow as, if not slower than, his dog, which was good for him. He was younger than the dog in dog years, but not by much. The snow had been falling heavily, but that was all right with him; he had been drinking heavily. He didn't notice the cold or the snow very much. His dog, also named Rufus, was in front of him.

Rufus, the man, couldn't wait for his dog to stop, so he sauntered over to a bare tree and pissed. Steam rose into the snow-filled night air. Rufus, the dog, looked back over his shoulder, coughed a dog cough and waited.

Once finished, which took some time, they continued up the road. This was their nightly walk. Rufus, the dog, had to make it count. By the time they got home, he'd have polished off the half-pint in his pocket and he'd be sleeping like a baby. 'Cept later than any baby he ever knew of.

Three-quarters of the way to the top of the road and the train yards, Rufus, the dog, stopped dead in his tracks. The dog got stiff and then brought his nose down to the ground.

The dog veered from the road and plowed into the snow-covered field.

Rufus, the man, yelled. Rufus, the dog, smelled the ground and then began to bite at a mound of snow.

Rufus, the man, came over to grab the old dog but had to walk carefully in the icy ruts. As he got closer, he could see the dog had something in his mouth and was tugging on it with all his weight.

"Goddamnit, what is you doing?"

He walked closer and squinted. His eyesight wasn't nearly what it had been. Then he saw that his dog was pulling on the ankle of a man. An ankle that had a bare blue foot attached to it.

"Goddamn!"

Chapter 38

A Call for Macbeth

0150 Hours—Monday

Hagen sat alone at the desk. He had called Nicholas Rosetti, the Tactical Lieutenant, at home. Rosetti had been asleep but was glad he had been called. He'd said that the commander would want answers in the morning. Hagen turned up the volume on his radio, hoping to hear some news from the street.

The intercom buzzed twice. He picked up the phone.

"Tac. Hagen."

"Pick up three-zero," said the tired voice of the midnight desk officer. Hagen didn't respond, just punched the button on the phone. "Eighteen Tac, Hagen," he said, reaching for a message pad. I'm a damn secretary, Hagen thought, shaking his head in disgust. I've traded all my street skills for secretarial ones.

There was silence at first. He could tell by the static on the line that the caller was on a cell phone. "Macbeth?" the voice on the phone asked.

"He's on the street," Hagen said, not able to place the voice. "I'm his partner. Can I help you?"

"Yeah. You be telling him that bitch Gibbons ain't

gonna be making no more motherfuckin' calls."

The line went dead with an abrupt crackle and pop. Hagen reached for the radio.

Chapter 39

The Minuteman

0150 Hours—Monday

Javier Ricardo Fernandez pulled his neon yellow IDOT International four-ton straight truck onto the shoulder of the southbound Dan Ryan Expressway behind a stalled car. The IDOT Minuteman Service provides roadside assistance to the expressway in the Chicago area. It's really important in winter, when a lot of vehicles fail their owners. The area has a lot of underprivileged that drive cars and trucks even more underprivileged than they are.

Fernandez sat up high in his truck. The plows had gone through regularly and the road was in fairly good condition, despite the snowfall. The heater was spewing hot air onto his legs. It could never be hot enough in weather like this.

He was second-generation Mexican-American but could speak only a little Spanish. He hated the winter months but loved his job. He'd been a mechanic at a car dealership on the north side but saw no real challenge or advancement. He was a people-person and enjoyed helping those in need. He was a natural.

He pulled on his fluorescent orange gloves, after radioing in his location to the State Police dispatcher. His orange hat was on and his jacket zipped up. He opened the door and hopped out onto the shoulder, careful not to step into traffic. He walked in front of his truck. The lights coming from behind and above lit up the car in front of him.

"Hello!" he said over the rush and scream of southbound traffic. It was hard to hear on the highway. He waved his gloved hand at the people in the car. "Hello!"

After a half hour, he was back in the truck, warming his cold fingers in the wash of hot air blowing out of the dash. A lot of work had to be done with his bare hands, and in this weather that was downright dangerous. This time it had been a battery, sapped by a shitty electrical system.

He watched as the car pulled away when a lull of traffic allowed. He felt good, cold but good. As the car accelerated, kicking snow and salt backward in a rooster tail, he noticed several objects sticking out of the snow on the shoulder. In the dim light, he couldn't make out what they were exactly. He thought they might be some sort of metal rods that were sticking out of the roadway.

He pulled his gloves on and climbed back down from the truck, walked over and turned on his flashlight. He had to get real close before he recognized a bulky garbage bag mostly covered by plowed snow. Whatever was sticking out of the snow was attached to the bag by something. He knelt down, perplexed. He stared at the objects, four broken blue and white objects. They weren't metal rods.

He stood. His mouth was dry and his stomach convulsed. He dropped on his ass and turned, vomit spraying the pile of plowed snow next to him. He got into his truck and called in his gruesome discovery. He looked back out the window into the cold glare of his headlights, where the four blue and white fingers of Robert Starr, Jr. stuck out of the packed snow, waving goodbye.

Chapter 40

Identifications

0240 Hours—Monday

Ryan stood in the lobby of 1150 North Sedgwick, directly across the parking lot from the burnt-out Toyota Camry. A detective from Area Three stood at his side, taking notes. "My guys," said Ryan, "Ketchum, Hampton and Barnhill, eighteen sixty-four Adam, were out on the street when they heard several gunshots. They radioed the shots in and started over here. On the way over, they heard an explosion. They called that in, too. Just seconds after that, Ketchum came over the air with the person trapped in the car." He pointed toward the yellow crime scene tape snapping in the cold wind. "We taped off the area when the firemen said there was nothing else that could be done. I looked around a little and found no spent cartridges, but I wanted the crime scene clean for you guys. No one has come up with an identification, at least that I know of."

"I haven't heard of any either," Detective Al Toomer said. "Thanks, Ronnie." Toomer was dressed in a long overcoat that was open, revealing a dated sports coat and wide, colorful tie. A half-smoked cigarette hung from his mouth, bobbing up and down as he spoke. "Your guys can go if they want, or they can hang out. I don't care, as long as they don't get in the way."

"We're already on overtime," Ryan said. He knew his men would want to beat the bushes a little.

Ryan knew Area Three Detectives frequently called his tac team when they were looking for someone in Cabrini. Nobody spent as much time in these projects as his guys. "A couple of my guys have good contacts in here. Let's see what they can come up with."

"No problem. We could use the help."

Macbeth had his back to the crime scene, the frigid weather forgotten thanks to his northern upbringing. He scanned the crowd that had gathered to watch the police work. The windows of the projects that faced the parking lot were filled with people, many of whom had their windows open and were hanging out, despite the time and temperature. He looked for familiar faces, but didn't see any. He suspected someone in 1150 knew something, but he had serious doubts whether anyone would come forward with anything useful. It wasn't too unusual for gangs to intimidate people into giving false information. He figured Ketchum might stand a better chance at getting a good tip. Ketchum had a well-established system of informants he'd been working on for years.

Macbeth's attention was diverted by Toomer waving Ryan over. The detective was standing next to the driver's window of the burned-out wreck. Ryan ducked under the crime scene tape and walked up to him. They talked and then Toomer, who had put on rubber gloves, showed Ryan something about the handcuffs. Ryan bent closer and took his flashlight out.

His sergeant stood looking around. He called out to Ketchum. Ryan and Toomer walked over and met Ketchum at the edge of the crime scene. Toomer lit another cigarette, flicking the old one well outside the tape. Toomer showed Ketchum his notebook. Ketchum shook his head, looked over at Macbeth and motioned him over.

Macbeth walked up to Ketchum, who was looking at Toomer's notebook again.

"Didn't you know a security guard named Chaney?" asked Ketchum.

"Yeah, he worked the 624 Division building." Macbeth reached for the notebook. "Why?"

" 'Cause the detective says his name is on the handcuffs." Ketchum pointed his thumb over his shoulder at the burnt car.

"No shit?" Macbeth looked at the notebook page in his gloved hand. It read: W. Chaney # 84 Chicago Security.

"That's him," Macbeth said, remembering his one-time informant. "First name starts with a *W*, not William, but something like that."

"We still don't have an ID on the body, though?" Ryan asked Toomer.

"No idea, but one of the crime lab guys thinks it's female."

"Hey, Stace!" Zito shouted from the lobby doorway where he was holding the door open. "Timmy says you got to call the office right away. Says it's an emergency."

Macbeth gave the notebook back to the detective, turned and walked to his car. It was snowing again. The car was still running and Zito had left the heater on full blast. He turned it down. Reaching into the small canvas bag he kept on the front seat, he removed his cell phone. It chirped, reminding him that it needed charging.

"Eighteen Tac. Hagen."

"Timmy, this is Macbeth. What's up?"

"Listen, Stace. I just got a call," Hagen said quietly, as if he were trying to prevent someone from overhearing. "The caller said Latricia Gibbons wouldn't be calling you no more."

"Shit. You thinking that the body in the car is hers?"

"Yep," said Hagen. "That's exactly what I'm thinking."

"Aw, fuck." Macbeth closed his eyes.

"That's exactly what I said."

"I'll let you know," Macbeth said. It wasn't so bad when the roasted flesh didn't have a name to go with it. "Don't go nowhere 'til I call."

"I'll be here." Hagen hung up.

Macbeth approached the burnt-out car from the driver's side. He was followed by Toomer and Ketchum. The temperature was falling and the wind whipped hard, biting at any exposed flesh. Except, of course, the charred flesh of the car's occupant.

Macbeth brought his Mag-light to bear on the remains of the body in the backseat. From this close, the flashlight had the power of a spotlight. He looked closely at the blackened flesh that had shrunk and split from the skeleton.

The body's head was thrown back, arms shriveled and crisp, the mouth wide open, as if when she had screamed, her jaw unhinged. The pose, burnt taut from fire, spoke of unbearable agony. There were several rents in the flesh that exposed bright red meat. Macbeth could see the slim remains of some kind of material that had been used to bind the hands. He tried but could not positively identify the body. He couldn't say for sure that it was her. Whatever clothes she had been wearing were burned away. He shook his head and stepped back, but he knew in his heart that it had to be her.

"I don't know, it could be," he said. Ketchum looked

through the window. "Maybe. The face is awful distorted, though."

"Right now, it'll stay a Jane Doe, but we'll look into Latricia Gibbons. It gives us someplace to start," Toomer said. "Hell, she's probably upstairs right now asleep, drooling on her pillow, while we're out here freezing our asses off."

"What do you think, Teddy?" Macbeth asked.

"Fuck if I know," said Ketchum. "I know where her momma stays, though. She can take a look at this thing and, if that don't work, I'm sure she'll have an extra key, as much as she baby-sits those kids."

"This'll be a dental identification," Toomer said. "I doubt the ME will even let a family member see that thing."

Chapter 41

624 West Division

0300 Hours—Monday

Macbeth parked their unmarked Caprice in front of the white cinderblock building at 624 West Division Street. All the buildings in the Cabrini projects north of Division Street were white. Those south of Division were red brick. He put the car keys in his belt buckle for easy access. He and Zito locked the doors before walking up the hundred feet of poorly shoveled sidewalk to the building.

Cabrini Green had been modified since the Dantrell Davis shooting in 1992. The little second-grader had been shot and killed by a sniper's bullet. Since his death, the Feds had provided money, and all the buildings were locked down, equipped with iron gates, metal detectors and twenty-four-hour guards. The lobbies were no longer open. By federal mandate, a significant percentage of the security personnel had to be residents. At first, this sounded good. But when gang influence was figured into the equation, it became readily apparent, except to the Feds, that local residents were easily intimidated. After all, they had to live in the buildings where they were working. A gang member wouldn't have to go far to find an off-duty guard.

Zito reached the double-doors first and pulled them

open. He walked into the entryway. Directly in front of them was a metal detector, with a steel door directly to the left that was used as an exit. Macbeth walked through the detector and heard nothing. Zito stopped and looked around the back of the machine. It was unplugged. Zito kneeled down and plugged the cord back into the outlet. When he walked through, the machine squawked.

In the lobby, Macbeth pressed his face against the dark security booth. He shined his flashlight inside and saw the two guards fast asleep. He rapped hard on the Plexiglas with the back end of his flashlight. Both men opened their eyes, but only one got to his feet to let them in.

Macbeth stood in the doorway while Zito was in the office on the phone with Hagen. The junior guard, Maurice Jones, the one who'd gotten up to let them in, was back out in the lobby monitoring the metal detector; the senior guard, Bobbie Ross, stayed in the booth with Macbeth and Zito. "How long have you worked here?" asked Macbeth, recognizing that Ross had the look of a hardcore gangbanger.

" 'Bout four months," said Ross.

"Did you know a guard by the name of Chaney?"

"No."

"How long have you worked for Chicago Security?" he asked.

"Four months, there 'bouts."

Zito hung up the phone and looked back at Macbeth, then at Ross. "Timmy says this is definitely the place." Zito played with the phone cord. "I wonder what your supervisor's going to think when we tell him you guys were asleep with the metal detector shut off?"

"He gonna be pissed off," Ross said.

Macbeth backed out into the lobby and closed the door.

There had been no traffic in the five minutes since they'd arrived. Jones had his black nylon coat on, zipped up, with his hands stuck in his pockets. Jones wore a black knit band around his ears.

"How long you worked this account?" Macbeth asked, walking around the lobby until he had Jones between himself and the guard booth.

"This my second week."

Macbeth noticed that Jones half turned and looked out of the corner of his eye toward Ross. "Did you know a guard named Chaney?"

There was hesitation. Jones looked over at Ross again. "No," Jones said.

Macbeth looked into the booth and saw Ross was talking to Zito. Zito was still sitting in the chair, facing them, with Ross standing, his back to them and the lobby.

"You in a gang, Maurice?"

"No," Jones said without hesitation or apparent thought.

"Who unplugged the machine?"

Jones looked fully into the booth at Ross' back. "I . . . I don't know."

"Quit lying, Maurice." Macbeth almost felt sorry for the kid.

"Man, I don't know. It was on the last time I looked." Jones didn't sound too sure of himself.

"Is Ross in a gang?"

Jones looked toward the floor and shuffled his feet. "You'd have to ask him."

"Listen, Maurice. We're not here to get you guys in trouble. We just need some answers, okay?" Macbeth looked into the booth again. "Ross can't see you. Just nod your head. Give me a side-to-side for yes. It'll look like a no, okay?"

Jones looked up at him, his eyes filled with tears. He shrugged his shoulders and gave an up and down shake of his head. "A'right."

"Did Ross turn off the machine?"

Jones looked out of the corner of his eye again before he shook his head side-to-side.

"Is Ross a gang member?"

There was no hesitation this time. Jones shook his head from one side to the other, leaving no room for doubt. A tear ran down Jones' cheek; he must be figuring that his ass was as good as fired. Macbeth nodded. Zito caught his eye and held his gaze for a second.

"Get in the booth, take off your coat and roll your sleeves up," Macbeth said to Jones. Jones looked at him. "Come on, I don't have all fucking night." He put a hand on Jones' shoulder and gently turned him. Jones stepped forward and opened the door to the booth.

"Mike, this asshole is fucking me around," Macbeth said. "He might be a GD."

Jones looked at him as if he had been double-crossed, but he began to remove his coat. Jones threw the coat on a chair and unbuttoned his shirt. Ross moved away from his fellow guard. "You can roll up the sleeves," Macbeth said.

"I've got on long underwear," Jones said, quickly stripping to his waist. He had no tattoos of any kind.

"Dress," Zito said. He'd apparently picked up on Macbeth's game.

"Okay, now you," said Zito, looking at Ross. Reluctantly, Ross began to peel off his jacket, shirt and long underwear. He stood in the booth, wearing his black pants and gun belt. As expected, his upper torso was covered in tattoos. All of them were of the amateur, homemade variety. The six-pointed star and the pitchfork of the Gangster Disciples street gang dominated the inked markings.

"You're a GD," Macbeth said.

"No, that was when I was kid," Ross said unconvincingly. He started to get dressed.

"Okay," said Macbeth. "Let's see your tan card."

The tan card is the State of Illinois' permit to carry a weapon. The card identifies the person, weapon and circumstances under which a person can be armed. It's a crime to not be in compliance with the conditions listed on the card, including the specific make, model and serial number of the handgun.

Ross pulled out his wallet and began to search through identification cards, bills and receipts. He found the permit and handed it to Macbeth.

Macbeth read the card. "Let's see your weapon."

Ross unsnapped the holster and looked over at Zito. His eyes widened when he saw Zito's Beretta in his lap. Ross carefully removed his own gun and gave it to Macbeth.

"You got a problem, Bobbie," Macbeth said. "This is a Colt Python. Your card reads a Smith and Wesson Model 19. I wonder what other discrepancies we'll find?"

"Officer Macbeth," Zito said, "you got a nasty grin." Zito handcuffed Ross. He sat Ross down and said to the other guard, "Call your supervisor, Officer Jones. Ross, here, is going to jail."

Chapter 42

Processing

0400 Hours—Monday

Bobbie Ross was in more trouble than either Macbeth or Zito had previously imagined. When they ran the gun through the gun desk, they were told it had been stolen from the house of a deputy sheriff in Lake County, Indiana. That was another charge: Possession of Stolen Property. The biggest discovery came when Bobbie Ross turned out to not be Bobbie at all. He was actually Milton Gerald Ross, Bobbie's older brother, a Gangster Disciple and convicted felon. That was a felony charge: Unlawful Use of a Weapon by a convicted felon.

When the Chicago Security Supervisor, Lester Stantly, arrived, he was very upset. At first, he couldn't believe that one of his men had been arrested. He implied, at first, that the charges had been fabricated somehow. Zito seemed to enjoy explaining to him how, over the last couple of months, it had become increasingly difficult for the police to operate in the 624 building. The Chicago Security Guards had something to do with those difficulties, something Zito would be more than happy to put to the Chicago Housing Authority. That is, if he didn't receive some cooperation from Mr. Stantly. Luckily, Stantly didn't recognize it as a bluff.

The problem, Stantly said, was beyond his limited control. He contacted his supervisor. When Macbeth asked about Chaney, Stantly said that he usually worked the south side accounts and didn't know Chaney.

After getting the arrest report signed by the watch commander, Macbeth went behind the front desk to use the photocopier. Out of the corner of his eye he saw a large, dark, security officer walk up to the front desk. He had bronze oak leaves on the lapel of his navy blue nylon jacket. Macbeth saw the Chicago Security patch and figured the oak leaves designated him as some sort of big shot. When the guard spoke, his voice was deep and controlled, "I'm here to see Macbeth or Zito."

"Hang on, I'll be right there," Macbeth said flipping the case report over in the copier. The officer stepped back against the wall and waited. Macbeth collected the papers as the machine spit them out. He retrieved his originals, shut the lid and walked around the copy machine.

"How you doing? I'm Macbeth." He offered his hand. "Thanks for coming down."

"Donald Freeman." They shook hands. "No problem."

"I've got a couple things I need from you," Macbeth said. "Well, actually one I need."

"Shoot," said Freeman. They walked toward the back of the District. Macbeth paused at the base of the stairs.

"First, I'll tell you about your guard, Bobbie Ross," Macbeth said in his official tone. "His real name is Milton Ross. He's a gangbanger and convicted felon. Gun he's carrying is stolen. He's going to jail."

"I see," Freeman said. He put one foot on the bottom stair and placed his large hand on the painted metal banister. "He's unemployed as of now, too."

"Thought you might say that," Macbeth said. "By the way, the other kid at that account, Jones, seems like a good kid. He wasn't mixed up with Ross that we can tell." Freeman nodded. Macbeth continued, "I'm also looking for another of your guards. Stantly wasn't able to help me and it's an emergency."

"Who?"

"Chaney. He used to work 624."

"That makes three of us that'd like to talk to Wendell." Freeman straightened and buried his hands in his pants pockets. Macbeth could hear change rattle.

"What do you mean?"

"Yesterday Wendell didn't show up for work. I ain't heard from him. Why are you looking for him? Is he in some sort of trouble?"

"I'm afraid so. Did you call his house?" asked Macbeth.

"Yep, woke his wife up," said Freeman. "I don't think she's slept since, calls me every few hours. Shit, she called me just before Lester did. I think she filed a police report."

"Chaney isn't the kind of guy with a drinking or drug problem or girlfriend, is he?"

"Shhhit! Wendell, are you crazy?!" Freeman said, shaking his head. "Anybody but Wendell. Shhhit. Wendell ain't missed work in years."

"That's how I remember Chaney, too, squeaky clean." Macbeth looked up at the top of the yellow tile walls that were stained brown from dust and dirt. The custodians apparently couldn't reach past six feet without a ladder or chair. "Where's he work now?"

"Over at the old folks' home on Clybourn, midnights. We moved him over after he helped the police over at 624. We were concerned for his safety."

189

"You got Mrs. Chaney's number?" Macbeth began to climb the stairs.

"I only got it 'bout eight or nine times on my beeper." Freeman followed Macbeth up.

Macbeth led Freeman to the second floor. When they walked into the office, Macbeth was surprised to see Ketchum and Hampton sitting on either side of Ross on the prisoner's bench. Macbeth sat at an empty desk.

The conversation in the office came to a stop. Freeman crossed the room and stood silent for a second in front of Ross. "You're fired. Give me your ID," he said flatly.

"Here you go," Zito said, holding up a plastic identification card. "We got to inventory his tan card, though."

Freeman took the card from Zito. "This is all I need. Thanks." He took his pager from his shirt pocket and walked over to Macbeth. He read the number to him. "If that's all, I got rounds to make."

"Thanks, Freeman," Macbeth said.

Zito removed Ross' handcuff from the ring in the wall. He cuffed both hands behind Ross' back. Hampton followed Zito, Ross and Freeman out of the office and down the stairs to the lock-up.

Ketchum stood and walked over to Macbeth as he was about to dial Chaney's number on the phone. "Macbeth, Latricia Gibbons' mother ended up being brought in. Somehow she was able to identify the body," he said in a soft, overtired voice. "I guess she did it from her teeth. Lonnie had just knocked out one of the front ones."

"Aw, fuck."

Chapter 43

A Crowded Shoulder

0400 Hours—Monday

James Patrick O'Boyle pulled in behind the assortment of State Police vehicles on the shoulder of the southbound Dan Ryan Expressway near Eightieth Street. The old, unmarked Chevy Caprice had yet to warm up. O'Boyle and his temporary partner, Josef Greizedicht, had been the only dicks free when the call came in from the State. They'd been in the office doing the paper on an Aggravated Battery from earlier in the morning.

O'Boyle opened the car door and got out quickly, to avoid being run over by the traffic speeding southbound, despite the weather. He wondered if it would ever stop snowing. He looked at his partner, the amiable Joe "Greasydick," Mr. Personality. Greizedicht stayed in the passenger seat, trying to get more out of the overworked heater.

O'Boyle approached from behind, trying his best to avoid getting snow on his dress shoes. By the time he had walked past two unmarked state investigator cars, two crime scene processing station wagons, three state patrol squad cars and one massive Minuteman International truck, his shoes were packed with snow. He walked carefully toward a small crowd of State cops who were watching the crime scene techs crawl around a mound of snow on the shoulder. They were measuring a pile of snow atop a garbage bag that had broken open, spilling its contents onto the shoulder. The leak, an arm, to be more accurate, complete with four blue fingers at the end.

"Hello," O'Boyle said.

Two state troopers at the rear of the group turned to face him.

"This is a crime scene, you'll have to . . ." The nearest trooper began.

O'Boyle stopped the lecture by producing his detective identification.

"I'd be happy to leave, but you guys called me." He put his ID away. "What have you got here?"

A short man stepped away from the front of the group, partially into traffic. One of the troopers guided him back onto the shoulder. The short man was wearing a heavy winter parka, mittens and a cap with folded-down ears. His nose was bright red and there was clear snot running into his mustache. "I'm Sergeant Todd Weatherby from Investigations."

"Jim O'Boyle, Area One Dicks. How you doing?"

"I'm freezing my ass off. Glad you could make it," said Weatherby. "This might be one of yours. Looks like he was wrapped up and dumped here."

"I see," O'Boyle said. "Actually, this is Area Two's section of town. When you called, you said you were farther north."

"Yeah, ah . . ." Weatherby said. "One of the troopers got his cross-streets mixed up. We should know pretty soon what we got."

"I'd say you already know." O'Boyle recognized

Weatherby's type. One thing a detective developed was a good bullshit indicator, and his was going off strong as he looked at the State Investigator.

"What?"

"Looks like you got a dead body on the highway. Until you can prove otherwise, it's yours. See ya." He turned on his heels and walked back toward the car. He waved at Greizedicht who was high-stepping through the piles of plowed snow on the passenger sides of the gathered vehicles. "They don't need us, Joe."

O'Boyle stopped by the last state patrol car, where a trooper sat behind the wheel. "Who made the call for Chicago?"

"Sergeant Weatherby," the trooper said through the open window. O'Boyle could hear the heater blowing full blast. Farther back, Greizedicht got in the car and closed the door.

"Figures."

"Yeah, he's from downstate," said the trooper. "He did less than a year on patrol before getting a promotion and a nice spot in investigations. He's a politician. Couldn't find his asshole with both hands."

"That's just fucking great."

Chapter 44

Can't Sleep

0430 Hours—Monday

Sharron Chaney was startled by the phone. Hours ago, she had given up hope that Wendell would be calling. The gangbangers weren't after money. They wanted revenge.

"Hello," she said.

"Mrs. Chaney?" a voice asked. She knew right away that the caller was white.

"Yes."

"Mrs. Chaney, I'm sorry to bother you at this hour," the voice said. "I'm with the Chicago Police. My name is Macbeth. I used to . . ."

"I know who you are." She was awake now. "I know who you are, Officer Macbeth."

"Have you heard from Wendell?"

"No, and I hold you responsible." The anger began to rise in her breast. Here on the phone was the man that she told her husband would get him into trouble.

"Excuse me?"

"You heard me," she said.

"I don't understand."

"Because of you, my Wendell could be dead."

"Mrs. Chaney . . ."

"Don't give me that! If it wasn't for you and your damn police business, I would have my Wendell." She felt the anger climbing from her breast to her throat. If it reached her head, she'd lose it and wake up the children. She tried to calm down. There were several moments of silence.

"Mrs. Chaney, did you make out a police report?"

"Yes."

"Did you and Wendell have a fight or anything like that?"

"That's what the other officer asked," she said. "No one will listen to me. There was no fight. There have been no marriage problems. Wendell left for work early that night and was probably killed by those gangbangers he put in jail for you. Why won't you people listen to me?"

"Why did Wendell leave early for work?" asked Macbeth.

"I don't know. He didn't say."

"Wendell was in a car then?"

"Yes," she said.

"Did the officer take that down?"

"Yes, she did."

"Do you have a report number?"

"Yes."

"Can you give it to me?"

"You're the police, you should have it!" The anger was becoming harder to control. "Why are you asking me for all this?"

"I'm trying to figure out where to start."

"Why don't you start with those gangbangers that he put in jail for you!"

"Mrs. Chaney, that doesn't happen as much as you might think . . ."

Sharron slammed the phone receiver down. She was certain she had woken up the baby, but she couldn't take any more. Why won't they go out and find her husband? Wendell should have listened to her. She walked into the hallway toward the baby's room.

Macbeth stared at the receiver that had gone dead in his hand. Somehow, he couldn't bring himself to be mad at her. He even felt some guilt begin to churn his stomach. He hung up the phone, but picked it back up again. The Fourth District should still have the report at the desk. If not, he'd have to call Missing Persons.

Chapter 45

Back to the Shoulder

0435 Hours—Monday

Greizedicht was on his second double cheeseburger when O'Boyle squeezed into the chair across from him with a cup of coffee. O'Boyle didn't have any food, not because he objected to the food, but he reserved White Castle for drunken binges. Greizedicht ate loud and fast, like he thought someone was going to snatch the food from in front of him. O'Boyle was sure that, with his chewing and lip-smacking, he'd wake up the drunk who had passed out on the other side of the restaurant.

Greizedicht was fat. He dressed in polyester, and his outfits were completely uncoordinated. At roll call, O'Boyle had suggested he look for the "GrrrAnimals" tags in adult sizes. The comment bounced off Greizedicht like a rubber ball off a brick wall. It had got a laugh from the other dicks, but just a wet burp from Greizedicht.

No one in the Area wanted to work with him. He hadn't had a regular partner for years. He was a curse given to detectives when their regular partners went on furlough. He was so bad that a number of detectives took their vacations together so as to not stick each other with him. O'Boyle wasn't that lucky. His partner was young and got shitty furlough picks. O'Boyle got better ones, but was stuck with . . .

He tried to not watch Greizedicht eat. No matter how hard he tried, just like with horror movies, he couldn't help but look.

O'Boyle's pager went off. Thankful for something to do, he got out of his seat, went to his car and got his cell phone. The office. What'd they want now?

"Area One. Sergeant Miller."

"Yeah, Sarge. It's O'Boyle."

"Listen, take Greasydick back to the scene on the Ryan."

"Sarge, that's Area Two's, not ours."

"Yeah, well, they got some big retirement party tonight and we gotta cover 'em," Miller said. "Besides, Greasydick ain't doing shit. That shooting from earlier is yours."

"Yeah, but I'm on my way to Christ Hospital to see how he's doing," O'Boyle said.

"He's still in surgery and still a John Doe," Miller said. "Now get over there."

"Fine."

"Hey, O'Boyle!"

"Yeah."

"Make Greasydick get out of the car and do some fucking police work for a change."

"Yeah." O'Boyle stabbed the End button with his index finger.

Chapter 46

Late, Late Night

0440 Hours—Monday

Macbeth shut off his Jeep after he pulled into the rear fire lane in the east parking lot of the twelve-story, brick senior complex at 1533 North Clybourn Avenue. He didn't see Zito's headlights anywhere. He got out and locked the door.

He put his keys in his inner coat pocket as he walked up the ramp. No sign of Zito. Should be finishing my last beer, he thought. The door was locked and chained. He leaned toward the glass and cupped his hand to look through the quickly-forming frost. Inside the lobby, a black security guard was talking to Zito. He must've parked in front. Macbeth knocked hard.

The guard walked over and took out a set of keys, unlocking the chain. He was wearing only his navy blue uniform, no coat, as he pushed the door open.

"What the fuck you park in back for?" Zito asked.

Macbeth shrugged his shoulders and took off his gloves, offering his right hand to the guard. Macbeth saw that Zito still had his Chicago Police star hanging from a chain around his neck.

"Hi, I'm Macbeth," he said, shaking hands.

"Moore."

"Officer Moore here," Zito said, "was telling me that he knew Wendell. And that Wendell didn't come to work tonight or last night."

"Chaney mention anything about being scared or something happening or anything?" asked Macbeth.

"Not since he first came over to this contract from Cabrini. But that was months ago," Moore said. "When he first started, he used to talk about the GDs wanting to get him over testifying, and all. But he hasn't said nothing since."

"Never talk about being followed?" asked Zito.

"No," Moore said. "Not that I can remember."

"Are there any Mickey Cobras in the building, or any that visit?" asked Macbeth, wondering how the handcuffs got into the parking lot of the Mickey Cobra building.

"Not that I'm aware of."

"Wendell have any friends in the police department?" asked Macbeth. "Anybody that he talked to?"

"Yeah, Wendell used to talk about you, but he hasn't in a while. He sometimes would talk about a guy that works the projects, name of Farmer."

"Terry Farmer?" asked Zito.

"Yeah, that's him," Moore said.

"Why was Chaney coming into work early on Saturday?" asked Macbeth.

"Beats me."

"Wendell ever mention losing a pair of handcuffs?" asked Zito, zipping his coat.

"No, not that I can remember," Moore said, picking up his Detex clock. "I gotta make some rounds. If you want to stay, I'll be about fifteen minutes. If you want to go, just make sure the doors close all the way. Otherwise, we'll get some frozen pipes."

Moore left the lobby by way of the service elevator. As the door dinged shut, Zito turned to Macbeth. "I think Chaney lost his cuffs and they got found by the Cobras."

"If they'd been used by GDs maybe, but there are no Cobras where he used to work," Macbeth said.

"He might of lost those cuffs long time ago," Zito said. "Who knows? This is all probably coincidence. Those gangbangers ain't gonna retaliate against no security guard."

"Who's over at Public Housing?" asked Macbeth.

"Only the special employment people," Zito said, his hand on the crash bar of the front door. "Terry went home a long time ago."

"Aw, fuck it. This has been a long night. Probably just coincidence," Macbeth said, walking across the lobby. "A beer would have been nice, too."

Chapter 47

Back at the Office

1400 Hours—Monday

Rachel Westing sat behind her desk; the office door was shut and the lights were off. She had only arrived back in Chicago less than an hour ago. Her concern for Robert Starr had been well-founded. He hadn't been seen or heard from since late Thursday afternoon, when he'd left for home. There'd been no messages on her machine, on her desk or anywhere. No word from Bob whatsoever. There was definitely something very wrong.

Robert Starr, Sr., the company's president, had come to work and locked himself in his office. He'd left word he wasn't to be disturbed for any reason short of his son's return.

Rachel sat in her office until everyone but a handful had left for home. She couldn't motivate herself to drive anymore today. It had taken her three hours yesterday to travel forty miles of lonely, skinny Wisconsin back roads in the storm and five hours this morning. No way she could bring herself to negotiate the Eisenhower traffic feeling like this. Queasiness made it hard to stand or sit comfortably.

She called a nearby hotel and made a reservation. She stood and blew her nose into a Kleenex she found in her purse. She grabbed her coat and decided to try and settle her stomach with something to eat on the way to the hotel. Then it was a bath, followed by bed.

Chapter 48

After Roll Call

1845 Hours—Monday

Macbeth sat in the front passenger seat of the Caprice with Hagen in the back. Zito was driving. Zito pulled out from behind the Eighteenth District station slowly. The snow had quit, but the property management truck had yet to plow the small lot. Snow still clogged the smaller side streets and parking lots. They were on their way to eat at the Golden Cup Restaurant on North Clark Street.

"Why didn't you call from the office? You know, let your fingers do the walking?"

Hagen said, "Ryan expects me back in an hour."

"It's on the way," Macbeth said. He hadn't slept well after he had gotten home. He kept seeing Latricia Gibbons' charred face screaming in front of him. Was there something he could've done to prevent her murder? "It won't take long. I want to talk to Terry Farmer for a minute."

Public Housing North was located in the Cabrini Green Projects, in the 365 West Oak Building. There were parking spots for police vehicles along the building's front drive, but they were under at least ten inches of snow. Zito let Macbeth out and idled the car in the middle of the driveway.

Macbeth pushed through the lobby door and walked around to the Housing North offices. He had to knock on the door to get the attention of the fat, white desk officer, Walter Deacon.

Deacon had worked Public Housing forever. He'd survived commanders and had become such a regular fixture that the residents of 365 West Oak had come to expect to see him sitting behind the desk. Deacon would usually be eating. If a resident wanted a report, he'd point to the pay phones across the lobby and tell them to call the cops. When he was reminded that he himself was a police officer, he'd tell them he didn't write reports of any kind. If they insisted, he'd mouth off, calling into doubt the residents' heritage and hearing ability. Few residents asked him for reports anymore.

Deacon stretched his fat arm over and pressed the button with a finger that had to be greasy. Macbeth shouldered his way through the office outer door. He'd worked a project car before joining the tactical unit. He and Deacon had clashed on several occasions over the desk officer's inability to do what he was paid to do. Macbeth walked past Deacon toward the tactical room without saying a word.

Macbeth knocked on the half-open door and stuck his head in.

Sergeant Joseph Calderon looked up from the *Sun-Times*. "Hey, Stacey. How're you doing?"

"Good, Sarge. I don't suppose Terry's in, is he?"

"No. Can you believe he's in Vegas?" said Calderon. "Should be back tomorrow or Wednesday, I think. Something I could do for you?"

"Nah, I need to talk to him 'bout a guy," said Macbeth. "Mind if I leave him a note?"

"Go ahead. I'll put it in his mailbox for you."

After knocking a dead cockroach off of the seat, Macbeth sat across the table from the sergeant and wrote a quick note about Chaney. He folded it up and gave it to Calderon.

Zito and Hagen were waiting in front, the unmarked squad car facing the opposite direction from when they had dropped him off. Macbeth climbed in, noting the heater was on high.

"Well?" asked Zito.

"The fucker's in Vegas." Macbeth said, as he closed his eyes and saw Latricia's charred eye sockets staring at him.

The van's brake lights lit up as Dedrick Dease pressed the pedal to shift into drive. He slowly rolled out of the parking spot in the back of the lot of the apartment building. He turned right. Dease didn't turn the headlights on until he was on St. Charles Road. Just like the past four nights. Another night wasted. Ten hours spent waiting for a bitch who didn't show.

Chapter 49

After Work

0300 Hours—Tuesday

Macbeth tipped the pint glass up and let the remaining Guinness flow into his mouth. It tasted good, a little warm maybe, but good all the same. He set the glass on the bar. Ryan, Zito, Hagen and Ketchum stood next to him. They'd all gathered at The Boss Bar after their shift. Hampton and Barnhill had other plans. Alternative rock was blaring from the jukebox, so conversation was difficult up close and impossible from a distance.

"Ready for another one, Stace?" asked Ryan.

"Yeah, I got it," Macbeth said. He looked over at Monica Alexander, the bartender, who was washing glasses behind the bar. She had a gorgeous face and a figure she loved to show off. She was nice to look at but, if you didn't watch her like a hawk, she'd steal you blind.

Macbeth held up his empty glass. Alexander leaned her head so close to him that her bleached-blonde hair fell over his arm. Her physician-enhanced cleavage threatened to spill onto the dark, wet wood of the bar top.

"Another Guinness?" she asked.

"Yep, and Ryan needs another Lite," he said. "Why don't you back everyone up, while you're at it?" She looked over to see what everyone was drinking. Macbeth watched closely.

She began to set upside-down shot glasses, representing drinks paid for, to those who still held fresh drinks. She put down a Lite and another pint of Guinness and withdrew several dollars from the kitty on the bar.

Ryan poured his beer from the bottle into a plastic cup and looked over at Macbeth. "Let's not get melodramatic about this, Stace," he said.

"What?" asked Macbeth, wiping the beer foam around his mouth.

"There wasn't shit you could do," said Ryan. "So, quit running all those scenarios. Okay?"

"Yeah," Macbeth said.

"Yeah, nothing," Ryan said. "Did she call you? Tell you she was in trouble?"

"No." He took another drink.

"Did anybody else call and tell you?" asked Ryan.

"No. It's just . . ."

"Come on," Ryan said. "Don't be a jagoff. Latricia Gibbons was over twenty-one and she knew what she was doing. Right?"

"Yeah."

Ryan leaned closer. "She was a player and she got herself killed. You didn't get her killed. You feel bad? Go catch the fucker that did her."

"Yeah." Macbeth took another pull of his Guinness. "Hope Chaney don't end up a crispy critter, too."

"You might be right about that." Ryan sipped his beer. "You call Toomer in Area Three about Chaney?"

"Yeah. I paged him. He called back from the morgue. They were pulling rounds out of Latricia."

"Well, then, I guess you can enjoy your days off," Ryan

said. Their whole team had the next two days off. "Find the guard when you get back, if he's still missing."

"Yeah," Macbeth said. "I guess."

"Doing anything tomorrow?"

"Nah, Erin's working."

Hagen walked over and offered Macbeth a pool cue. "Might go by The Exit. I got some friends playing there from Minneapolis."

"No shit," Ryan said.

"Yeah, Arcwelder," Macbeth said. "They're opening for Jesus Lizard." He took a large gulp of his Guinness. He chugged the rest. Ryan laughed and backed away from the bar to let a female patron by. Macbeth held up his glass for the bartender to see. He turned back to Ryan to explain the band names.

"Stacey, I don't want to fucking know," Ryan said, still laughing.

Chapter 50

Leaving Early

1040 Hours—Tuesday

Rachel couldn't stop crying. How could this be happening? she kept asking herself. Rosemary and the children must be devastated. But how could she be thinking of them? How could she not? Rachel sobbed. She looked out the window; even the Chicago skyline couldn't lift her. She'd slept very little last night and what sleep she got was alcohol-induced. She woke up with both a hangover and cottonmouth and couldn't shake either.

At ten forty-five, Bob's secretary came in and told her that Bob's father had called and said to go home. He knew.

Rachel figured he had known about her and Bob for months. Bob, of course, didn't think so. She'd never had the heart to tell him about the passes his father had made toward her. Even after she suspected he knew about her and Bob.

Rachel started the BMW and backed out of the parking stall. How odd that just a week ago he had given her this car. She'd been so excited, she couldn't wait to tell her parents. Rachel Westing had finally arrived. Now, she just wanted Bob back. Forget the car.

She drove to Lombard on autopilot. She parked in her

building's heated garage. In the elevator, she felt a load of pressure settle in her. So many people missing in this country were never found. How many times had she seen news reports about them? Now, Bob was one of those people.

She lay down on her bed fully dressed, rolled over and cried.

At eight thirty the next morning, she called the office. There was no news. She asked for the day off and was told to talk to Starr Sr. It was several minutes before he came on the line.

"Rachel?" he said. "How're you, darling?"

"I feel terrible." She sniffled. "How's Rosemary and the kids?"

"Holding together. I understand you want the day off?"

"Yes," she said, reaching for another Kleenex. "If that's all right."

"Take the rest of the week, if you want. Just stay by the phone, in case we need you."

"Okay, I just can't face going out this morning." She blew her nose quietly. "Excuse me. I'll be in tomorrow or Friday. I've got so much to do."

"All that can wait, darling," he said. "Come in when you feel like it. I'll have Cheryl call if we need anything from you, okay?"

"Okay. Thank you."

Chapter 51

Waiting

1700 Hours—Wednesday

For the seventh night in a row, Dease pulled the red van into the lot in Lombard, parking so they could see the front of the apartment building and the garage entrance. They didn't want to push their luck. Other than not finding the car they were looking for, it had not gone too poorly. They settled down for another night of watching. Boo had stayed at home. Boo would've much rather been with them, because he was waiting to hear from Lonnie. There was no doubt that Huggins would be pissed off, to say the least.

Donna Collins recognized Lonnie's voice immediately, after accepting the charges for the collect call from the jail. She wondered how much trouble her son would be in if she'd simply hung up. She almost smiled, until she saw Boo's expression when she called him to the phone. She knew he was a liar, a gangbanger who had probably shot and killed someone by now. But when she saw him come out of his room, she thought she could briefly recognize her little boy; there was fear in that stare, and he didn't chew his thumb tonight, he sucked on it.

Even after all that she'd been through with him, she had

a difficult time stopping herself from hugging him. She was scared, too. She knew whatever trouble Boo was in could be brought right to her doorstep. She went into her bedroom and began packing.

Boo was surprised at how calm and soothing Huggins' voice was over the phone. Then again, he knew too well how dangerous Huggins was at those times. Boo was thankful Huggins was locked up; deep down, though, Boo knew that being behind bars didn't stop his power. Huggins could reach out from his cell. Boo was an example of that kind of power. And there were any number of bangers waiting for the chance to prove themselves to Huggins.

"You motherfuckers better be getting my shit back," Huggins said. "I don't want to be hearing no more bullshit. Take your niggers down to this bitch's motherfuckin' crib and camp out, dig?"

"A'right," Boo said around his thumb. "We on it."

"Better be, else I be on you," said Huggins. "Like flies on shit, motherfucker. Like death on Latricia's dumb black ass. Get what I'm saying?"

"A'right."

Chapter 52

Called Away

The Exit was a bar on the east side of Wells, just south of Eugenie. The patrons were the alternative crowd, mostly young college types, many sporting weird haircuts. The most popular color for attire was black. Black T-shirts, jeans, combat boots and leather jackets, often old Chicago Police jackets minus the police patch. A police jacket with the official patch is a misdemeanor a lot of cops felt compelled to enforce, especially when the jackets were worn with multiple earrings, body piercings, tattoos, bald heads or spiked hair. The right shoulder could still sport the city flag.

The Exit was harmless, unless you lived near it in the north side neighborhood of Old Town. Living near the bar meant occasional loud music and boisterous patrons wandering the streets after closing. The Exit had a number of sizable bouncers who kept the trouble at a minimum, even outside. The bar was for dancing and had a world-renowned dance pit. Known to be the throne of the "Counter-Culture," many cutting-edge bands liked to play there. The bar's manager, Joseph Czarczk, kept the big shows low key.

When Joe C. did have a big show, he hired extra security. Because of the liquor license the bar held, it kept off-duty police officers from working. A couple of friends were able to get around some of the technicalities of the departmental rules. Macbeth was one of those who'd be around when needed, though not officially on the payroll. He and Joe C. had met playing hockey. Macbeth had always been a part of the counter-culture, with an earring, tattoos and a deep love for the music, especially loud guitar. That was probably why he always went to see his friends' band, Arcwelder. The band thrived on a guitar-driven sound that couldn't be played loud enough.

Macbeth cheered with the crowd as it roared its approval as Arcwelder launched into its second encore of the night. "Cranberry Sauce" was an instrumental of legendary proportions. Macbeth felt his chest throb with the bass and the beat, as if the music had taken over pumping his blood. He grinned. It felt good. Here he could grin. On more than one occasion, he had been told that his grin was frightening. He'd stared at his own reflection, trying to figure where it came from. He'd decided it must be from a couple of scars, his crooked nose and his cold blue eyes.

A vibration brought him back to the real world. He barely noticed the slight vibration in the sonic atmosphere of the live music. He hoped that it would be Erin calling to say she had gotten off work early. He wanted to rendezvous. He looked down at the pager on his belt. No luck. The number belonged to a CPD phone he didn't recognize.

He lifted himself off the heavy black table that supported the band's sound and light boards. He felt the tug of the .45 tucked in the back of his ripped blue jeans, and felt it to be sure it was secure. A loose T-shirt covered it. He sat his beer bottle on the table. The beer was his first and had yet to be touched. He pushed through the sweaty throng toward the office fifteen feet away.

A black-shirted, muscular bouncer stood in the doorway, wearing his blonde-green hair in starch-plated spikes that dipped and swayed to the beat. He nodded as Macbeth approached. Macbeth put his hand to his ear, as if he were making a phone call, then pointed into the office. The bouncer slid out of the way.

The office was supposed to be soundproof, but Arcwelder had a way of testing things. Joe C. was at his desk and was trying to talk on the phone. He was a large, pale, six-foot-four white guy. His blonde hair was cut into a rigid, heavily-starched flattop that added several inches to his height. He had a big, combat-booted foot on the desk edge, his legs covered in maroon long underwear that disappeared under cut-off blue jean shorts. He wore a muscle shirt with a small German flag on the chest. His arms bulged with muscle, the kind you get from hard work, unlike Macbeth, whose muscle was built by years of weight training. Czarczk also had tattoos covering both arms, mostly skulls. He held up a finger, letting Macbeth know he would be a minute. Macbeth repeated his hand-to-ear gesture, which brought a nod of approval.

When Joe C. got off the phone, Macbeth sat down and called the number on his pager.

"Public Housing North. Deacon." Macbeth recognized the fat desk officer's voice. He figured there could be only one reason for Housing North to be paging him.

"Terry Farmer in?" He raised his voice to be heard over the music. Arcwelder had begun another song.

"Hang on." Deacon must've had a mouth full. Whatever he was chewing couldn't be as greasy as his personality. Macbeth waited.

"Farmer."

216

"Yeah, Terry. Macbeth." He put a finger in his free ear as Joe C. stepped out of the office into the crowd.

"Hey, Macbeth. How's it hanging?"

"Not bad."

"Listen, I got your message about Chaney. I would've paged you sooner, but I thought you were at work."

"Don't worry. How'd you do in Vegas?"

"Ah, I ain't quitting," Farmer said. "What's that tell you?" Farmer paused before he began again. "Stace . . ."

"Yeah." Macbeth wondered what it was that he was having trouble saying.

"This ain't going no further, right?"

"No man, between you and me. Promise." Macbeth had to listen intensely through the background music. "I'm just trying to find Chaney. Want to meet in person? I'm not far away."

"No, I just don't want this shit to get out is all. Know what I mean?"

"No further than me, Terry."

"All right, it ain't that big a deal anyway. Ain't like I made money or nothing," said Farmer. "Wendell calls me the other day."

"What day?"

"Mmmmm, Thursday night, real late," said Farmer. "Said he'd been in an accident and couldn't afford to report it to his insurance and so forth. He asked me to run a plate for him, so he could talk to the owner and get some money to fix his ride."

"His wife told me he left for work early, but didn't mention a crash or anything about collecting money," Macbeth said.

"Don't know. Maybe he didn't tell his old lady," Farmer said. "You know she don't like him playing police much."

"She doesn't like the police much, either." Macbeth didn't feel like laughing at his own joke. "He tell you about the crash?"

"No, but I still got the plate. Want it?"

"Why not? Give it to me." Macbeth rummaged through the desk drawers for a pen. He scribbled the number on a free drink card. "Chaney mention anything about gang-bangers, Gangster Disciples, or anything like that?"

"No," Farmer said. "I haven't talked to him for weeks, except about the plate."

"Thanks, Terry. See you 'round." Macbeth grabbed his old police leather off a chair before he left the office.

He found Joe C. by the front door. Joe was hanging out with the bouncers as they collected the cover charge and stamped hands.

"Joe." Macbeth pushed through the people coming in. Joe C. turned around and raised his eyebrows. "I gotta go to work for awhile. I should be back."

"Okay," said Joe C. "You're gonna miss a great show."

"I hope I'm back for some of it," Macbeth said, pulling his coat on.

Chapter 53

At the Desk

2330 Hours—Wednesday

Macbeth took the stairs in the garage at the rear of the Eighteenth District two at a time. He knocked the snow out of his hair as he opened the door and walked through the hallway toward the front desk. His pager went off. The number, one he didn't recognize, had a suburban area code.

He paused at the citizens' side of the front desk long enough to call the number. Busy. He walked around to the police side and looked at the computer screen. It was up and running, a miracle. He typed the plate information he'd received from Farmer on the vehicle inquiry form and hit Enter. The screen went blank for several seconds, then popped up, filled with orange type. The car wasn't in the city hot desk system.

He punched the button to call up the Secretary of State information, and waited as the screen went blank again. His pager shook on his belt. Looking down, he noticed the same suburban number. Must be Erin.

"Hi." He watched the computer screen come up with no hits in the LEADS system. The plate wasn't wanted in the Chicago area, or nationally. "Where're you at?"

219

"I'm in Palos at my aunt's house," she said. "I'm snowed in, tiger."

"No shit. Snowing that heavy out there?" He asked the question absentmindedly, as he waited for the next screen to pop up.

"Yeah, real heavy," she said. The Secretary of State returned and he turned the printer on. It hummed and spit out a copy of the info, with a south side address.

"How'd the car do, babe?"

"Fine, but the roads are horrible." Macbeth almost missed recognizing the tone in her voice because of his concentration on the computer. She apparently was just as disappointed to be snowed in as he was. "I should be out of here tomorrow. Don't you think, Uncle Billy?" He could hear Uncle Billy launch into what promised to be a lengthy diatribe about snow removal.

The dissertation was interrupted by a pair of beat cops dragging a drunk into the station for the Rush Street detail. The drunk was screaming about the injustice of it all, as well as using profanity and a liberal amount of spit. The desk sergeant, who was about to begin his dinner, stood quickly. Macbeth had never seen the man move so fast. "Don't be bringing that jagoff back here! Take him straight to the goddamned lock up!" The sergeant dropped his fork. "Goddamn it!"

"Where are you at?" Erin asked from Palos.

"At work. I gotta go. Page me when you wake up."

"Ok." Then she said in a lower voice, "I'll be thinking about you."

"Me, too, baby." Macbeth hung up. He looked at the printout and then at the computer. Why not? Couldn't hurt. He shrugged his shoulders and called up the screen. He typed in Chaney's plate. He didn't expect to find anything. There hadn't been time for the information to get into the system from Missing Persons.

"What the fuck?" he said aloud, as the computer screen responded in brilliant orange. Towed. The hot desk said Chaney's car had been towed from somewhere on the south side. "Towed," he said to himself out loud. The Eighteenth District desk crew didn't seem to notice him talking to himself.

He printed the information from the screen. He ran the plate a couple different times, using the plate and the Vehicle Information Number. The plates hadn't been recovered, but the computer confirmed that Chaney's car had been towed from 835 West Fifty-First Place, an apparent steal. That was the Ninth District. He looked up the number and dialed.

"Nine, Sergeant Richards," a gruff voice said after the second ring.

"Sarge, my name is Macbeth." He used his official tone. "I work tac in Eighteen."

"Yeah, what can I do you outta?"

"You guys recovered a car at 835 West Fifty-First Place either Sunday night or early Monday morning," Macbeth said. "You still have the report on it?"

"In review." Sergeant Richards' voice grew suspicious, as if he could anticipate extra work about to be requested.

"I got the R.D. number. You think you could pull it for me?"

"It important?"

"Yeah, as a matter of fact."

"All right," Sergeant Richards said, as he let out an exasperated breath. "Give me your number." Macbeth gave him his number.

"I'll have someone pull it and call you back."

Macbeth's "Thanks, Sarge" was wasted on an empty telephone line.

Chapter 54

Out South

0001 Hours—Thursday

Macbeth's midnight blue Jeep bounced through the snow, spitting waves of snow behind each tire. Macbeth actually wore his gloves, despite the heater being on high. The snow got heavier as he drove south on the Dan Ryan.

He got off at Thirty-Fifth Street, where Comisky Park dominated the western skyline. The White Sox had changed the name a few years back to collect on some big bucks advertising revenue, but to Macbeth it would always be Comisky. He drove west past the park, then under the railroad viaducts beyond the ballpark. His headlights bounced off the stalactites that constantly grew from the water runoff on the railroad tracks above.

Several blocks later, he pulled into the bus stop opposite the Ninth District. He locked the Jeep and walked across the street. The door to the Ninth District was on Lowe, and the District shared its south wall with the firehouse next door. Macbeth climbed the four marble steps that had ruts worn down the center. He pushed open the door and entered the small lobby.

Macbeth stepped up to the front desk on the left. A sergeant sat at a desk in the corner, almost out of sight. Three uniformed officers were back there as well. A female officer was on the phone and another female officer read the paper at a desk across from the sergeant. A male officer was making copies. No one looked at him when he stepped up. Macbeth figured someone must've watched him park and come across the street, taking him for a cop.

"How you doing?" Macbeth asked of no one in particular. No one looked up, as if each expected the other to do it first.

Finally, the sergeant looked at him. "Can I help you?"

"Yeah, Sarge. I'm Macbeth. I called earlier."

"Okay, right." He pointed to the female officer on the phone. "That's Lucy. She'll help you when she gets off." Macbeth nodded and waited. He didn't have to wait long. She hung up and the sergeant pointed at him. "Luce."

She turned and said, "You Macbeth?"

"That's me." He read her nametag, Moreno. She was pretty cute, nice figure, too. She took a copy of the tow report from in front of her and brought it to the front desk. She was barely five-foot-two and had long, black hair pinned up on her head. Several strands had fallen onto her shoulder. She had an olive complexion and large, dark eyes. She smiled as she handed him the sheet.

"Here you go, Officer Macbeth," she said.

"Thanks. It's Stacey."

"You're welcome, Stacey. I'm Lucy."

"I appreciate you digging this up for me." He was beginning to feel warm inside.

"No problem," she said. "I gotta stay awake somehow. Hey, isn't Stacey a girl's name?"

"Not necessarily. Stacey's actually my middle name."

"Really?"

"Really. Really. I don't much like my first name,"

he said seriously.

"Why not?"

"You know, Lucy, you'd make a great detective."

"I know," she said. "That's what I keep telling them, but they don't listen." She giggled and it struck straight at his heart. "So, what is your first name?"

"I'm not telling." He caught himself about to grin. "Are the guys who took this working tonight?"

"Let me see." She rocked up on her toes to see the sheet. He spun it around to face her. "Donahue and Tomanewski. Marty is." She pointed to Donahue. "Marty's Tomanewski's recruit."

"Marty on the street?"

"Nope. Roll call. The watch commander just went down," she said smiling.

"How long, do you think?"

"Half-hour." She wrinkled her nose. "He's kind of long-winded."

Macbeth whirled the report around to him and looked to see if it had been towed already. No indication. A couple days since the recovery, the car could still be there. If it was, he could drive over to get his answer and be on his way back before roll call was over. He glanced at his watch, twelve fifteen. "Shit."

"What?" Lucy asked with a devious-looking smile on her face. "You don't have enough time for a cup of coffee? My treat."

He looked at her and let himself grin.

"As much as I'd like to, I have to pass," he said. "How about a rain check?" She began an exaggerated pout. It was a look that could melt the most resolved. He nearly changed his mind on the spot.

"I suppose," she said with her lip still drooping. He

turned to leave and was almost out the door when she called back to him. "So, are you going to tell me your name?"

"Stacey," he said laughing.

"No . . ."

He knew he could get into a lot of trouble with this woman.

Chapter 55

Fifty-First Place

0025 Hours—Thursday

Macbeth turned west from Halsted onto Fifty-First Place, his Jeep jumping through the slushy, snow-filled ruts. Large, fluffy flakes made it hard to see in the dim streetlights. He slowed almost to a stop in the middle of the block and looked to his left at the white frame house, flanked on either side by a vacant lot. The porch light was off. He squinted. The glow of the streetlight was inadequate to see the address. Finally, he made out handwritten numbers to the right of the door: 833.

He rode the clutch and idled slowly forward. He looked hard at the back of the lot. There were a lot of trees on the back of the property, most bare, but he couldn't see any vehicles. He gassed the Jeep and shifted into second.

He bounced into the alley south of Fifty-First Place. It offered a jolting ride. His gun dug into his back above his kidney, but he enjoyed himself. This was about as close as the city could come to northern winter driving. He felt good for a moment. Then he stopped and shifted into neutral.

In the headlights, he could see a short groove worn in the snow where a car had been dragged out of the lot. He picked the report off the seat next to him and held it near his feet, then turned on the light under the dashboard. Burned. The car had been burned. He hadn't looked closely the first time. He immediately moved his eyes to another section of the report, noting the trunk had not been marked.

He couldn't help but think about Latricia Gibbons. But he'd be holding a different kind of report, if they'd found a body in the trunk. If they'd found it. This was Chicago and bodies did turn up in trunks now and then. "Shit," he said to himself. "I hope you ain't in the trunk, Wendell."

He turned his phone on and dialed the number for the Ninth District. Before his call went through, the phone chirped, telling him he had a message in his voicemail. It'd have to wait.

"Nine, Heiben."

"Officer Moreno, please."

"Hello, this is Officer Moreno."

"Lucy, this is Stacey."

"Oh, hello," she said. "I didn't expect you to call quite so soon."

"Are they out of roll call yet?"

"This is business, huh?"

"Unfortunately."

"Fine," she said sighing. He could feel that flirting pout all the way through the phone. "No, but they should be shortly."

"I gotta couple questions for them. Could you ask them to come over to 835 West Fifty-First Place when they're done? I'll wait."

"I could do that for you," she said. "I suppose."

"Thank you, Lucy," he said. "How 'bout I upgrade that coffee to dinner?"

"I would like that."

"Thanks again," he said. "Good-bye."

"Goodnight, Merlin."

Chapter 56

Beat 934

0050 Hours—Thursday

Macbeth parked in front of the vacant lot. He didn't know if the squad car could make it through the alley and didn't want to find out. Lucy must've looked him up in the department Alpha File. It listed every officer by name, star number and unit of assignment. That was the only way she could have found out, short of knowing someone who knew him or calling the Eighteenth District. Only his closest friends knew his real first name.

Finally, a squad car turned westbound down Fifty-First Place and eventually pulled alongside. Unlike his Jeep, which was covered with snow, the police car was in constant use and clean of snow, except for the wheel wells. They were clogged with packed, brown snow. The driver's window rolled down and an older policeman with receding gray hair looked over at Macbeth.

"Donahue?" Macbeth asked. The driver scrunched back into his seat and the passenger leaned forward. He couldn't make out a face, only a hand that waved. "Donahue?" he asked again.

The passenger reached up and turned on the dome light. It was much too bright, causing Macbeth to flinch and the driver of the squad to turn his head away. Marty Donahue couldn't be more than twenty-two. Macbeth couldn't see anything other than her exposed face. Everything else was out of view under a coat, vest and uniform, all of which did nothing to compliment the female figure. She shielded her eyes. "Hi. I'm Marty Donahue," she said. "Luce said you wanted to talk to me?"

"Yeah, the other night you recovered a car from this lot—suspected steal, burned out."

She nodded and waited.

"The car belonged to a friend of mine who is now missing."

"Sorry."

"There was no info about the trunk given in the report. Do you remember if it was opened?"

"I think so," she said. "I think the fire department opened it. I forgot to mark that, huh?"

"Yeah. I'm just hoping my friend wasn't in the trunk."

"Oh, good Lord. I hope not."

"The car went to Pound Three?" he asked. She shrugged her shoulders and said something he couldn't hear to her partner.

"Yeah, Three," her partner said. "That's the one by Seven." Macbeth knew. He'd worked the Seventh District for years.

"Okay, thanks." He began to roll up his window.

"Wait!"

"Yeah." He leaned over, holding onto the window crank.

"Lucy said to give her a call." Macbeth saw the driver roll his eyes and shake his head. He could see in the man's eyes that he didn't like what his department was becoming.

Chapter 57

Pound Three

0105 Hours—Thursday

Macbeth turned south on Halsted, then west on Garfield Boulevard. Outside, the night was dark and cold; little moved except thick, falling snowflakes that were stirred slightly by the wind. There were very few vehicles on the four-lane road at this time with the storm in full swing. Macbeth picked up his cell phone again and punched in his message retrieval code. He brought the phone up to his ear as Erin's voice said, "Hi, tiger," in a low purr. "Just wanted to tell you that the only thing I have to snuggle up with tonight is a stuffed teddy bear and that just ain't gonna cut it. He's cute and all, but he isn't hard in all the right places. You know what I mean?"

He shook his head as he pushed the End button. She must be telepathic. He put the phone in the console compartment of the Jeep and took a left on Racine Avenue. Minutes later, he parked at the curb in front of 6120 South Racine. The Seventh District was a brick, two-story corner building, surrounded by brick homes and flanked by two Arab-owned groceries.

Macbeth walked around the outside of the station to the garage across the driveway. It was constructed out of the same orange brick as the district building. The vehicle pound took up the south side of the property, including a fenced-in half-block lot that once was filled with recovered vehicles and towed cars. Now that it was scheduled for closing, there were only a handful of vehicles stored there.

He walked up to the garage door and looked through a window. It was dark. The soft sound of a TV show came from somewhere in the back of the garage. He knocked hard on the garage door. Nothing. He waited and pounded again. He cupped his hands against the window and looked for any movement. He knocked again, this time with less conviction.

A light went on in the back. Macbeth reached down and removed his star from his belt. He could see the figure of an older man step out from behind a wall in the rear of the garage and walk slowly toward the door. He had on dark overalls and a baseball cap. As he got closer, Macbeth could see that he was white and walked with a slight limp. Macbeth held his star against the window and waved with his free hand.

The door opened, and the man let him into the garage. "Too cold to be standing out there," the man said. "What can I do for you?"

"Sorry to bother you. My name is Macbeth. I work Eighteen Tac." He held out his star for the man to see. "A car that got towed the other night belonged to a friend of mine who's now missing."

"I see."

"I was hoping to get a look at it."

"No problem. What car?"

"Ford Escort. Should of come in Monday, about this time of night."

"Oh, that car," he said. "Ain't gonna do you much good, though."

"Why not?" Macbeth asked.

"It's covered in snow and ice," the man said. "But you can look at it. I don't see no problem with that. What you looking for, anyway?"

"I'm hoping my buddy isn't in the trunk," Macbeth said flatly.

"I don't rightly think so." The man rubbed his chin. "Fire department tore open the trunk to put out the fire."

"Well, I gotta check," Macbeth said. "The police report doesn't mention it."

"No problem." The man turned toward the back and motioned for Macbeth to follow him.

As they walked into the rear of the garage, Macbeth could see a card table had been set up with an old black-and-white TV, and there was a paper plate with balled-up cellophane wrap on top of it, probably a 7-Eleven sandwich. A napkin sat untouched next to the plate. The garage attendant paused by the door and pulled on a navy blue winter parka that had grease stains on it. "My name's George. George Roehmer. I've worked this garage for twenty-some years. They tell me I gotta move later this summer. Might just retire. I don't want to go no place different."

Roehmer opened the door and the snow blew in gently. Outside, Macbeth could see several oversized lumps. In front of one was a groove in the snow that showed it had arrived more recently than any of the others. Macbeth wasn't surprised when Roehmer walked over to it and turned to face him. "Here you go. See what I mean?"

"Yeah. Shit," Macbeth said. The car was completely covered in snow and ice.

"Don't do you no good, right?"

"You're right about that." Macbeth walked around to the back to see the trunk. He brushed off the snow to reveal a layer of ice on the car. He could plainly see the pry marks of the fire department iron bars and it looked as if they had gotten in. He still wondered, remembering some of the trunks he'd seen. It wouldn't be too hard to miss a body in a trunk full of junk.

Roehmer shook his head and looked at his watch. "Listen," he said. "I ain't supposed to do this, but what the fuck. What're they gonna do, fire me? Let me pull it inside and let the snow and ice melt off."

Macbeth looked over at him, relieved. "I would really appreciate that. How long 'til I would see anything?"

"Couple hours, at least," Roehmer said. "I could put the heater on it."

"George, you're a lifesaver. This car was in an accident, too. I'd like to see what kind of damage was done. Out here I can't see shit."

"Told you." Roehmer walked back toward the garage. "Come on and help me get the truck ready." Macbeth followed him into the garage.

Chapter 58

Old Friends

0135 Hours—Thursday

It took Roehmer about twenty minutes to bring the car inside and put the gas heater on it. The snow began to melt and the water ran down the floor to the drain. Macbeth walked over to the table and looked at the TV. The picture was grainy, but it was obvious late-night TV hadn't changed. He couldn't stomach the idea of a career full of all-night TV. Roehmer fixed a pot of coffee and asked him if he wanted any. Two unmarked squad cars pulled past the garage door windows; Macbeth declined the coffee and told Roehmer he'd be back, as he walked out the door.

Macbeth watched Stephen Kurtz pull his hood string tight around his face before getting out of the squad car. Kurtz opened the back door of the tac car and motioned for his prisoner to get out. The prisoner stared straight ahead; to Macbeth it looked like he was trying his best to ignore the request. This apparently succeeded only in annoying Kurtz, who reached in and unceremoniously dragged him out by his arm. The prisoner got to his feet, staring off into the distance. Kurtz's partner, Kenny Christian, was leaning into the trunk of the car, probably getting their gear bags.

The second car was parked farther into the lot, with its

lights off. Macbeth could make out Joey Orissom and Ray Jackson sitting in the car, but doing who knows what.

Kurtz pushed his prisoner forward, and they walked around the car into the driving lane behind Christian. Macbeth followed. Christian opened the side door to the Seventh District and held it for them. Kurtz removed a glove with his mouth and reached into his pants pocket. He pulled out a key and was reaching for the door lock, when Macbeth swatted his shoulder. Kurtz turned and looked.

"What the fuck are you doing here?" Kurtz asked with a grin.

"Asshole's probably here to bond out his girlfriend who got caught over on Sixty-Third giving blow jobs," Christian said, laughing and shaking hands with Macbeth.

"How you guys doing?" Macbeth asked. "Glad to see somebody around here can still do police work."

"What the fuck is this shit, old homey week?" the prisoner asked. He was immediately rewarded with two solid cracks to the back of his head, one each from Kurtz and Christian.

"Get in there, shit-for-brains," Kurtz said, spinning him into the dark office. Kurtz stepped behind the prisoner and shoved him into the corner as the lights went on. The prisoner sat on the bench and curled up. Macbeth and Christian stepped in.

"Keep your smart-ass mouth shut except for what we ask you, and nothing will happen other than you going to jail."

Kurtz walked over to the prisoner, uncuffed one hand and fastened the free cuff to a metal ring jutting from the wall. Kurtz pulled his hood down and unzipped his coat. Taking it off, he threw it on the back of a nearby chair. Christian shook off his parka and hung it on a hanger from the lopsided coat rack in the corner.

"Where's Wolcott?" Macbeth asked.

"High Yellow?" Christian said, referring to his sergeant and Macbeth's old sergeant, George Wolcott, by his infamous nickname. "Where else?" The black team members started calling Wolcott "High Yellow" to his face because of the yellowish tint of his light complexion. But the white officers used the nickname to emphasize Wolcott's complete lack of courage.

"On his beeper?" asked Macbeth. He looked around the office where he had once worked.

"Damn near every day." Kurtz dug some paperwork out of the vice report drawer. "Rest of the team took time and split hours ago."

"What's Joey and Ray gonna do?" Christian asked.

"They're outta here," Kurtz said. "Going to the gin mill to meet up with everybody else."

"It's a fucked-up night out there," Macbeth said. "Can't say I blame them for hitting the bar early." He hooked a finger in the direction of the prisoner. "What's this desperado done?"

"Old Reggie here?" Kurtz nodded toward his prisoner. "Got him with a pack."

"A twenty-pack," said Christian, digging a plastic bag from his jacket pocket. He held it up for Macbeth to see. It had a number of small, resealable, blue-tinted plastic bags inside, each containing a white rock of crack cocaine.

"Nice," Macbeth said, looking wistfully at the contraband. "In the Greens, I'd be perfectly happy with a twenty-pack. There are so many damn coppers in Cabrini, the assholes are paranoid. A lot of spots won't have more than ten bags at a time. They go out west and bring them in; more times than not, they cut those in half. The projects are harder than hell, compared to this shit out here."

"No fucking way?" Christian snorted a laugh.

"I shit you not," Macbeth said. "We play a lot of games to get what we do."

"It's slowing down a little here, too," Kurtz said. "We still do good, though."

"I'm sure you do," Macbeth added.

The tactical office door swung partway open and Ray Jackson stuck his large, freckled face in. "Hi, Macbeth! How the fuck are you?"

"Not bad, Ray. How they treating you?"

"I ain't complaining," Jackson said. "Wouldn't matter no way. Want to come out for a taste?"

"Thanks, Ray, but I can't."

"Alright," Jackson said. "You guys straight?"

"Yeah, we're set," Kurtz said. The door shut before he finished his sentence.

"So," Christian said to Macbeth. "You said you were here for what?"

"I got a friend missing. Well, actually an informant of sorts. Ninth District recovered his car over on Fifty-First Place, burned out. I'm waiting for it to thaw."

"How long's he been missing?" Kurtz asked, spinning a report into the typewriter.

Christian searched the prisoner thoroughly, piling the contents from his pockets on the long table in front of the bench.

"What's today?" Macbeth asked, as he counted in his mind. "This would be the fourth day, I think."

"He just run out or meet with foul play?" Christian asked, as he sorted through the debris on the table. He picked up a Bic lighter and threw it in the trash. "Take your shoelaces out and your belt off," he told the prisoner.

"This guy is as clean as they come," Macbeth said. "Has to be foul play."

"His car in the pound, huh?" Kurtz hooked a thumb over his shoulder in the direction of the auto pound.

"Yep."

"What you gonna do 'til then?" Christian asked.

"Fuck if I know," Macbeth said. He sat on the edge of the desk closest to the door.

"Hey!" Kurtz said, looking over at his partner. "Didn't they get a John Doe body on the Ryan the other night?"

"Yeah." Christian said. "They did."

"No shit," Macbeth said.

"Yeah," Christian said. "In fact, O'Boyle was telling us in court the other day the State Police tried to give it to him. I guess they had some little weasel asshole running their investigation for them. Tried to dump it on Jimmy."

"Jimmy O'Boyle, Area One?" Macbeth asked.

"That's him," Kurtz said. "Do you know him?"

"Oh, yeah," Macbeth said. "We worked together for nearly a year here on tac. He was my first partner on tac, before they finally let Louie and me hook up again."

"He's working first watch in Area One. I'd call him, if I was you," Christian said. Macbeth picked up the nearest phone and dialed the Detective Area by memory.

"Sergeant Miller, Area One."

"Sarge, this is Macbeth from Eighteen Tac. Is O'Boyle around?"

"No, on the street. What'd you need?"

"He had a body the other night that wasn't ID'd?"

"Yeah."

"I got an informant missing," Macbeth said. He was getting tired of explaining his situation. "His burned-out car turned up over on Fifty-First Place the other day. I thought this body on the Ryan might be my guy."

"That's the State Police's investigation," Miller said.

"O'Boyle's John Doe comes from an Aggravated Battery over in Seven. The body the State got is a John Doe, too."

"An Agg Batt in Seven?" Macbeth seemed surprised. "Either body been ID'd yet?"

"I know the shooting victim hasn't been," Miller said. "I don't know about the Ryan body. What's the description of your friend?"

Macbeth described Chaney from memory. "Male black, about thirty, five-foot-ten or -eleven, one hundred fifty pounds, give or take."

"Body on the Ryan is a white male," Miller said. "Let me see." Macbeth could hear the rustling of paper. Kurtz and Christian began typing reports and asking the prisoner questions. Macbeth pressed the phone receiver to his head.

"Could be the Agg Batt victim, though," Miller said. "Nothing but a goddamned body."

"How come you can't ID this guy?" Macbeth asked.

"He was stripped naked, shot and left for dead," Miller said. "And he's still in a coma."

"No shit?"

"No shit."

"Where's he at?"

"Christ, ICU."

Macbeth was about to hang up when he thought to ask for the report number. He wrote it on his hand and thanked Miller. "You got a review office key?" he asked Kurtz as he hung up the phone. Kurtz smiled and tossed his ring of keys at him.

"It's the one with a red border."

"Thanks."

"Hey, Macbeth," Kurtz said. Macbeth stopped at the door and turned. "If you hear some . . . strange sounds coming from the courtroom . . ."

"Yeah?"

"Don't intervene." Kurtz's face broke into a broad smile. "It's only Lieutenant Waterford and Sergeant Big Tits doing their thing on the judge's bench."

Macbeth laughed as he opened the door.

Thirty minutes later, Macbeth was on Southwest Highway, driving through the ever-thickening snowstorm. He'd told Roehmer he would either be back or call.

He'd easily found the report in the Agg Batt file and made himself a copy. The report, however, did little to shed any light on the possibility of the John Doe being Chaney. All it said was that a man walking his dog had found a naked male black who had suffered several wounds that appeared, at the time of the writing of the report, to be gunshot wounds. He had been taken to Christ Hospital and admitted into the Emergency Room in critical condition. There was no explanation as to why he'd been shot.

Chapter 59

Christ Hospital

0230 Hours—Thursday

The parking for the Emergency Room was actually underneath the ER itself. Macbeth found an empty spot and stopped by the guard booth on his way to the elevator. He showed his identification, and got directions to the Intensive Care Unit.

It took a few minutes to find the right elevator bank. He got turned around once or twice, but the elevator was fast. The doors opened to a bright hallway; the lights made him squint. He couldn't believe it was two thirty already. Directions to the ICU were posted on the wall on colored plastic placards.

A minute later, he walked up to the large nurses' station. The desk was nearly chest-level. He held up his star as the nurse looked up. Another nurse was standing with her back to him, watching a variety of monitors. Even though it was quiet, there was a tension that you could almost see.

"Yes?" the seated nurse asked. She was pretty, with dark blonde hair worn short and the most piercing blue eyes. Her nametag read: Melissa.

"I'm looking for a missing person," he said, looking into the eyes of Nurse Melissa and enjoying himself. "A sergeant from Area One told me to look at a guy that was brought in here the other night."

"You must be talking about Bob," she said.

"Bob?"

"Yeah," she said. "That's what we call him. It's better than John Doe."

"How's he doing?"

"About the same, really." She stood. Macbeth leaned on the counter and glanced down at the desktop. The Southwest Suburban section of the *Tribune* was spread out next to a half-eaten sandwich and a can of Diet Coke. She walked around the end of the counter.

"I didn't mean to interrupt your dinner," he said. "Just point me in the right direction."

"Don't worry about it. Nicole," she said over her shoulder to the other nurse. Nicole turned. "I'm going to take this officer to look at Bob. Be right back."

"Okay." Nicole turned back.

"My name is Stacey." Melissa looked at him as she walked toward a cubicle several beds away. He looked at the patients as they walked by. Each bed was surrounded by machinery that hooked up one way or another to the patient. It looked like a bad science fiction movie and gave him the creeps.

"I hope you can put a name to Bob," she said. "He's been here since Monday. Everyone else has some kind of visitors or family. That will sometimes have an effect on people coming out of comas. Bob has no one. It's sad."

They stopped at an opening in a curtain. Macbeth looked at Melissa, who turned to look at the patient. He followed her gaze to the bed. After a second, she said, "Well?"

He just stared. The black man lying in the bed had a tube in his mouth and a hose leading from his nose. An IV was taped to one arm. An EKG was wired from pads on his chest to one of several machines. Two machines had electronic readouts that Macbeth assumed were fed to the nurses' station. He saw the ragged lines of sutures and staples covering the man's stomach, his head, parts of his chest and most of his left arm. His right foot was heavily bandaged, as well.

"Stacey?"

Macbeth snapped out of his stare and said, "His name is Wendell Chaney."

Chapter 60

Midnight Caller

0300 Hours—Thursday

James Middleton felt but did not respond to the first of his wife's three elbows. He was tired. His wife gave a fourth and final push. "James, wake up."

"Huh," he said rolling over. He brought his hands out from under the covers to rub his eyes. "What, honey?"

"Phone," she said. "Sharron Chaney. She's hysterical."

He sat up in the bed. One of his flock needed him. All thoughts of sleep and grogginess vanished. He took the phone. "Hello, Sharron?"

"They found him! They found him!" Sharron Chaney said.

"They found Wendell?" he asked.

"Yes! Yes!"

"How is he?" He feared the worst.

"He's in a coma," she said.

"Where?"

"Christ Hospital." Sharron Chaney sounded like she was about to break down.

"Is someone going to drive you there, Sharron?"

"I don't have anybody to call. The police say they can't come and give me a ride."

"They're most likely busy, Sharron," he said, getting out of bed. He dragged the phone cord across his wife. She sat up as he walked the phone around to the closet and opened it. She got out of bed herself. "How about the kids?" he asked.

"I don't have anybody to watch them either," Sharron said. She sounded like she was having a hard time breathing.

"Relax, Sharron," he said. "Relax, everything is going to be all right; take some deep breaths. Just give me a couple minutes. My wife and I'll be right over. We'll take you and the children over to the hospital."

"Ohhhh, thank you, Reverend. Thank you!" Sharron said. "I've got to get the kids ready."

"Yes," he said. "Get the children ready. We'll be right over."

Chapter 61

Long Time No See

0415 Hours—Thursday

Macbeth sat by himself in the police room at Christ Hospital. He was leaning back in the padded chair, his feet on the counter, eyes closed.

Sharron Chaney and her children had been escorted into the ICU earlier. The fact that she harbored no love for the police was obvious. Her stare spoke volumes about her feelings. He couldn't blame her. She had little to thank the police for today.

Her Reverend had brought them to the hospital. He was a nice man and had come back to explain Sharron's situation. He didn't think she meant to offend. He had thanked Macbeth and they shook hands. Macbeth knew Reverend Middleton was sincere, and told him he understood and sympathized with Mrs. Chaney. Macbeth left the floor to the nurse and the emotional family. He went to the police room to call Area One.

Macbeth didn't know how long Jimmy O'Boyle had stood in the doorway of the police room, looking at him as he slept. When O'Boyle sat his notebook down on the counter next to his feet, he came fully awake. But, as one who was used to nodding off in the presence of others, he didn't flinch or open his eyes all the way. After O'Boyle stepped out, Macbeth opened his eyes and found his notebook. It was blue, with the Chicago Police Star in white and Detective Division scrolled across the top. When O'Boyle returned, carrying a Pepsi and Diet Pepsi, Macbeth had the notebook open and was reading the reports.

Macbeth closed the notebook and stood. "Good to see you, O'Boyle." Macbeth offered his hand. O'Boyle sat the pops on the counter next to his clipboard, before shaking.

"How you doing, Stacey?" O'Boyle asked. "Little tired?" He pointed at the can of Diet Pepsi. "You still drinking the watered-down stuff?"

"Thanks." Macbeth picked up the can and popped it open. "I'm all right." Macbeth took a sip. "It's my day off. I missed a great concert, so I could ID your victim for you."

"And I appreciate your efforts." O'Boyle yawned as he opened his can. "He out of his coma yet?"

"Nope," Macbeth said. "But his family's upstairs with him. His wife brought her pastor, too." O'Boyle rolled his eyes. "No. The guy's all right. He won't give you trouble."

"I hope not."

"Who're you working with?" Macbeth rubbed his neck, trying not to look at O'Boyle. Sergeant Miller had already told him.

"Don't ask." O'Boyle sat. "You know, you got one evil-looking grin." He dragged a hand across his face.

"So I've been told," Macbeth said, feeling a little sadistic. "Who?"

"Fuck you," O'Boyle said dejectedly. "It's not permanent. Kenny's on furlough and will be back in a day or two."

"You're working with Greasy Dick, aren't you?"

"Like I said, fuck you and the horse you rode in on."

As if he had just been given his cue, Josef Greizedicht stepped through the doorway. "Ain't there no more fucking chairs?" he asked. "Hey, where'd you get the pop?"

"How're you tied up with Chaney?" O'Boyle asked, ignoring his partner.

"Damn near a year ago," Macbeth said, "Chaney testified against some GDs in a case I had. Several went to prison for a lot of years. Wendell's part was really small but pretty crucial. His wife's convinced that this is all retaliation against him."

"That's TV shit," O'Boyle said referring to his notebook.

"Yeah, that's what I told her," said Macbeth, taking a sip of his Diet Pepsi. "They had an accident on the Dan Ryan. Friday night, I think. They suffered some damage to their car and couldn't afford to report it to the insurance company. I guess Wendell planned on stopping by to see if he could collect something from the other driver."

"Stace," said O'Boyle. "How did Chaney know where the other driver lived?"

"I'd rather not say," Macbeth said. "I looked into it and it's of no relevance."

"No?"

"I didn't give it to him," Macbeth said, looking back at him. "I talked to who did, and I'm telling you. It isn't going to have anything to do with what happened to him. I promise. I'm assuming he left for work early Saturday night to talk to this other driver, though."

"Talk to him yet?" O'Boyle's stare never left Macbeth.

"Nope. Would've been my next stop had I not come over here." Macbeth took the computer printout from his coat pocket and handed it to O'Boyle: "5326 South Bishop."

O'Boyle said, looking at the printout, "Not that far away from where he was found."

"Couple miles," Macbeth said.

"Connected by a major artery," O'Boyle said. "I'll go over there later, see what we can turn up."

"Readout says a van," Macbeth said. "I didn't get to talk to Sharron to confirm if that's the car involved in the accident, though."

"Why not?"

"She hung up on me."

Chapter 62

On the Way Home

1630 Hours—Thursday

Robert Starr, Sr. drove his Mercedes Benz 500 SL through the rush hour traffic as if he was on autopilot. He didn't even comment on the driving of the other commuters. He ignored the weather. He had the radio on, but didn't listen. All he thought about was his son, Robert Jr., and his family. What he wouldn't give to have him back.

The car phone rang. At first, he didn't recognize the sound for what it was. By the third ring, he reached for the receiver mounted on the car's transmission hump. Pressing the speaker phone button, he said, "Yes," toward the microphone mounted on his visor.

"Mr. Starr." It was his secretary. "The police are on the line from your son's house."

"Have they found him?"

"They won't say. But Rosemary can't speak. They say she is too emotional at the moment."

He knew what that could only entail. "They're at Bob's house, right?" His voice nearly broke from the emotion churning in his stomach.

"Yes," she said. He knew she was crying on the other end of the line. He couldn't hear her, but he knew full well;

252

he felt it, and it brought tears to his eyes as well. She must know, as he did, that Bob was dead. Some people have a sense about things. He had struggled to deny what he knew in his heart. His head had been denying it for days, but his heart knew. He disconnected.

He hit the speed dial for Bob Jr.'s house. It rang twice before it was answered by a male voice. "Hello."

"Hello." Starr's voice was firm and businesslike. It was the only way he could conduct himself without breaking down. He had to stay in control, at least until everything was in order. "This is Robert Starr, Sr. With whom am I speaking?"

"Hello, Mr. Starr. I'm Lieutenant Childress. I'm with the Winnetka Police Department."

"Yes, sir," Starr said. "What is it you want to tell me?"

"News like this is best given in person, I'm afraid."

"Don't give me that, Lieutenant," he said. "You're going to tell me that my son is dead."

"Well sir," Childress said, "that's not exactly the purpose of my visit."

"Say what you've got to say, then."

"A body has been recovered and we suspect it's Robert," said Childress. "We need someone to go to the Medical Examiner's Office and make a positive identification. Mrs. Starr is in no shape to do that."

"No, she isn't," Starr said. "I would rather spare her that task. I'm on the road now. Where do I need to go?"

"The body is currently being held at the Cook County Medical Examiner's Office," Childress said. "I can give you the address, sir."

"Let me get something to write with." He pulled his pen from his suit pocket and had to swivel the top off with his mouth. He found a pad of paper in the glove box. "Give me the address."

After giving him the address, Childress said that Rosemary wanted to speak to him.

"Robert . . ."

"Yes, Rose." He made a quick merge to the right on the Edens Expressway. He'd have to turn around and head back into the city.

"I want to come and see for myself."

"I don't see how that could be helpful." A tear broke free from his eye and rolled down his face. "I can make the identification. You don't have to go there." He could only guess what a morgue looked like. He saw no reason that his daughter-in-law or his grandchildren should ever have to walk into such a place.

"I must," she said. "I must. It can't be Bob. It just can't be Bob."

"Rose . . ." he said, "what would you do with the children?"

"My mom and dad are here." She was crying. He couldn't put his foot down, as much as he wanted to. He didn't have the stomach to argue with her. He knew she'd never listen to him, anyway. She'd always had a mind of her own.

"If you think it's necessary. I'll wait for you there."

"Bye," she said, hanging up.

"Goodbye."

Chapter 63

Back to Work

1800 Hours—Thursday

Macbeth practically had to pull himself up the stairs; his legs were thick and weren't responding. He was stiff, too. It reminded him of the midnight officers in the Ninth District. Zombies. Sleep-deprived. His head throbbed. He had gotten to bed after six in the morning, and what little sleep he'd had, after a number of beers, was almost worthless. A half hour ago, he'd looked in the mirror on the way out of his apartment. He had two days' growth of beard, and there were dark rings under his eyes.

He walked through the office and made a beeline to the prisoners' bench. He sat, his back making a thump against the wall. Then, slowly he slid to his side, until he was lying flat. Even the stab of his gun into his kidney failed to get him to sit up. The bright office lights stung his eyes, so he brought an arm, still in his leather jacket, around and over his face.

Ryan looked over from his desk. "Hard days off, Stace?"

Macbeth was only able to grunt.

"Must've spent the whole time looking for your razor. Would've been easier to go out and buy a new one."

Macbeth made no response. Hagen and Zito walked into

the office and began laughing.

"What the fuck happened to him?" asked Hagen.

"Must'a took one big, mean, fuckin' cat to drag this motherfucker in," Zito said. Ryan laughed.

Macbeth lifted his arm and peered at the three of them with one bloodshot eye. "Fuck you all."

"Late night, Stace?" asked Hagen. "Or early morning?"

"Both." He tried to sit up. He was hung over, but he hadn't had that much to drink. Was there a chance that the emotions of the last few days were starting to catch up with him? "Found Chaney last night."

Ryan and Zito spun around. "You did what?" asked Zito.

"I found Chaney," Macbeth said, tilting his head back against the wall. "I found Wendell."

"Where?" asked Ryan.

"Christ Hospital. Seems Wendell was the victim of an Aggravated Battery. He was shot, stripped and left for dead. Only he didn't die. He's in a coma."

"Dicks got anything?" Ryan asked.

"No. I know the dick handling it, though. A friend of mine from Seven. I'll call him later. See what they turned up."

"Did you call Toomer in Area Three?" asked Ryan.

"Not yet." Macbeth didn't want to get up to walk all the way over to a desk to use the phone. "I will before I hit the street."

It took another ten minutes before he built up the strength and courage to move. Then he called Area One first. O'Boyle wasn't in but was expected before midnight. Area Three said Toomer wasn't at work either. The Area Three sergeant asked him to complete a Supplemental Report, after hearing his story. That took another ten minutes to type, after he found the report.

Macbeth and Zito ran a copy over to Area Three before stopping at R. J. Grunts for dinner.

Chapter 64

2121 West Harrison Street

1900 Hours—Thursday

Robert Starr, Sr. had been led to a viewing room, a bag had been opened, and the thing exposed. He knew he'd never forget the sight and even harbored a cold dread that it might follow him into the next world, if he even believed in such a thing anymore. The head lay flat on the metal gurney, as if it were some kind of stretched-out, empty balloon. It vaguely had the face of his son, grotesquely distorted by a gaping hole. But it was his son all the same.

Starr Sr. sat alone in the front lobby of the Medical Examiner's Office. It was officially known as the Dr. Jack Stein Institute for Forensic Medicine. He was the only person in the lobby. Whatever receptionists were there, were behind glass. The sofa he was on had gray cushions. Starr rested his head in his hands and stared at the floor. How could that thing be his son? The horrifying wounds. Had he suffered? Now, it was a soulless mass of meat. Good thing his mother wasn't alive. This would surely have killed her. She'd always been so fond of their only child. Little Bobby.

The lobby was warm and comfortable, compared to the working area. In the lobby, there were plants and plaques, and the atmosphere was actually pleasant. Back there, where they kept Bobby, was cold, metallic and sterile. Back there, the lights were bright but gave off no warmth. Starr had come in through the entrance for the living but had been brought back to the other side, where the living catalogue the dead.

He barely heard the lobby doors open. When he looked up, he saw Rosemary pushing behind a smaller, older woman whom he didn't recognize at first. She was petite. Her hair was gray, shot through with white, her face wrinkled from too much sun. When they came through the second door, he recognized Rosemary's mother, Ruth. Ruth Gambell had extraordinary eyes and a fierce personality that burned behind those amazing green eyes. She must have driven her daughter from Winnetka, leaving her husband at home with the grandchildren. It didn't surprise him. He knew Rosemary must get her feistiness from her mother. It had been that trait that had initially attracted his son to her.

Starr stood and hugged his daughter-in-law. He didn't even let go when she gently tried to break the contact. Eventually he relented and stepped back. He looked at Ruth. He saw the hope and desperation in their eyes. He could only shake his head and look to Ruth Gambell for support.

"Rose," Starr said. "Honey, you can't go back there." His son's wife would not look at him. Ruth came up behind her and put her hands gently on Rosemary's hips. She tried to steer her daughter to a seat. Rosemary allowed herself to be controlled. Tears escaped her eyes as moans came from her throat. Her mouth was no more than a tight slit in her face.

"Nooooo," she said quietly.

"Come on, baby" said her mother. "Come on, now."

"You just cannot go back there." Starr sat down next to Rosemary. "I've seen. There's no reason for you to have to view the body. It's Bob. You know I wouldn't make a mistake."

"I've got to see him," she said. "Please, please, I have to see for myself." He looked to her mother.

"Ruth," he said, "if she goes back there, it will haunt her for the rest of her life. I'm telling you, it's the most awful thing I've ever seen. I don't know if I could go back there again." He turned and pleaded with his daughter-in-law. "Let me carry that burden, Rosemary. Remember Bob the way you saw him last, not like that. Please."

"Come on, honey." Ruth reached up and stroked her daughter's hair. "Listen to what Robert's saying. It's for the best. Please."

Rosemary turned to her mother with tears streaking her cheeks, her eyes red, bloodshot and unfocused. "Momma," she cried, with the word rising in pitch and volume. The daughter wailed and collapsed into the arms of her mother. She wept for her husband. Starr, who had stared into the face of death minutes earlier, looked away. He couldn't bear to look at this, either.

Rachel couldn't stop crying. There was nothing she could do but let the tears flow. She thought she'd be able to drive and had told Starr Sr. she could, when he asked her to come to the office by eight thirty that evening. He said he had news about Bob. She knew it couldn't be good. She'd tried to get him to tell her over the phone, but he wouldn't. He'd said Starr Markets was a family business and he would share the information with the family when they were all together for support.

She pulled a pair of old jeans over her long underwear and a sweater over her black turtleneck. In the bathroom, she spent ten minutes putting on her makeup, only to decide to wash it off and go without. She found her keys in her purse, picked up a full box of Kleenex, and grabbed a winter jacket before she left her apartment. She headed for the elevator and the heated garage below.

Chapter 65

Patience Is a Virtue, Isn't It?

1955 Hours—Thursday

Dedrick Dease was sitting at the wheel of the van when the silver BMW pulled out of the underground garage. "That it?" he asked Boo, who had spun around in the seat next to him.

"That's the motherfucker!" Boo said. "Get behind the bitch."

Pookie and Melvin Early sat up in the backseat. They'd been dozing off.

"Let's fuck that bitch up," Pookie said.

"Slow," Boo said. "Just get behind her. Do like I say."

"A'right," Dease said. He easily pulled into traffic a car behind the BMW.

Traffic on St. Charles Road was light. Rush hour was over. It was not snowing and cars were moving well on the plowed and salted streets. The temperature was actually a bit warmer than normal. No wind stirred, making it rather pleasant outside. There were a few white, puffy clouds in the sky, which was lit up brightly by the full moon. Maybe this trip to the office won't be so bad, Rachel thought, driving-wise, at least. She pulled a Kleenex from the box and wiped her eyes for what seemed like the thousandth time.

She stayed in the lane that brought her onto the eastbound Eisenhower Expressway. Her lane merged with other eastbound lanes coming off the tollway; they were separated from westbound traffic by concrete barriers. Slowly, as she drove east on the expressway, the sparse suburban landscape gave way to the crowded cityscape of tall, rundown three-flats. The roadway dropped down between steep banks, flanked by the old brick buildings of the West Side of Chicago.

Rachel blew her nose and wiped her eyes. She wasn't paying much attention to the road, other than trying not to run into anything. The tears in her eyes were making that a little difficult when it got crowded, but thankfully that wasn't much of a problem. There weren't that many people on the road, and she was keeping to the right.

Boo counted off the exits and entrances as Dedrick drove past, waiting until he was on familiar ground. Once everything was in place, all they had to do was wait until he gave the word. He'd prove to Huggins that he was worthy. He'd been about to give up. Ten minutes ago, his confidence had been slipping. He took his thumb out of his mouth. "Fuck this bitch," he said under his breath. "She got Lonnie's car. Bitch is messin' with his future."

Rachel had just passed the Kostner exit when she felt her car lurch forward. It took a second for her to realize she had just been in an accident. There was only a set of headlights in her rearview. She continued eastbound and tried to make out the driver of the van behind her, but she couldn't. She knew she had to pull over. "What the hell?" she said to herself, frustrated with the delay this was going to cause. She hit the steering wheel with her fist. "Why me?"

"Why don't the bitch pull over?" asked Early from the backseat.

"Stay behind her," Boo said. Here it was, right in front of him, all that they'd been working for all along. "Bitch is scared." Boo fingered the gun in his pocket, thinking that she had a lot to be scared about.

"Hit her again!" Pookie yelled anxiously from the backseat.

"Shut the fuck up," Boo said. They had a plan and all they had to do was stick to it. Worst it could get was that they'd have to ditch the bitch's body and, hell, that wasn't no problem. Dease started getting closer to her bumper.

"Just follow her," Boo said.

Her turn signal came on before the Independence Boulevard exit. "Follow her," Boo said nervously. This wasn't part of his plan. She should have pulled over on the highway. Keep cool, he kept saying in his head.

"What if she go to the poh-leece?" asked Dease.

"Then we keep driving," Boo said. "Just keep cool on her tail."

"A'right," Dease said.

"Get her on the ramp!" Pookie said.

"Shut the fuck up, Pookie," Boo said, never taking his eyes off the BMW. "Nigger, you be ready to run. Catch her at the light."

Rachel coasted to a stop at the light. The van was coming up behind her. Across the four divided lanes of Independence Boulevard was a well-lit gas station. There didn't seem to be any customers in the station, but there must be an attendant. The light turned green before the van stopped behind her. She stepped on the gas and the back end of the BMW slipped on some ice. Rachel noticed that the entrance to get back on the expressway was closed off. Great, she thought. How deep into this neighborhood would she have to go to get back on? The West Side was kind of notorious. She moved over to the right lane and turned into the station, thinking maybe the driver would know how to get back on the highway.

She sat in her car and watched the van in her rearview mirror. She was hoping the driver was as scared of this neighborhood as she was. Maybe they could even handle this somewhere safer. Maybe even down at the Hancock Building. Surely, the police could make a report out there.

"Melvin, you see anything?" asked Boo. He hated having to trust Melvin to anything, as bad as he fucked up the plate thing. But everybody else had something to do. Melvin could at least look out for the police.

"Nah, we cool," Early said.

"A'right," Boo said. "Fuck this bitch."

As Dease stepped on the gas and moved across the intersection, Boo and the others ducked out of sight. The van bounced and kept bouncing until Dease came to a stop behind the BMW. Dease got out of the van slowly. Boo was giving him orders, but he wasn't paying any attention. He was the clean-looking one, so he had to be outside, taking all the chances. That shit was played out. He heard the side door of the van rolling open. Boo was right. The bitch wasn't getting out. He felt the weight of the pistol in his waistband. It was a last resort.

Rachel looked over her right shoulder. She could only see one person in the van, a young man. When he got out, she was reminded of the kind of young, black man that was always on the news, accused of this crime or that. But he also looked like the guy who worked in the mailroom at Starr Markets. She didn't know his name, but knew he was nice. He wouldn't hurt her. It wasn't right that she would first think of the driver of the van as some kind of criminal, just because he was black. Did that make her a racist?

Was he injured? He was moving so slowly toward her car. But he wasn't limping, or holding his side; something wasn't right. She checked her door. It was locked. He stopped at her rear bumper. She felt for the button to her window; she'd roll it down when he came alongside, but only a little bit. She turned. What was taking so long? He was looking around. That was odd.

Pookie eased out of the van and looked over at the gas station attendant behind the bulletproof glass. He was looking Pookie's way, but didn't seem to be paying much attention. He wasn't making no phone calls, at least. Did he have an alarm button? No reason to press it yet, even if he did have one. Pookie was just a man getting out of a van. The attendant had no idea what Pookie was going to do.

Rachel felt like she was going to throw up. Even through her grief, she saw that he was looking for witnesses. He wasn't no nice mailroom guy, he was some asshole about to rob her. Wasn't she the stupid one for feeling guilty! She ripped the gear shift into drive and stomped on the gas. She was out of there. Her hair flipped over the headrest behind her as her tires spun, sending the back end around before it caught on dry pavement.

"Shit!" Dease was torn between running up to the window to shoot her in the head and running back to the van to go after her. He froze.

Coming around the front of the van, Pookie saw the woman freak out and drop the car into drive. It took a second for her to start pulling away. The back end of the car swung toward him. He had to do something. The police station was only a couple blocks away.

Pookie jumped toward the car, near the passenger side window. He brought his hand out of his coat pocket.

As Rachel felt her car straighten out, the window to her right exploded. Small glass particles showered her. She screamed and tried to cover her face with her arm.

The shattered window filled with a huge dark shadow, with eyes and hands grabbing at her. She slapped and elbowed at the shadow, while trying to straighten out the car and get the hell out of there.

Dease's legs began to move after the car pulled away, with Pookie's feet hanging out the passenger window. He ran for the van and saw Boo's head bob up from under the dash. Dease jumped into the driver's seat and shifted, with the door still swinging open.

"Motherfucker!" Boo shouted and pounded the dash. The van pulled off.

Rachel tore out onto the street, still picking up speed. The man hanging halfway in her car was trying to grab the steering wheel and the shift lever. She fought with him as she tried to swerve and dump him out. But he was too far in. He got hold of the steering wheel and yanked down hard. The BMW came around. The rear tires lost traction. The car spun out of control in an arc, going up on the curb. The guardrail smashed the front and prevented it from careening down the embankment onto the expressway. Something was hung up on the guardrail; the rear wheels just spun on the slushy road.

Boo bounced about in the passenger seat, wanting the van to go faster. Early rolled around in the back with the garbage. Dease drove right into the rear bumper of the BMW.

Pookie was jolted by the crash but not thrown from the car. He grabbed hold of the dashboard and shook his head. As he lay across the front seat, he heard the woman struggling in front of him.

Rachel had seen the rail coming toward her and braced for the impact. She was thankful she had her seatbelt on. She frantically undid the belt and clawed the door open. Cold air hit her face. Freedom. She could hear the expressway below. If only she could get down the embankment. She bolted up from the driver's seat as the man lunged for her. He missed.

"The bitch is getting away!" screamed Boo. He fumbled with his door.

Dease kicked his door open, but knew she'd get over the rail before he could get to her. Once she got down to the highway, it'd be over. If she took the keys with her, they'd be fucked.

★ ★ ★ ★ ★

Rachel pushed away from the BMW toward freedom. There wasn't anyone who would be able to catch her.

Pookie saw that she was about to jump over the guardrail. He knew they'd never get her once she was over. He lunged hard and caught a handful of hair. Wrenching it backward, he pulled with all his weight. Her legs went out from under her, as she was ripped back. Her head slammed against the edge of the convertible's frame. She fell and didn't move.

Boo and Early carried her to the van. Once she was inside and the door was closed, Boo hopped in the passenger seat. Dease pulled up behind the silver car, until he made contact with the rear bumper. Pookie got in the driver's seat of the BMW and steered the car to the right. Dease nudged the small car until it bounced back onto the street. It only took a few seconds to free up the car.

They circled the block until they were on Independence. No police, yet. Good. They cut to Kostner, then got back on the eastbound expressway, heading toward the Dan Ryan and home.

Boo allowed himself to smile. Adrenaline was pumping hard. Huggins would be happy, very happy, very motherfuckin' happy. He had got his shit back for him. Boo looked in the rear of the van at the woman. She was as good as dead. No problem. Hell, might even be fun, killing her. She sure had fucked up his life for awhile. Now it was his turn.

Dease drove the van while Pookie and Early taped her up. Dease drove like an old white man all the way to the south side. Nothing happened.

Once in the Raspberry neighborhood, they parked the BMW in the garage of the abandoned building. Boo and Early took the woman into the basement and left her in the room with the boarded-up window. Dease and Pookie parked the van in front.

They met up in Pookie's bedroom to watch the last half of the Chicago Bulls game.

Chapter 66

Disappointment

2220 Hours—Thursday

"Come on Teddy." Macbeth looked at his watch for the hundredth time. "What the fuck's keeping you?"

Zito looked over at him from behind the steering wheel of the unmarked Caprice. "Give it some time, Stace," he said. "Teddy and Frank got to give it a few minutes to see if they come back up."

"They've been in there long enough," Macbeth said. He and Zito were parked just outside of Cabrini on Clybourn Avenue. They were waiting to hear from Ketchum and Hampton about a dope spot on the ground floor of 1230 North Larrabee. Another tac car was out of sight on Cleveland.

"We'll give them a couple more minutes," Zito said. "You got to relax, you know."

"What?" asked Macbeth.

"You heard me, man," Zito said. "You been edgy for days now, ever since that broad got killed."

"Yeah." Macbeth leaned back into the seat of the car. "I know. I just got a lot going through my head. I can't seem to get this whole fucked-up thing out of my mind."

"You found Chaney," Zito said. "Didn't you?"

"Yeah," Macbeth said. "I wish O'Boyle'd call, let me know

271

what they got over at the address I gave him. Had to be what happened. There wasn't anything else it could've been."

"Yeah." Zito rolled down his window. He removed a pack of Kool cigarettes from his inside jacket pocket and banged on the bottom of the pack. "Maybe." One cigarette fell halfway out. He picked it out and put it in his mouth. He pulled a lighter from his jeans pocket and lit up. "You talk to Toomer, yet?"

"No. I gotta get hold of him. I can't believe these two incidents aren't somehow related."

"*Zito,*" the radio that sat between Zito's legs squawked.

"*Go ahead, Teddy.*" Ketchum and Hampton had snuck into the 1230 North Larrabee and climbed the stairs to the eighth floor. They were hunkered down in an abandoned apartment conveniently kicked open. They waited in a back bedroom with their radios off, to prevent radio traffic from giving away their positions.

"*Zito.*"

"*Turn the volume up, Teddy!*" Zito shouted. The plan was to have the assist cars pull up after the dope spot was back selling. The dealers would try and run up the stairwells, only to find Ketchum and Hampton on their way down.

That was the plan but, like usual, Ketchum had turned his radio on, but it was on the lowest setting and he couldn't hear shit! They'd been on Teddy about this shit for a year, at least.

"*Go ahead, Teddy,*" Zito said again.

"*I think they shut down,*" Ketchum said.

Zito looked at Macbeth. "They saw you guys sneak in is more like it," Zito said. Then into the radio, "*We'll hit the lobby again in three minutes, give you some time to go out the back. Start down now.*"

"*Ten-four.*"

No one had been in the lobby except the security guards, but after the other night, that didn't make anyone feel too good. Zito and Macbeth drove away from Cabrini in silence. After Sunday night, they both wanted to run criminal backgrounds on the guards. Macbeth asked Zito to drive to the office, so he could call Areas One and Three.

"Where's Ryan?" Zito asked as they walked into the office. Hagen was plugging away on the computer, but there was no sign of their sergeant.

"On the street," Hagen said. "Stace, some girl called for you."

"No shit?" Macbeth sat down at Ryan's desk.

"Yeah, Lucy something, I think, from Nine."

"She at work?" Macbeth looked through Ryan's desk drawers for a phone book.

"No, she gave me her home number, though. Said to call her whenever, that she would be up. She sounded cute," Hagen said. "But that's usually a bad sign."

"Not in this instance." Macbeth found the book and flipped to the page for the detective areas.

"Her number's in your mailbox," Hagen said.

"All right," Macbeth said, while dialing the phone. "Yeah, Sarge. This is Macbeth from Eighteen Tac. Is O'Boyle in yet? . . . Yeah, I can hold." It was a minute before the sergeant came back on the line and told Macbeth that O'Boyle was in the watch commander's office. Macbeth gave him the number to the tac office and hung up.

By the time O'Boyle called back, Macbeth had called Area Three and was told Toomer had taken the night off.

"Stace," said O'Boyle. "How're you doing?"

"Better, now that I got some sleep," he said. "What'd

you find at the address on Bishop?"

"Nothing," O'Boyle said. "Nobody home. Place was dark. Day crew went out today and the neighbors said the resident, Liberty Collins, left to visit relatives on Sunday morning, or something like that."

"No shit. I was hoping something would bust loose."

"That makes two of us," O'Boyle said. "Some neighbors said they deal dope out of the house or out front, but they were pretty vague. Either it's a subtle operation or they're scared out of their minds."

"Scared," Macbeth said, knowing there was no such thing as a subtle dope operation, at least not on the street-level end of things.

"Yeah," O'Boyle said. "I've gotta run. The State was able to ID that body on the Ryan. I've got to ride with Greizedicht down to the morgue. I guess it's going to turn into some sort of task force. Stiff must have been someone with some pull. What fucking fun this is going to be. I not only gotta work with Greizedicht, but that other dickhead from the State."

"All right, O'Boyle," Macbeth said. "Take care."

"You, too."

"Stace." Hagen looked up from the computer as Macbeth hung up the phone.

"Yeah, Timmy."

"That girl, Lucy. Her number's in your mailbox."

"Oh." Macbeth threw the phone book back in the drawer.

"I didn't think you heard me before."

"I was dialing." Macbeth reached up to the stack of in-baskets that passed for mailboxes; each sergeant's desk had a stack of them for his team. Macbeth reached up and removed several pieces of paper, looking for Lucy's number. "Thanks, Timmy."

Zito was still on the other phone line, talking with someone from Chicago Security. Macbeth thought about calling Erin. She'd paged him twice, and he had yet to call her back. He just didn't feel like talking. He'd only come to work thinking he would hear from O'Boyle that they'd cleared the Chaney shooting. Guess not.

He didn't really feel like talking to Lucy, either. Though, the thought of her smiling face sparked a warm feeling inside. The thought of Erin did, too. Lucy was just new and a little different. But she was a police officer. And he had a rule that he wouldn't date cops. He'd broken that rule once and it led to some serious . . . complications. He figured he'd use the time that Zito was on the phone to clean out his mailbox. It would at least get Ryan off his back, since he was always complaining about the paper piling up in the boxes.

He found some property tracers he had filled out, a notice that a defendant had pled guilty, a lab report confirming the presence of cocaine in some powder recovered in an arrest and a page pulled from the desk calendar with last Sunday's date. There was writing on the back. Timmy Hagen's writing.

He remembered asking Hagen to check the two numbers he had been paged with. "What the . . . ?" Below each phone number, written in the careful Catholic school-taught script of his partner, was an address. He sat back in his chair and ran his hand through his hair. Standing, he thrust the paper into his pants pocket. The first address read: 5326 South Bishop—Collins, Liberty. The second address was not far away: 5515 South Sangamon—Raspberry, Willie.

Chapter 67

Permission

2240 Hours—Thursday

Ron Ryan sat in a booth in the rear of the Golden Cup Restaurant on North Clark Street. His back was toward the wall and his dinner was in front of him, untouched. He looked at his pager. The number was a direct line to the tac office, followed by Macbeth's star number and a nine-one-one. He knew Macbeth didn't declare emergencies often. He scooted out of the booth.

The pay phone was bolted to the wall between the two front doors. He dug the thirty-five cents from his jeans pocket and dropped the change in the coin slot, dialing the office.

Hagen answered and handed the phone to Macbeth.

"What's up, Stace?" Ryan looked over to the table, where his meal was growing cold.

"The night I played hockey," said Macbeth. "I had Timmy run these two weird pages I got. He threw them in my box. Well, I was just going through my mail a few minutes ago and I found them. The first one comes back to 5326 South Bishop."

Ryan didn't make the connection. "Yeah?"

"That's the address the van came back to, 5326 South

Bishop," said Macbeth.

"What van?"

"You know, the van that was involved in the accident with Chaney."

"No shit?" Ryan's appetite vanished.

"Yeah, no shit. I gave it to O'Boyle. The day crew from Area One went over there, and the neighbors said the resident left town on Sunday. Chaney used to have my pager number. I think he went to the address on his way to work Saturday night. He must've paged me when he got there. Remember Terry Farmer was in Vegas."

"Sounds reasonable," Ryan said. "What about the other address?"

"That's 5515 South Sangamon. Chaney must've gone there next," Macbeth said. "And it's new to me. The pages came shortly after one another."

"All right. What do you want to do?"

"I'd like to take a ride."

"Sounds reasonable." Ryan looked at his watch: 2250 hours. "Make the notifications. Tell Pat I gave you permission."

"Okay, Sarge. Thanks."

"Hey, Stace."

"Yeah?"

"Be careful. And call if you need anything. Don't forget to let Seven know you'll be in their neighborhood."

"Ten-four," said Macbeth, hanging up.

Zito could tell by listening to Macbeth's end of the conversation that they were headed south into the Seventh District. Macbeth ran downstairs to get the watch commander's approval. He'd okay it once Ryan did.

Ketchum and Hampton pushed an arrestee into the tac

office, a young black male with his hands cuffed behind his back. He wore a Dallas Cowboys starter coat that hung down past his knees. The kid was about five-foot-five and weighed probably one hundred twenty pounds. He looked maybe sixteen or seventeen.

Hampton walked him to the westernmost wall and sat him down. Hampton took his own coat off and threw it over the back of a nearby chair. He pulled a chair out from under the table and sat directly in front of the youth. "How old are you?"

"Huh?"

"How old are you?"

"Huh? Fifteen," said the youth, looking around.

Ketchum looked over at the kid. "Is there somebody at your house that could confirm your age?" asked Hampton.

"Huh?"

"Is anyone home that can prove to us you're only fifteen?" asked Hampton.

"Huh?"

Ketchum walked over from the other side of the room. "Listen, you little motherfucker." He thrust a bony finger into the kid's face. "Say 'huh' one more time, and I'll knock you into next week. Now the question."

"Huh? What was the question?" The kid flinched as Ketchum stepped toward him.

"Is there," said Hampton slowly, "someone at your house that can prove how old you are?"

"Uh." The kid looked between his legs at the dirty floor. "I'm seventeen. I turned seventeen last week."

Zito began to put on his coat. Ketchum looked over at him. "You going out?"

"Yeah," Zito said. "Macbeth's got some information on a house in Seven. It might be related to that Chaney thing."

278

Ketchum looked at Hampton and the prisoner. Hampton was putting one of the kid's cuffs on the wall ring. "Where?" Ketchum asked.

"The 5500 block of Sangamon," Zito said, tossing a piece of paper at him. It landed halfway between them and the desk. Ketchum looked at it and handed it back to Zito. Then Ketchum picked his spiral notebook off the desk. He flipped to the front of the notebook and began running his finger down the page.

"Raspberry," Ketchum said. "Anthony Raspberry, also known as Pookie. He's a Cobra, too. I hear he lives out south. That could be him. Cobras are all over that area."

"You got to be kidding me," Zito said with a laugh.

"No," Ketchum said. "That other address, Collins. I could be wrong, but that could be Antwan Simms' aunt."

Zito looked at the clock, almost 2300 hours. The night was more than likely shot.

Chapter 68

The Drive-By

2330 Hours—Thursday

Boo stood in the basement of the abandoned house, looking down at the woman taped up like the guard had been. Dease stood next to him. A grin hadn't left Dease's face since they'd parked the van. Boo knew the woman was still alive. Her chest moved up and down. She wasn't making too much noise, though. There was a little wheeze when she breathed, but that might be because of the way her face was taped.

"That shit was cool," Dease said slapping his back.

He looked over at Dease. "Fuck that. It ain't over 'til I see the shit," he said, beginning to chew on his thumbnail. He set the sawed-off shotgun in the corner.

"Pookie and Melvin have that tire here in no time," Dease said, still smiling.

"Shit better be there," he said. "I'm one dead nigger if it ain't."

Since he knew the Seventh District, Macbeth drove. He turned southbound down Sangamon Street against the one-way sign. A red van was parked in front of the Raspberry house, the first house off the alley on the east side of the street. He asked Zito to get the plate number as they drove by, while he looked at the house.

The house was a tall three-flat. The alley ran along the north side of the property, and an abandoned building abutted the property on the south. There were three floors aboveground and one halfway underground, probably a basement. There were lights on all over the house.

Zito turned to look at him.

Macbeth stole a look out of the corner of his eye at his partner. "That the van?"

"That van," Zito said, "has Chaney's plates on it."

Chapter 69

Responding to a Call for Assistance

2350 Hours—Thursday

Ryan was at his desk across from Ketchum and Hampton and thought about the situation. Macbeth and Zito were sitting on the van. The van, at the very least, had stolen plates. And it might have been used in the shooting of Wendell Chaney as well. Macbeth had said they were in a position where they could see the van if it pulled off, but they couldn't see the house very well. Ryan looked at Ketchum; he was signing the case report. Ketchum and Hampton would be done soon. Henry Barnhill was downstairs. Petty had ducked out earlier. What about Hagen?

Fuck it, Ryan thought, if I need Hagen, my ass is in real trouble. If I don't, he stays in the car. How much trouble can he get into in the car? He was talking about Hagen, though. Didn't the saying go, "It's better to be judged by twelve than carried by six"? Hagen's gun might be the one that turns the tide in our favor. He goes.

Lieutenant Finnegan said he was aware of the situation, but apparently was none too happy. He had insisted that Ryan call the Seventh District and arrange for further support from their tactical unit. Not only as a courtesy, but it might come in handy. Ryan made the call and wasn't happy with what he had been told. The watch commander, Lieutenant Waterford, was unavailable. The supervising tactical sergeant, Wolcott, was on the street. Wasn't Wolcott the one Macbeth had always talked about? The one with no balls. Great. This was turning into a classic cluster fuck.

Chapter 70

Smoking a Blunt

0010 Hours—Friday

Boo took the blunt from Early and brought it to his lips. He sucked in hard. The cool smoke filled his mouth and then went down his throat. The room took a gentle spin. It'd been one fucked-up week. The weed worked fast. He took another drag before passing it to his left. He was a Cobra. Cobras always passed to the left, never to the right. That was for GDs.

Dease took it from him and took a hit. He giggled and couldn't hold his breath. The greenish-gray smoke leaked from his mouth. The others laughed and pointed. Pookie, on Dease's left, reached out as Dease tried to take another hit.

"Come on, motherfucker," said Pookie.

Dease gave up the blunt and started laughing. He pointed at Pookie, who had the blunt at his lips. "Did you see that nigga?" Dease said. "He be going down the motherfuckin' street, legs be hanging outta the bitch's car."

Pookie grinned, his mouth open. His teeth showed through the smoke. He laughed and the smoke came out his nostrils. "Shhh-i-i-t!" he said, blowing out the smoke. They all laughed.

"I couldn't see shit," said Early. "I was rolling around the back. I get up and all I see is Pookie's legs sticking out the window. Shhh-i-i-t, that's one crazy nigga!"

Boo took the blunt and held it in his hand before taking a hit. He took a drag, held his breath and passed it to his left. He exhaled, looking around. The girl was curled into a ball in the corner, covered by a blanket. He was fairly certain she was awake, but he was too high to care. It wouldn't matter anyway. Ten feet from her, the tire from the BMW leaned against the wall, separated from its rim. In front of the tire sat four bricks of cocaine, stacked up, wrapped in plastic and tape.

Boo looked back to their loose circle. Dease was packing another hollowed-out cigar with weed. Tobacco littered the floor. "Fire that motherfucker up, Dedrick," he said.

Rachel Westing lay curled up. Her head felt as if it had been split in two. Her arms, hands, legs and feet were numb. Her right side burned like it was on fire. She tried to roll over, but that only caused more pain. She heard voices. The voices raged through her head as if they were in her skull, kicking at the most sensitive spots. Why are they so loud? she thought. It feels as if they are right on top of me.

Then she smelled marijuana. She'd smoked enough in her college days to know the smell. After awhile, the pain in her head subsided slightly. She credited the pot.

She tried to listen to the conversation, but couldn't. Her head still hurt. She drifted in and out of consciousness. She wondered what was going on. Why had they picked her? She was cold and numb. Gradually, she began to put the pieces together. This is what happened to Bob. What was going to happen to her? Her mouth was gagged. She said a silent prayer.

285

Chapter 71

Decisions

0045 Hours—Friday

Snow was falling again, thick flakes settling over everything. Ryan pulled his unmarked Chevy up to Zito's. They rolled down their windows. Hagen sat next to Ryan, Barnhill in the back. Zito was by himself. Ryan's left sleeve was beaded with drops from melting snowflakes.

"I gotta hurry," Zito said. "Macbeth's over by the school, across from the van. He's got to be freezing his ass off."

"He loves this shitty weather," Hagen said. "The shittier the better."

"Yeah," Zito said.

"Did Stace talk to the dick yet?" asked Ryan.

"Nah," Zito said. "We paged him, but he didn't call back before I left to meet you." Zito reached for his dashboard and turned his car's fan up a notch. "I guess he had some big meeting to go to."

"What does Stace want to do?" asked Ryan.

"Hello," Zito said. "He would just as soon kick the door down and home invade the place. But I think I talked him out of that."

"Must be the surrounds," Ryan said laughing. "Makes

him want to go back to his old Seventh District ways."

"Yeah," Zito said. "I don't think we've got enough yet to get a warrant, not with Chaney laid up incommunicado."

Ryan shook his head. He agreed with Zito, but felt they were only a break away from getting enough to warrant a search of the house. At this point, what did they have? A missing person who had turned up in the hospital unconscious and shot multiple times. His car was found burned-out, not too far away. The plates of his car were now on a van that matched the description of the vehicle in the accident. But the van came back to a house several blocks away. The phone number to that house, and the house where the van was parked, had come up on the pager of one of his team members, a team member familiar with Chaney, and who had worked with him, too.

"Shit," Ryan said. He looked at Hagen. "Any ideas?"

"Nope," Hagen said.

For several seconds, no one spoke. They looked at one another. The snow kept falling. Zito picked up his radio. *"Stace."*

"Go ahead," came Macbeth's reply.

"I got Ryan and company over here with me. We can't come up with a plan. Have you got any ideas?"

"Just the one I told you before."

Zito looked over at Ryan and shook his head. *"No home invasions, Stace,"* Zito said into the radio. *"Did O'Boyle page you back?"*

"No," said Macbeth. *"Not yet."*

Ryan looked down at his belt, where his pager was shaking furiously. He pushed the button with a finger stiff from the cold and saw Ketchum's cell phone number blink across the display. He retrieved his phone from the glove compartment and dialed Ketchum.

As the Caprice sped down the Dan Ryan, Ketchum reached over his right shoulder and pulled down the seatbelt. He didn't wear it as much as he should, but now when Frank's driving got a little too enthusiastic, it was a must. Ketchum pushed the buckle until it clicked securely.

His phone rang and he picked it up. *"Hello?"*

"Teddy," Ryan said over a static-filled airway. *"What do you have?"*

"Well," Ketchum said, *"I don't want to say in court how or where I got this, but there's a Raspberry that's a Cobra all right. My guy tells me he lives by an alley just off of Garfield Boulevard, either on Peoria or Sangamon."*

"That helps," Ryan said.

"That address on Bishop," Ketchum said, feeling a smile twitch the corner of his mouth. *"That's definitely Antwan Simms' auntie's house."*

"Yeah?" Ryan said.

"You don't remember Antwan Simms? He's the one Lonnie Huggins was riding with the day Macbeth got him with the pistols. He goes by the name of Boo."

"Oh," Ryan said.

"Yeah. That's what I was saying."

By one thirty in the morning, Macbeth jumped in with Ryan, Zito and O'Boyle, who had finally gotten back from his task force meeting. Ryan had positioned his tactical cars and two more from the Seventh District around the van, so that it couldn't pull off without being seen. None of the cars were close enough to be spotted.

Macbeth felt they had to get into the house and everyone was in agreement. It was the method that caused the argument.

"Stace," said O'Boyle. "I know we did our fair share of home invasions in Seven, but I can't see jeopardizing this investigation by doing one here."

"We got to get in there," Macbeth said. He was getting more and more frustrated.

"We can get a warrant for the van." Zito rolled his window down. "We could approach the house, looking for the owner. Go from there."

"Yeah," Macbeth said. "But, what if no one answers or no one cooperates?"

"Well," Zito fished in his jacket pocket for his cigarettes, "then we settle for the van only." He pulled one from the pack and stuck it in his mouth.

"Sarge," O'Boyle said. "I say we write a warrant for the van. I don't see a problem with approaching the house to find the owner or driver. Once inside, we'll be able to justify whatever we need to do."

"Pretty weak," Macbeth said. "Time-consuming."

"Yeah," Ryan said. "But that's all we got."

"I say, do the van, like O'Boyle's saying." Zito pulled a match from a book, struck it and lit his cigarette. He blew the smoke toward the open window.

"I think that's the best bet," O'Boyle said. "Who knows? Maybe we'll get lucky and someone will bail out of the house with a gun in their hand and give us all sorts of reasons to be real thorough." He looked at Macbeth and winked. They all sat silent for several minutes while Ryan thought it over. It was getting late. This case was getting more and more complicated. More than likely, they were going to end up with shit for all their effort. But they were here and had to do something.

"Fine," Ryan said. He turned and looked at O'Boyle. "Write one for the van. We'll make sure it doesn't drive off.

Before we execute, we'll knock on the door. Let's cross our fingers and hope we get lucky."

Macbeth leaned his head back. "That's weak."

Chapter 72

Stoned

0220 Hours—Friday

Boo looked into the corner of the room in the basement. The girl was curled up in the blanket, quiet, but not dead. He knew he was high, really fucking high. This last week had been the worst. But he had the coke. Now all he had to do was take care of the girl. Then it would be over.

"Melvin," he said.

"Yeah?" Early struggled to his feet.

"Where you leave that .357?"

"At Pookie's."

"Go get it," Boo said. "I wanna get this shit over with right fuckin' now."

"A'right," Early said, walking over to the pile of coats. His was on the bottom.

"Hold up," Pookie said. "That motherfucker be in my house. So I go to get it."

"I don't give a fuck who gets the motherfucker," said Boo. "Just get the motherfucker."

"A'right."

Chapter 73

Waiting

0220 Hours—Friday

Jimmy O'Boyle stared at the search warrant complaint in the typewriter in the Area One Detectives' squad room. Sitting out in the cold with the tactical officers had made him think of his days in Seven. It seemed ages ago. He glanced at the clock. It would be another twenty minutes before Ryan called the judge. Then it would be a matter of getting his signature.

He'd already talked to the State's Attorney from Felony Review who was in the Area. She'd agreed to approve the warrant, after he'd explained the circumstances. When he got to the part about searching the house, she had held up her hands. She didn't want to hear about it. Now, all he had to do was type it out.

Ryan drove to the Seventh District alone, and parked on Racine Avenue directly in front of the side entrance. Above him, bloated clouds were spilling their flaky contents onto the city. Behind him, in the neighborhood, the snow gave even the harshest living conditions a pleasant coating.

He turned his back on nature's beautification project and entered the District building. He was looking for Lieutenant Waterford, Seventh District Watch Commander, First Watch.

Macbeth watched the van from the west alley through a gangway. Zito sat in the backseat next to him with his eyes closed and his head back against the seat. Barnhill and Hagen relaxed in the front. Frustration was mounting, despite things slowly moving forward.

"*Steve, Kenny,*" Macbeth said into his radio, "*you see anything?*" There were several moments of silence before they responded. Kurtz said, "*No. Nothing but snow.*"

"*Did Wolcott call you yet?*" Macbeth asked.

"*Are you kidding?*" Kurtz said. "*We only paged him an hour ago.*"

Macbeth had to laugh as memories of trying to get hold of his old sergeant came back to him. High Yellow was always off doing something, never police work. If you needed him, you had to page him. He never listened to his radio. There had been times when the watch commander had demanded to see him and they had covered for him. Those had made for some intense times.

Lieutenant Waterford actually surprised Ryan by his eagerness to be involved and his willingness to let Ryan handle everything on the street. Waterford told him to fill in Sergeant Wolcott, when and if he showed up. Wolcott would be the Seventh District representative.

Macbeth wouldn't take his eyes off the van or the house. The temperature outside was harsh, frigid cold, appropriate for the dead of night.

"*Macbeth?*"

Macbeth recognized Ryan's voice on the car-to-car frequency. He said, *"Yeah."*

"We're all set with Seven," Ryan said. *"We hear from O'Boyle yet?"*

"Nope."

"How about Wolcott?" Ryan asked.

"Not last time I checked," he said. *"Steve?"*

"Nothing, Stace."

"Hey, Sarge," Macbeth said.

"Yeah."

"I want to take a quick walk around the house to see if I can see anything. Do a quick recon."

"You aren't planning on seeing a man with a gun and kicking in the door, are you?" Ryan asked.

"No." Though the thought had crossed his mind.

"Take a couple guys with you," Ryan said. *"Not you, Timmy."*

Macbeth looked over. Zito seemed to be sleeping, despite his upright position. Both his eyes were closed, his breathing deep and even. "You're a jagoff, you know that?" Zito said.

Macbeth took his fingerless gloves out of his pocket. "You don't have to go."

"Yeah, right. And be as big a jagoff as you? I don't fucking think so." He dug his own gloves from his pockets. "Call Teddy. He knows a lot of the players."

Five minutes later, Macbeth and Zito were squeezed in with Ketchum in the back of Ryan's car. Ryan turned in his seat, making direct eye contact with Macbeth when he gave his next order.

"No cowboy shit," Ryan said. "Okay? I'm fucking serious."

There was a long silence. Macbeth didn't know whether he should smile or get mad. Finally, he smiled. His sergeant knew him too well. "No cowboy shit," he repeated.

"You know," Ryan said. "You got one fucking evil-looking grin."

"Yeah," Macbeth said opening the back door. "That's what my mom used to tell me."

Chapter 74

Fetch Them Guns

0230 Hours—Friday

Pookie left the chilly basement and did a quick circle of the garage. Nothing. After all, it'd be fucked-up to have some two-bit thief stumble onto Lonnie's car and all that dope. Not after all they'd done to get the motherfucker back. When he finished, he went into the house to get the gun.

When he passed his sister's room, he saw a light under the door. She must still be up. When he opened the door to his own room, he found the TV on and his little nephew, Pee Wee, in his bed.

"Man, what the fuck is you doing in my room?" He shut the door. Pee Wee clenched his eyes shut and curled up into a knot. The G.I. Joe bed sheets were wrapped around his legs.

"Man, get the fuck up," Pookie said. "I ain't gonna hit you."

Pee Wee cracked his eye open a hair to look up at him.

"Why ain't you with your momma?"

"Rob is over," Pee Wee said. "She say I had to get lost for awhile."

Pookie shook his head. He hated when his sister did that. "That shit ain't right," he said. He heard a thud

296

against the wall, followed by some moaning and bed squeaks. Her man must be over. Pookie and Tami had had arguments about how she raised her son. But Tami didn't want to hear what he had to say. Pookie spoke his mind, because he played with Pee Wee more than anyone else besides her.

"What you watching?" he said.

"TuPac," said Pee Wee, his eyes lighting up.

"He straight." Pookie sat on the edge of the bed. Pee Wee began to untangle himself. "Cold motherfucker there."

"He be a bad motherfucker, just like you," said Pee Wee.

Pookie chewed on his lip for a second. Out the window, he could see the abandoned house and garage. He knew he had to get back to Boo and the boys, but what could a couple minutes hurt? This was family shit. "Maybe, but you ain't fittin' to be in no gang," he said. "Stay in school and listen to your momma, a'right? Gangbanging got TuPac killed. And I don't want you getting hurt, either."

"A'right," Pee Wee said, shrugging his shoulders.

Pookie leaned back and unzipped his coat. He could spend a few minutes watching some rap videos with the kid.

Pee Wee smiled as he leaned back against the bedroom wall.

Pookie tried to put the low moans and squeaking springs out of his mind. He bit down hard on his lip and reached over to turn the TV up.

Chapter 75

On The Way

0230 Hours—Friday

George Ronald Wolcott routinely visited his girlfriend's third-floor flat on Hoyne Avenue while he was working. His wife was too demanding of his time when he was off-duty, and he was never able to break away to visit. He began making more frequent visits while he was working, once he had been given the responsibility for a tactical team that was full of hard-working police officers who needed minimal supervision.

He came out of Brenda's building and climbed into the unmarked Chevy Caprice down the block, all the while trying unsuccessfully to keep the snow from getting in his shoes. His squad car lurched down the street. He didn't want to be too conspicuous. After he had turned on to Damen Avenue, he reached over and took the police radio out of the glove compartment. He turned it on and began to drive to the Seventh District.

Wolcott had called the tac office from his girlfriend's house. Ray Jackson had informed him that Macbeth and some other Eighteenth District officers were sitting on a house. His crew already had overtime approved by Lieutenant Waterford, starting at one-thirty in the morning.

Wolcott took advantage of this opportunity to spend extra time with Brenda. Getting paid overtime for a piece of ass, now that was living. But now, he took his time driving into the Seventh District to see what kind of case his boys had been dragged into.

Chapter 76

Into the Cold

0235 Hours—Friday

Macbeth wore his Carhart jacket, black fingerless gloves and a dark knit skullcap. Zito's receding hairline was left exposed, including bright red ears. Ketchum had the hood of his winter coat pulled tight against the cold. He also wore thick arctic gloves and heavy winter boots.

Macbeth led them north in the alley behind the Raspberry house. He wanted to get an idea of the layout of the house. As they walked, Ketchum put his gun in his coat pocket. Macbeth and Zito kept theirs holstered. Macbeth explained to Zito that once they got to the house, to hang back behind the garage, since it was easy to see he was white. Zito grunted and zipped his jacket halfway up.

Before he crossed Fifty-Sixth Street, Macbeth stood a moment at the mouth of the alley and looked around. No one was out. He could hear traffic on Garfield Boulevard, but none came down Fifty-Sixth Street or Sangamon. He stuck his hands in his pockets, stepped out of the alley and quickly crossed the street. Ketchum and Zito were on his heels.

He stopped on the alley side of the garage, behind the abandoned house. They'd only been out in the weather for a few minutes, but he could feel the cold. It was strangely exhilarating.

Ketchum's hand on Macbeth's shoulder stopped him as they approached the abandoned building's garage. Ketchum pointed to a boarded-up basement window. It was a bad board-up job and probably did little to keep the wind out. It did nothing to contain the light. They stopped behind the garage.

Macbeth cupped his hands around the radio. *"Sarge,"* he whispered. His breath spilled white clouds out, to be dispersed by the wind.

"Go ahead, Stace," Ryan said. His voice had an uncomfortable edge to it.

"We got lights in the abandoned building basement next door." Macbeth looked from the corner of his eye at the garage. He didn't want his voice to carry.

"What do you think?" asked Ryan.

"Probably some wineheads," Macbeth said. Ketchum nodded in agreement. Zito stared at the basement from around the garage corner. *"We're going to go down and remove them."*

Sergeant Ryan thought about what Macbeth told him. He didn't like his guys creeping into an abandoned building this late at night. It might be the bums that Macbeth suspected, but any number of things could be in that basement. But, if they were going to be doing a search warrant soon, they didn't want any surprises, either. It was a hard call, but he couldn't afford to be indecisive; they needed to get going. *"Be careful. You don't want to alert the neighbors of your presence."*

"Ten-four," Macbeth said.

Zito turned away from the abandoned house and faced

Macbeth. Ketchum gave him thumbs-up. Macbeth stepped up and looked at the basement entryway. The dark hole of a stairway yawned at him. There were four or five steps before he got to the door. No matter how hard he tried, he couldn't see past the darkness.

Chapter 77

Come On, Pookie

0245 Hours—Friday

In a corner of the basement, the cold had started to gnaw on Early's high. He looked up to see Boo standing in front of the tire. Boo just stared down at the four bricks. Motherfucker, Early thought, that's the most shit I've ever seen.

"That's an awful lot of shit, ain't it?" Boo spoke without turning. "Lonnie's gonna love this shit. I'm gonna be big time."

"You the man," said Dease from the corner. Dease picked up the shotgun and aimed it. "Boom. Boom. Die, bitch."

Boo looked at Dease as he aimed the shotgun at the girl. She rocked ever so slightly, easily mistaken for breathing. She was humming under her breath.

"Your turn, Dedrick," Boo said. "We all done our part." He walked over to Dease and took the shotgun out of his hands. "You gonna use the gat, though, not the gauge."

"A'right." A grin spread across Dease's face.

Boo looked over at the boarded-up window, as if he could see Pookie's house. "Come on, Pookie. What the fuck? He better get his black ass down here soon with them guns."

"Please, Father. Save me," Rachel chanted under her breath. "Please, Father. Save me. Please, Father, save me . . ."

Chapter 78

Forward

0245 Hours—Friday

Teddy Ketchum pulled his hood as tight as he could. He couldn't hear as well, but he didn't shiver as much. He poked his head around the corner of the gangway south of the abandoned building. Wind howled through the narrow passage between the front and back of the houses. He had to face the wind to see Macbeth and Zito. His eyes teared and he was afraid the tears would freeze in his eyes, instead of on his cheeks.

Ketchum wasn't happy he'd been chosen to watch the back, but it wasn't his call. It was Macbeth's. Zito couldn't stand outside for any length of time because he didn't have a hat. Macbeth couldn't stand outside because he simply refused to. That left him. It was Macbeth's thing, anyway.

He watched Macbeth and Zito sneak around the far side of the garage and creep to the back wall of the abandoned building. The newly-fallen snow suppressed the crunch of the frozen layers underneath. He'd taken his gloves off and had to breathe into his cupped hands to keep his shivering to a minimum. He hopped from one foot to the other, trying to keep his feet working. The weight of his revolver pulled his coat pocket down, keeping that side of his coat stiff and unyielding to his arctic dance.

Macbeth paused at the top of the stairs. From his angle, he could only see the first couple steps. There was no sound or light. He balanced with his arms as he crept forward and down. His fingers felt the cold as they flexed.

When he got to the bottom, Zito followed. Macbeth stood to the right, while Zito stopped to the left of the door. A new clasp was on the door, but no lock; he knew that this wasn't just some wineheads. There was still no sound. Macbeth nodded toward the door and knew he wasn't turning back.

Ever so slowly, Macbeth pushed the door open. What little light existed from the night sky spilled into the basement. He could see the glow from a light emanate from a curtain hung in the doorway toward the front of the house. As he took his first step, he noticed the vague, wet outlines of footprints on the floor. He looked back at Zito, who had drawn his Beretta from its holster. He heard the click as Zito thumbed the safety off.

Macbeth stepped in and to the right. He stopped and Zito came in to the left. Macbeth drew his .45. They walked slowly toward the light.

Chapter 79

Diversion

0246 Hours—Friday

"Go get me something to drink," Pookie said to his nephew.

Pee Wee turned to look at him. "Huh?"

"Go downstairs and get me something to drink." Pookie stood.

"What you want?" asked PeeWee, scooting to the edge of the bed. He jumped off and landed on his stocking feet.

"I don't know," Pookie said. "Anything. Just get your ass moving."

"A'right." Pee Wee ran from the bedroom.

Pookie reached under the mattress and got out the Ruger. He stuck it in his waistband. He reached in again and pulled out the Taurus. He put it in his coat pocket, along with the extra bullets. Pee Wee couldn't have even opened the refrigerator before Pookie was coming down the stairs. Pookie knew in his heart what he was doing was wrong, but he chose to do it anyway. He loved Pee Wee and didn't want the kid to follow in his footsteps.

A minute later, Pee Wee took the stairs two at a time until his short legs stumbled. He had his uncle's orange pop. At the top of the landing, he passed his mother's room. He could still hear noises.

He stopped in his tracks. He looked at the door to the bedroom and knew his uncle wasn't there. He had fallen for the same line his mom used on him. Why do grownups keep trying to get rid of me? he thought. Why they always ditching me? He hung his head. His bottom lip got heavy and hung from his face. The toes of his socks doubled over as he shuffled up to the door, dragging his feet.

Pee Wee pushed the door open. The hinge squealed. The room was empty and the mattress had been moved. He went to it and heaved it up as much as he could, knowing what he was going to see. The guns were gone. Only minutes before Pookie came in, he'd had the mattress up in the air, so he could look at the guns.

He stood next to the bed with his head down. The mattress settled back onto the box spring. The pop was about to slip from his hands, but he didn't care. Tears began to fall from his eyes. He turned to the window. He put the pop on the windowsill and split the curtains with his face. He knew where Pookie was going.

Pookie had decided to look the garage over one more time and had stopped when he saw new footprints in the snow. He pulled the Taurus from his pocket and reared up on his toes. Reaching under his coat, he took out the Ruger.

He turned toward the abandoned house and brought the guns out in front of him. He took a step, and then another, stepping in his old tracks to avoid noise as he crept toward the stairway. At the top of the stairs, he could see the door was open more than it should be. This is no fuckin' good, he thought, looking left and right. He stepped onto the first step.

★ ★ ★ ★ ★

Pee Wee watched his uncle pull out the guns. Cool. He didn't remember ever seeing Uncle Pookie walk so carefully or slowly before.

Chapter 80

Freeze

0248 Hours—Friday

Teddy Ketchum stopped breathing when he heard the muffled crunch of the snow. It was barely audible, but unmistakable. He peeked out. It didn't sound as if it had come from the stairwell itself, so he didn't think it was Macbeth or Zito.

He spotted a figure sneaking toward the back of the abandoned house. Male. Ketchum couldn't make out much detail. He wasn't sure whether the man was looking at him or the basement door. The figure had stopped at the top of the stairs. Ketchum was able to focus enough to realize the man held a gun in each hand.

Ketchum mentally inventoried the Seventh District officers. No way. This couldn't be one of them, not with two guns out. The man began to walk down the stairs slowly. Ketchum pulled his revolver from his coat pocket. The figure disappeared into the darkness.

Ketchum stepped out of the gangway and trotted to the top of the stairs. He moved as quietly as he could without sacrificing speed for silence. The man was already on the bottom step.

Pookie concentrated on the basement door. Then he

heard a noise from the top of the stairs. He turned his head. Pee Wee? No way. Could it?

Inside the basement, Macbeth was moving his legs so slowly that his thighs burned. Thanks to the surgery years ago, his knee cracked. The only way he could combat the noise was to take short, painfully slow steps. The cold was forgotten. Sweat soaked under his hat.

Zito moved around the furnace and waited. He had a good position to cover Macbeth. Once Macbeth reached the curtained doorway, Zito figured he would move up to the other side. But even from where he was, he could hear muffled voices coming from the other side of the curtain.

Ketchum stopped at the top of the stairs and looked down. Whoever he was, he was not a police officer. His baseball cap was cocked to the left, Mickey Cobra style. Ketchum focused on the barrels of the two handguns the man held. The man looked back at him.

Ketchum pushed his revolver straight out in front, feeling like he was moving in slow motion. It seemed to take forever.

"Police!" he shouted, spraying spit into the frigid night air. His finger began to squeeze.

Pookie couldn't believe it. Where did this asshole come from? The man at the top of the stairs brought a gun up with both hands. A cop!

"Motherfucker!" Pookie yelled. Everything went slow motion.

Pee Wee saw the stranger point a gun down into the

blackness that had engulfed his uncle minutes earlier. Then, bright blue and orange fire shot out of the man's gun. Three times. Pee Wee jumped with each explosion. His eyes closed, then jetted open, and kept opening farther with each loud crack. He couldn't breathe.

Pookie felt the bullets tear through his body as the flames from the gun shot toward him. The first bullet punched his arm and shoulder. He dropped the Ruger. The second shot hit him high in his back, blowing out the front of his chest. The third bullet hit him in the back too, but down low, on the right. It glanced off something and blew out his belly.

It was funny, he thought, that he wasn't knocked down. He remembered the security guard being thrown down by his shots. There wasn't any pain. Instinctively, he squeezed the trigger of the other gun. He felt it jerk, but didn't hear the explosion. The bullet went into the basement door.

Pookie turned toward the shooter as best he could. Have to get the guy that shot me, he thought. He wasn't at the top of the stairs now. Had he run? Pookie fell forward and crawled up the stairs.

Ketchum ran. His back felt exposed. He spun around and threw himself on the ground, facing the stairway. The man was coming out of the shadows. Ketchum waited in the snow.

Macbeth fell to the concrete floor of the basement before he even registered that there were shots being fired. He moaned as the wind was forced from his lungs. He rolled to his right, trying to get next to the cinderblock wall.

Zito covered his head and curled toward the cinderblocks, his pistol next to his ear. He knew he was shouting at Macbeth to see if he was hit, but he couldn't even hear his own voice, let alone an answer to his calls.

Ryan had held the radio to his ear. He'd barely heard Macbeth's transmission about lights that were on in the basement. He knew the three out on foot were trying to be quiet, but that didn't make it any easier on him. Then all hell broke loose. Gunshots erupted a block away. It had to be the abandoned house. Ryan knew it in his gut. Ripping the shift lever down, he brought his radio to his mouth.

"SHOTS FIRED! SHOTS FIRED! GO! GO! GO!"

Dedrick Dease dove for a corner of the room and crashed heads with Early, who picked the same corner. Boo jerked and crouched with the shotgun held out in front of him. He raised the shotgun and pulled the trigger, blasting the curtained doorway with buckshot. He went deaf. He jacked another cartridge into the chamber. The empty shell bounced noiselessly on the cold floor.

"Fuck!!!" Zito screamed as the curtain blew out with a bunch of holes and tears. Someone had a shotgun and it wasn't the good guys. Macbeth was belly-crawling toward the front wall.

Pookie climbed out of the stairway and stood. He looked for the cop who shot him but didn't see anyone. His legs were weak and shaky but there was no pain, only numbness. By the time he spotted the dark lump in the snow, it was too late. As he tried to bring his gun up, he saw a tongue of flame reach toward him again. This time he heard a queer splash as the bullet tore through his neck.

The round hit him just above the collarbone at his throat. The next thing he knew, he was lying in the snow. This was more like what he thought getting shot was supposed to be. He was surprised that there was no pain, no feeling at all. His head fell back and he opened his eyes. There was a hole in his neck. He couldn't breathe. His hand wouldn't bring the gun up. The stars twinkled. No, that was snow falling in his face. He blinked.

There was a light above him, a shooting star? No, just someone in the window of his house. Pookie forced his eyes to focus. Pee Wee. It was the last thing he saw as a black spot grew and ate his sight. He tried to speak but blood gargled out of the hole in his neck. His last breath died in his chest, drowned in his own blood.

Boo let go another shotgun blast on the doorway. The curtain was shredded. Then he backed against the boarded-up window on the north wall. He motioned with his head to Dease and Early to join him.

"Fuck this," Zito said. After the second shotgun blast, he was tired of getting showered with pellets. He brought his gun around and fired a series of shots through the wall on the left of the curtain into the room. Macbeth was almost to the wall on the right of the curtain.

"Pull these fucking boards off!!" Boo shouted as bullets hit around them. Dease crawled like a crab to where Boo was frantically trying to pull the boards off the window with one hand. He stood and grabbed at the boards that were nailed into the wooden window frame. Early came out of his trance, stood and ran over to the window to help.

Boo kept one eye on the doorway. A board started to

come loose as another spray of rounds came toward them, tearing chunks of concrete out of the wall.

Boo used the sawed-off butt of the shotgun to try to pry the board from the opening. What was left of the wooden stock cracked as the board fell to the ground and clattered across the floor. Boo jacked another round into the chamber and fired again, this time through the wallboard.

The blast ripped through the wall above Macbeth as he got to his knees. Zito fired more rounds through the door. Macbeth brought his .45 up and punched it through the doorway, letting go several shots.

Boo tossed the shotgun through the now-open window. He boosted himself up and through the opening. Early started after him as more rounds pounded the walls, splashing him with shards of concrete.

Macbeth grabbed what was left of the curtain and yanked it down as Zito crossed to the left side of the doorway opposite him. Macbeth peeked around the door. It was a low and unexpected angle. He saw the feet of a man going out the window with another man impatiently waiting his turn. Once out of the window, the man ran toward the front of the house.

Macbeth yelled, "FREEZE, MOTHERFUCKER!"

Zito slammed a fresh magazine into his Beretta.

Chapter 81

Freeze, Motherfucker!

0249 Hours—Friday

Dedrick Dease froze in mid-step and watched Early turn and run down the dark gangway. Slowly, he raised his hands over his head. There was a gun aimed at his back. He knew it. He felt it. It was as if some kind of bug was digging a hole between his shoulder blades. He was scared.

"Step away from the window, motherfucker!"

Dease took a step back. Strong hands grabbed him from behind and threw him up against the bullet-scarred wall. As he was being searched, he saw someone boost himself out the window. The hard barrel of a handgun pressed into his skull behind his right ear.

"I'd like nothing better than to blow your fucking brains all over this wall," said a gravely voice. "So, be careful when you put your hands behind your back."

Dease knew the threat was real. "I'm cool, man," he said. "Take it easy." He slowly put his hands straight out to his sides. The gun was removed from the back of his head. His left arm was pulled behind him roughly and cuffs were snapped on.

"Give me the other arm, asshole."

He brought the hand back slowly, until it touched the

cold steel of the handcuffs. The handcuffs closed and tightened around his wrists in a moment of pain.

Zito heard a low groan behind him as he tightened the cuffs. He froze. Fuck. He reached up and grabbed his prisoner by the back of his neck. Spinning the prisoner around in front of him, he went down on one knee, drew his Beretta and searched for the threat.

He saw a crusty bundle of blanket, hair and duct tape. He stood, pushing the prisoner in front of him. He heard another moan and bent over to drag the blanket away. Underneath he discovered a girl. Next to her was a tire and what looked to be about four kilos of cocaine.

Dease was flung against the basement wall and spun around. The cold steel of the gun cracked his cheekbone. The front sight tore his face open. He fell against the wall and onto the concrete floor. His arms were pinned beneath him. He had beaten enough people to know what followed. Powerful kicks ran down his head and body. He wondered when a bullet would explode the back of his head, blowing his brains across the floor and putting an end to his bad luck.

Chapter 82

Panic-Stricken

0245 Hours—Friday

Teddy Ketchum reached for his police radio without taking his eyes off the body in front of him. Steam rose from its wounds and the blood, as it leaked onto the frozen ground. It seemed to Teddy that the man was trying to speak, but only bubbles gurgled out from his neck wound. Ketchum followed the dying man's gaze to the third-story window of the Raspberry house. He could see the silhouette of a little boy watching.

The sound of the gunfire had blasted his numb ears. He had dove into the snow when more shots erupted from the basement.

"SHOTS FIRED! SHOTS FIRED!" he shouted again into his radio. *"MAN DOWN! SHOTS FIRED!"*

Ketchum covered his head with his arm but continued to broadcast. *"SHOTS FIRED IN THE BASEMENT! GET US SOME FUCKING HELP!"*

Ketchum rolled toward the wall at the rear of the abandoned house. He hit the wall and looked up. Nothing but the body was in the backyard. He was surprised that he could still see the steam from the body rise up against the falling snow.

A young, black male ran from the gangway toward the alley. Ketchum focused on the shotgun he carried. Ketchum was so cold he couldn't get a shot off. As he radioed in a description of the man and his direction, he heard the big engines coming his way. They were being driven hard.

"HE'S GOT A FUCKING SHOTGUN IN THE ALLEY! NORTHBOUND!" Ketchum shouted into his radio.

Macbeth's ears were still ringing when he crawled out the basement window. The open air seemed to help. He could hear Ketchum yelling about a man with a shotgun. He remembered the shotgun pattern on the basement wall. He knew the one he'd seen get out of the window had run for the front and the street, not the alley. Someone must have gotten out before him, and he had the shotgun. That was who he wanted.

Macbeth ran toward the back. Coming out of the gangway, he saw a man running north. A quick peek revealed Ketchum against the wall, pointing at the man. Ketchum was yelling about a shotgun. Macbeth pulled his .45 and ran down the alley.

Shirley Pounds guided her Chevy Caprice down the alley east of Sangamon Street. She'd been on Wolcott's Seventh District Tactical Team for two months. It beat the hell out of driving a beat car around. She loved it. She was working with Gregory Reason, who had finally put on his seatbelt.

They had heard the shots. Pounds froze for a second, not knowing what to do. Reason shouted at her to roll. That was something she could do. Her foot stomped on the pedal as fast as the snow-filled streets would allow. She rode into the alley with her back end swinging to the right. It got dangerously close to a garage before she straightened it out. Snow slapped the rear wheel wells as they raced down the icy, grooved alley. Pounds heard the radio squawk about a man with a shotgun.

There he was right in front of them! Slipping and sliding, but running full-out. No doubt he was carrying a shotgun, sawed-off at that.

"That's him!!" Pounds shouted, stepping down harder on the accelerator. Reason drew his revolver and reached for the door handle.

Boo had made it to the alley running. Got to make it across the street, he thought. Maybe across the boulevard. He noticed his shadow dancing in front of him down the alley. "Damn!" he said under his breath. "Poh-leeces every motherfuckin' place."

He skidded to a stop at the T-intersection and turned. An unmarked squad car came at him. It was still three or four houses away. Snow whipped up behind the car. He brought the shotgun down and fired from his hip.

"Motherfuckers!!!" he yelled.

Shirley Pounds' heart jumped in her throat when the running figure in front of her turned around. By the time he brought the shotgun to bear on her, her heart was threatening to stop. Reason looked like he was trying to crawl under the dashboard.

She never heard the blast. She saw the brilliant orange and blue flash as it fired. She was blinded as she ducked to her left, jerking the wheel. The car slid, then drove left, as the lead shot exploded through the window. She felt a knifing pain as a pellet found the soft tissue in her right shoulder.

★ ★ ★ ★ ★

Macbeth ran toward the alley, focusing on the man with the shotgun. Macbeth watched as he stopped, turned, pointed and fired. Macbeth ran faster, bringing his .45 up. He fired a wild shot that picked at the snow five feet in front of the gunman. Macbeth saw him throw down the gun, turn around and run. Slipping and sliding, he disappeared around the corner of the alley. Macbeth forced his legs to move faster.

Macbeth never saw or heard the car in the alley. It struck him from behind on his right hip. He was bent over backward and thrown into several garbage cans.

George Reason heard, more than felt, the hard thump before a fence post caved in the front bumper and radiator, bringing the car to a stop. He called in the shooting on the Seventh District radio frequency. He demanded an ambulance for his partner, who had been shot and was screaming and bleeding all over the front seat.

Macbeth stood. His right hip was numb but held his weight. He gave the tac car a menacing look. His .45 was miraculously still in his hand. He set out after the shooter in a limping trot.

When the "shots fired" call came over the radio, George Wolcott had slammed on his brakes. Without hesitation, he did a U-turn in the middle of Racine Avenue and pulled back into the Seventh District parking lot. In the office, he forged the watch commander's signature on his Time Due Slip. Officially, he had never been at work tonight, and even his salt-stained Italian dress shoes didn't distract his whistling as he began the short ride home.

Tami Raspberry tore at the knob of her bedroom door, breaking several of her fake nails. She and her boyfriend had hit the floor naked when the gunshots erupted. She heard a scream. She knew it came from her son. She flung the bedroom door wide and ran into Pookie's room. Her son, Pee Wee, stood at the window looking down, his lips pulled back over his teeth and gums. He screamed with every bit of his being and then some. Tami cradled his head to her bare breast, still wet from lovemaking. With tear-filled eyes, she looked down into the backyard next door and saw police running around. Then she saw the body. It was dressed like Pookie. He had to be dead.

Pee Wee cried. He stopped only to breathe. His eyes burned. His throat hurt. The poh-leece had just killed his uncle.

Chapter 83

Stop

0249 Hours—Friday

Melvin Early knew he had to escape. As he ran, his eyes darted across the street. He had to get past the school to freedom.

Ryan gunned his unmarked Chevy in behind Hampton's, as they raced north up Sangamon. It seemed to him Hampton wasn't in control of his car. That thought was barely out of his mind when a black figure burst out of a gangway of the abandoned house. Ryan hit the brakes immediately. The anti-lock braking system pumped the pedal fast beneath the sole of his boot. Ryan saw the brake lights flicker on Hampton's car. He must've taken his foot off the brake when the anti-lock kicked in. Hampton's car slid. The figure ran.

"Stop!" yelled Ryan, wishing against all reason that he could force his will on the laws of physics.

There was a sickening thump and crunch as the Chevy's bumper mashed the figure. The front fender slammed the rear bumper of a parked car. The man was somewhere underneath. The screech of metal-on-metal had barely ceased before the screams began.

Boo ran like a man possessed. Across the T-alley, he jumped a backyard fence to the front of the house. The gangway was blocked. He ran to the other side of the yard. As he jumped the side fence, a ragged metal spur pierced his palm.

When he landed on the other side, the metal spur tore across his hand. He grunted in pain. Blood sprayed the ground. He vaulted three more fences before he got to Peoria Street, a block east of Sangamon. Across the street was an empty gangway.

Macbeth easily followed the tracks in the snow. He vaulted the backyard fence with little trouble from his numb hip. The tracks went forward and returned from the side of the house. He saved time by going straight to the side fence. He hopped it.

Blood showed pink in the snow under the beam of his flashlight. His quarry was hurt. That was good, almost amusing. He set off after him, limping but taking the fences efficiently. He took his eyes off the trail only to see where he was going. Across Peoria he reached in his vest pocket for his radio. Gone!

He looked back. He heard the muffled noise of the scene behind him. People yelling. Confusion. He couldn't afford to stop. You had to press a wounded animal, especially in this weather. This offender was capable of doing just about anything to get away.

Macbeth entered the gangway on Peoria at a jog, the .45 in one hand and the flashlight in the other. He loved to hunt and found he excelled at it. Conditions only added to the rush. He continued into the night that was as beautiful as it was deadly.

Chapter 84

A Cluster Fuck

0250 Hours—Friday

Ryan stood over the trapped offender and shook his head. He directed Hagen to call for ambulances, fire and help from Zone Six. He also knew that within minutes the area would be flooded with the police. Anytime a cop got shot at or had to shoot brought in the cavalry. He ran with Barnhill toward the rear of the abandoned house.

Negotiating the slick corridor of the gangway, Ryan said, "Fuck!" He couldn't see how anyone could build up any speed running through such ice. Then again, desperation is a mighty motivator.

He ran past the basement window into the backyard and saw a dead body. Beyond that, he saw Ketchum in the alley, helping another tac cop pry open the driver's door of an unmarked squad car wedged onto a fence post. Steam poured from the hood of the car.

"Teddy!" Ryan shouted. Ketchum kept tugging the jammed door. "Teddy!" Ryan was directly behind him. Ketchum turned to look at him. "Where's Mike and Macbeth?" Ryan asked.

"Zito's still in the basement," Ketchum said. "Macbeth's on foot after the fucker with the shotgun."

"Where?"

Without taking his hands off the doorframe, Ketchum nodded northbound. Ryan could see faint tracks in the dim alley light. He wanted to follow Macbeth, but he was the only supervisor on the scene of a police shooting. The rulebook said he couldn't leave.

"FUCK!"

Chapter 85

The Getaway

0250 Hours—Friday

Boo ran through backyards. He hopped fences from one yard to the next, sprinting through them. Hoping to double back to the street, he angled across one yard toward a gangway. He never saw the clothesline. He felt it cut across his throat. He thought his neck was sliced in two, as his legs went on without him. The fall slammed the wind out of his lungs in an explosion of pain. He curled into a ball.

He was as good as caught, if he stayed down. He got to his knees and tried to draw breath, but couldn't. The front of his throat felt glued to the back. He stood on shaky legs and staggered to the side of the house. Some air finally squeezed through. He used the brick wall to stay on his feet as he stumbled down the gangway. It was blocked. He turned back and made his way into another T-alley filled with ruts frozen in the slush.

He looked up at the church, its spire shooting into the sky. The cold air barely got past the crease in his throat. He began to move, leaning against the fence surrounding the church. He turned in the vacant lot and walked toward Garfield Boulevard.

His throat felt like it was on fire. He could hear sirens

over the throbbing in his ears. There was no way he could make it across the boulevard. He stumbled as he tried to jog to Green Street. He had to find someplace to hide while he got better or until he could breathe.

The marks in the snow warned Macbeth about the clothesline. That had to hurt. He kept looking to see if there were any squad cars he could flag down. There were none. Nothing to do but keep going.

Chapter 86

Fuck The Rules

0251 Hours—Friday

It took Ryan a minute to set up the scene. An ambulance and fire truck were called for the offender under the car. A second ambulance was requested for the injured Seventh District Officer. A third ambulance was ordered for the female found tied up. The Crime Lab was ordered, too.

Kurtz and Christian were in the alley with the Seventh District Officers. Ketchum had Zito's prisoner in the backseat of a squad car.

No one could raise Macbeth on the radio.

Shit, Ryan thought; then he grabbed Zito and started after Macbeth.

He wasn't about to let the rulebook endanger one of his team.

Chapter 87

Hunkered Down

Boo knew he couldn't keep going. His neck burned. His lungs burned. He looked down the street. He had to hide or his ass was cooked. Then he saw it, a burned-out house. The upper floors were charcoal black, with ice hanging from the second story. Windows and doors were boarded up, with holes gaping through the roof. He staggered for the abandoned house.

The rear door on the porch was nailed shut. The basement door had been pried open. He squeezed through and leaned against the wall. A second later, he slowly and quietly began to climb.

He stopped for several breaths on the first floor. The night air was getting harder and harder to breathe. He reached up with a bloody palm and felt his throat. There was a lump and a cut across the front of his neck. When he sucked in, he could hear a wheezing sound. The deeper he tried to breathe, the harder it was to get any air.

There was another floor. He pushed himself up the stairway. He should be safe up there. Once he stopped running and climbing, it had better be easier to breathe.

On the top floor, he went through the first door. It was

330

dark, but it looked like the fire burned away most of the walls. He could see blackened wooden struts.

He squatted down and rubbed his neck. "Fuck! That hurt!"

Macbeth relied on his instincts to track in the confused ruts of the sidewalk and then to the gangway of the boarded-up house. There still wasn't anyone to wave down, and he wished to hell he hadn't lost his radio. He took a deep breath as he moved into the dark gangway.

Macbeth came to the basement door and listened. Nothing. His ears throbbed from the shootout in the basement. He tucked his flashlight in his belt at his back, took a deep breath and stepped into the basement. The .45 felt cold and deadly in his hand.

Macbeth waited for his eyesight to adjust to the darkness and listened. Then he moved on.

"Watch out for this fucking clothesline," said Zito, picking himself up. He rubbed his throat as he continued after the tracks. Good thing he wasn't really running hard.

Macbeth took his flashlight out as he climbed the stairs slowly. He holstered his .45 and held three exposed fingers over the flashlight lens to mute the beam. There were bloodstains on the blackened walls.

He stopped on the first floor and listened. His ears still rang. There were more drops of blood on the floor. He scanned the area with the faint red light. There, on the stairs. He had gone up. Does he even know I'm behind him? He started up the stairs, following the blood trail.

Macbeth slid the flashlight into his belt again. Only one

more floor. The holes in the roof should provide some light. He climbed.

"East on the sidewalk," Ryan said, looking at the jumbled tracks in the snow. Zito was on the boulevard parkway and turned toward him. "Come on." Ryan broke into a jog. Zito ran after him. Ryan radioed Hagen where they were headed. "Look." Ryan pointed at the ground. "There's blood."

Macbeth stopped at the top of the stairs and strained his pounding ears. He swore he heard a wheeze. The more he strained, the more he couldn't hear. When he hunted, he never questioned his own senses, but this was different. He couldn't trust his ears after the shooting. He wasn't sure if he heard true, or if his hearing was playing potentially deadly tricks.

After another moment, he stepped onto the landing. A board squeaked. He froze. Anyone up there would have heard it. His heart thumped in his chest.

Boo heard a creak. Someone was sneaking up on him. He stood. Both his legs shook. He got dizzy and leaned against the wall. The floor creaked under him. Fuck! He looked down. Why couldn't I have stayed down? He took a small step. Another groan from the floor. Fuck! He looked at the doorway. It was only feet away. He needed a weapon. He reached for a board. Another squeak. Fuck!

Boo saw someone jump into the room. Had to be a pohleece. How the fuck did they find him?

Macbeth saw someone bending over, picking up a board. Macbeth charged, grabbed him by the throat, dragged him upright and slammed him into the wall. He jerked back and Macbeth lost his grip and had to step into him. The man swung a board up at Macbeth's head. Macbeth blocked it with his gun hand. The board struck behind his knuckles and drove his hand and gun into his head. He reeled. Numb fingers couldn't hold onto the .45. It fell to the floor.

The man swung the board again. Macbeth blocked it with his shoulder and thrust his other hand into his attacker's throat. He tried to crush it, while pinning the board against the wall with his arm. The man let go of the board and threw himself backward, kicking with his legs. Macbeth lost his hold and the man shot back, hitting the outer wall of the house.

Macbeth tried to follow but had to shake his head to clear his vision. He heard a loud crack. The wood splintered and gave way. Macbeth watched as the man pitched out of the second story and then disappeared, followed by a sickening crack of cartilage and bone.

Macbeth ran to the hole and looked down. He couldn't see the body. Across the street, he saw an old lady bundled against the cold. She was looking into the yard below him at the body on the ground. Her gaze followed the path of the fallen upward to Macbeth.

Zito had heard the crack and crunch of the breaking wood. He had looked from across the street and didn't see the body fall. He only heard the resounding thud and discernible crack as it landed. Ryan followed as he ran for the yard.

"Fuck!" Zito kneeled at the side of the twisted figure on the ground. The man's limbs had settled around him like a rag doll.

"Is he dead?" asked a voice from above. Zito's skin

Chapter 88

The Boss Bar

0200 Hours—Tuesday

Ryan parked his S10 pickup on the corner of Clark and Hubbard Streets, a hundred feet from the revolving door of The Boss Bar. He checked his rearview mirror before stepping out and locking the door. Now that the temperature was rising at the end of winter, the fruit hustlers would be out working the streets again.

He pushed through the revolving door into the bar. The only strong light in the bar hung over the pool table. He stopped and let his eyes adjust. Zito was sitting at the bar with Ketchum. Amanda Petty was playing pool with Macbeth, Hagen and Barnhill.

The bartender, Monica Alexander, brought out a bottle of Lite Beer with one hand and sat a plastic cup on the bar with the other. At least someone had been keeping an eye out for him. He made his way to where his beer waited, and sat.

Ryan pulled a crinkled envelope from his pocket and laid it on the bar. He flicked it toward Zito and Ketchum. Zito looked at the envelope as he lifted his beer to his lips. Ketchum glanced down and puckered as he turned toward the bartender, trying to get her attention. Zito sat his bottle down.

"So," Zito said. "They finally got around to you, huh?"

"Yep." Ryan picked up the envelope. It was labeled Office of Professional Standards, better known as OPS, in which civilians handled investigations of alleged police brutality. Ryan laid it in front of him.

"Stace know?" Zito asked.

"Yeah," Ryan said. "I showed it to him."

"They're acting like they got some kind of federal case or something." Zito picked at his beer label.

"Yeah." Ryan looked over at Ketchum. "They call you, Teddy?"

Ketchum reached for his glass of Crown Royal on the rocks. He sat it on the bar, stirring it with a yellow plastic spear and an olive. "Yeah, they got me already. But since I wasn't there when Boo went out the window, I couldn't tell them much." Ketchum pulled the olive off with his teeth and tossed the spear in the direction of the garbage can. He missed by a yard.

"My lawyer," Ketchum said through his teeth as he chewed the olive, "had to keep objecting to their questions."

"No shit?"

"Yeah. They kept asking me if I thought Macbeth would throw somebody out a window."

"No shit?" Ryan said again.

Zito shook his head.

"Yeah," Ketchum said. "I guess the investigator was disturbed that, as a black man, I wasn't outraged that a white 'poh-leece' officer might throw a brother out a window." He took a gulp of his Crown Royal. "Fuck him."

There was a shout and a cheer from the back of the bar. Ryan looked up to see Hagen pulling his money out. Ryan chuckled. When would Timmy learn not to bet that old hillbilly pool shark?

Amanda Petty came through the crowd toward them with her pool cue held in front of her. Hagen and Barnhill were arguing, probably some obscure point of eight-ball. She must be taking the opportunity to walk over and brag.

"We beat 'em again." She dug a Marlboro cigarette out of her purse. She put it between her lips and coated the butt with her red lipstick. She went back into her purse and continued to dig. She gave up and looked the bar over. She apparently saw what she wanted and reached across Ketchum for a matchbook.

"Oh," she said glancing at the envelope in front of Ryan. "What's this?"

"OPS wants to talk to Ronnie," Zito said, acknowledging her for the first time.

"What about?"

"The deceleration trauma suffered by one Antwan Simms."

"Huh?" She pulled a match from the book. "What's that?"

"The shortest flight in the history of man," Zito said.

"Flying? What?" Petty lit the cigarette with a puff of smoke.

"Come on! Trix," Zito said, "you know. Boo. His leap of faith and subsequent crash. The Green Street Air Show. What has two fangs, scales and no wings? A Mickey Cobra."

"Oh," Petty said. "You're talking about the guy Macbeth threw outta the window." Petty walked back to the pool table with smoke trailing behind her.

Ryan, Zito and Ketchum drooped and shook their heads in a synchronized gesture of defeat.

"Dumb fucking broad," said Zito.

"Yeah, and she's on our side," Ketchum said.

"Yep." Ryan ordered another beer.

Two hours later, The Boss Bar's overhead lights burned down on a few remaining patrons gathered in the corner of the bar. Last call had been made for civilians an hour ago. Now, with just the regular Eighteenth District coppers left, last call was sounded again. One last round was passed out.

"How's the case against Huggins shaping up?" Ryan asked.

"It ain't." Macbeth sipped through the head of the recently-pulled Guinness Stout.

"What?"

"Yeah," Zito said. "The State says they can't proceed without the testimony of a co-defendant. So, they're going to try and hammer him on the gun charges."

"What about the dope?" Ryan asked.

"No good," Zito said. "Too much time, too many people handling the car."

"What about the other two defendants?"

"Well," Zito said, "Melvin Early's lips are flapping. But he's trying to put everything on Boo and Pookie, the two dead guys. Anyway, he's putting himself on the scene of two murders, so I think he'll go away for a long time. Now, Deadrick Dease, he ain't saying shit. He's going to be a tough case."

"Chaney can't ID his shooter 'cause he was blind-folded," Macbeth said. "Mrs. Starr picked Early and Dease out of lineups, but that was only after picking two wrong guys on the first try. Dease ain't talking and has Gold for an attorney. No prints. No physical evidence."

"No shit." Ryan zipped up his parka.

"Yeah," Macbeth said. "But, it's the Lonnie Huggins shit that really pisses me off. He's responsible for all this shit."

"Yeah, it bothers the fuck out of me, too." Zito pushed his beer away. He reached into his coat pocket and pulled out a pack of Kools.

"I thought you were quitting?" Macbeth asked.

"Yeah," Zito said. "So did I."

"See you tomorrow." Ryan put his shoulder into the revolving door.

Zito grunted as he lit his cigarette. After another minute, Zito and Macbeth were the only coppers left in The Boss Bar. Monica Alexander was counting the till, while the barboy was collecting the garbage bags from several cans stationed around the bar. Macbeth stepped into the revolving door and pushed; Zito followed.

It was still cold, but warmer times were definitely coming. Something was in the air, but Macbeth couldn't put his finger on it. Zito took a drag and blew the smoke out hard, as he looked up one side of the street, then down the other.

"You know, Stace," Zito flicked his butt toward the curb, "Huggins's gotta get out of jail sometime."

"Ain't that the truth." Macbeth stuffed his hands in his coat pockets and turned toward his Jeep, parked on the corner. "And I'm going to be there, waiting."

About the Author

Dave Case is a decorated, nineteen-year veteran of the Chicago Police Department. Currently, he's a sergeant in the Special Operations Section, but he has worked in a number of different positions throughout his career, ranging from uniform patrol to plainclothes assignments. He lives on the southwest side of Chicago with his wife and kids, where he's working on the next Macbeth novel. Rumors persist that he likes both the White Sox and Cubs, and at this time the investigation is ongoing. For more information, visit www.davecasebooks.com.